The Detective Joanna Best Mysteries
Book 5

# The French Infection

## Cenarth Fox

The Detective Joanna Best Mysteries
Book 5
*The French Infection*

First published in 2019 by Fox Plays
www.foxplays.com
www.cenfoxbooks.com

Cover design by Oliviaprodesign

ISBN 978-0-949175-28-1

# Dictionary of Australian slang/language

Here are some of the mainly Australian words in this novel.

**billy** - kettle, (a billy is a round tin for boiling water)
**carked it** - died
**drongo** - a fool
**fair dinkum** - sincere, genuine
**frothies** - glasses of beer with a froth (a head) on top
**g'day** - hi, hello (short for good day)
**green top** - cricket expression, a pitch with a lot of grass
**GST** - Goods and Services Tax (akin to VAT)
**Kathmandu** and **Patagonia** - outdoor clothing outlets
**Maman** - French for mother
**motser** - large amount of money (UK)
**nature strip** - grassed area between gutter and footpath (sidewalk)
***New Tricks*** - UK TV show featuring retired police officers
**night watchman** - cricket expression, a lower-order batsman
**nup** - no
**OIC** - Office in Charge, boss
**Oz** - Australia
**ratbag** - trouble maker
**Royal South Street** - eisteddfod in Ballarat
**rozzers** - police
**Rumpolian** - Horace Rumpole was a fictitious London barrister
**SM** - stationmaster
**snibbed** - to snib a door is to lock a door
**SOG** - Special Operations Group, Soggies
**sparkie** - electrician (sparks)
**telly** - television
**tradie** - tradesman (or woman) such as a plumber, carpenter and tiler
**troppo** - gone troppo means gone crazy
**uni** - university
**ute** - vehicle with tray at rear often used by tradies
**wanna** - want to
**whinge** - moan, complain
**Wimmera** - large rural region in Victoria, Australia

For those who have read all
the Detective Joanna Best mysteries

# 1

---

MAKING A BOMB IS TRICKY. Making it alone is scary. One slip and it's Goodnight Vienna. You need the ingredients, the knowledge, the nerve and a lotta luck. Meet newbie bomb maker, Yousef Jlassi.

He knew about social media, texts, phone calls, snail mail and face to face meetings. But if he used these and mentioned the word *bomb,* every cop and spook online would find him instantly, if not sooner.

Yousef was shit scared because he knew nothing about bombs. He was scared of failure, of letting down fellow terrorists, and worse, scared of his big brother, Laris. Mind you, everyone was scared of him.

Living in the French capital, people referred to Yousef's older brother as Laris of Paris—but not to his face. Hell no. Big brother was a powerful criminal who controlled drugs, human trafficking and prostitution in the City of Light. Not a nice chap.

Having cops in his pocket helped. Corrupt police took cash so Laris could break the law with impunity. His serious income was laundered by a former corrupt cop, Émile Bastien, who once worked with police officer, Lieutenant Intern Pierre Richelieu. Years ago, Émile went to jail and Pierre went to Australia.

Yousef was not a part of his brother's criminal empire. Yousef avoided the warlord and kept his terrorism a secret. If Laris knew about Yousef's bomb plot, the crim's fury would be greater than any chemical explosion.

In a room in a mosque, Yousef began to explain his plan. 'Stop,' said the leader. 'Our best weapon is secrecy. Lone wolf attacks work when you tell no-one.'

'But I need advice.'

'The infidels read your emails and monitor your web browsing. Give them nothing.'

'But how will I know I've made the perfect bomb?'

'Trust in Allah. Remember the martyr's reward.'

Yousef hit rock bottom with no knowledge and no help. Looking online for bomb-making tips was not an option. This project could blow up in his face, literally.

Then his luck changed. He went to see his parents in their modest Parisian flat and by chance there was brother, Laris of Paris. The criminal rarely visited and when he did he showered his folks with gifts. His mother didn't want them and his father threw them away. They hated his criminal activities.

'Hey, bro,' said Laris to Yousef. 'What's happening?'

Yousef gave a respectful but lukewarm reply and kissed his parents. They loved him but knew nothing of his radical conversion.

'What is this occasion?' asked the father. 'Both my sons are here and I am not dying.'

Laris laughed. Yousef struggled to smile. It was a loveless reunion and when Laris left, Yousef followed. In the street, baby brother chanced his luck.

'Laris, I need your help.' The look on the criminal's face screamed scorn with his blood being thinner than water.

'You got some girl pregnant and her boyfriend wants to kill you?'

'No. A friend is being blackmailed. He can't pay and needs to steal the photos. But they're in a safe and we don't know how to make the right explosives to blow it.'

Laris roared. 'You, a fucking criminal? Don't make me laugh.'

Yousef became desperate. 'Laris, please. My friend has a good job and a family and he'll lose everything. Please.'

The hardened crim took pity on his wimp of a sibling and gave Yousef the name and address of a safecracker. 'Tell him I'm your brother. And if you fuck up, I don't wanna know.'

The next sound Yousef heard was a door closing on a top-of-the-range black BMW. Laris left to make more filthy lucre.

The safecracker wouldn't open his door. 'I don't know you,' he hissed. 'Piss off.' Then Yousef dropped the "open sesame" password, the Laris of Paris connection, and the door swung open.

'Why didn't you say? I heard Laris had a brother. Come in.'

Andre Chaput was short and thin and even his warts were tiny. He washed himself and his clothes on a regular monthly basis, and his flat was last cleaned when the Nazis fled Paris.

Yousef gave his spiel about a friend being blackmailed.

'Describe the safe,' said Andre.

Yousef couldn't. There was no safe. 'It's big,' he muttered.

'What make and model?'

'My friend only saw it from the corridor.'

'I can't give quantities and instructions unless I know the details. Different safes need different explosives placed in different areas.'

Yousef despaired. 'How about he packs a lot of explosives against the door and blows the thing to kingdom come?'

'Does he want the contents of the safe or to commit suicide?'

Yousef wanted to say *suicide mission* but instead played his trump card. 'Laris said you're the best and would definitely help me.'

Andre shook his head. *Bloody amateur*, he thought and drew up a list of ingredients which, if mixed and positioned correctly would open the safe, the wall next to it and the ceiling above. Yousef was rapt but kept his joy confined.

He knew it was a fatal mistake to buy a whole lot of bomb-making ingredients in one hit in one store so took his time. On his regular shop at his local Franprix supermarket, he bought a small amount of one ingredient in amongst his other groceries. He didn't stand and stare at the shelving but went straight to the item and dropped it in his basket, as if it was a natural thing to do. This process went on for weeks. His stockpile of bomb-making material grew. Anyone studying CCTV inside the supermarket would see nothing suspicious. He hoped.

17,000 kilometres away in Melbourne, Australia, Detective Senior Constable Joanna Best was under pressure. She was the cop who captured the so-called religious serial killers. It was big news. The murders continued for weeks, the police struggled, and the media went troppo. When the killers were finally nabbed, naturally the media wanted a piece of the clever cop.

In a previous case, Jo and her friend, IT whiz Michael Chan, copped a paparazzi onslaught when they found a kidnapped toddler. They discovered how invasive the press could be. He hated publicity and she wanted to be left alone. So Jo knew what to expect when she and Michael captured the serial killers.

She asked her boss, DI Elly Rose, to shield her from the media. But they persisted, and foot-in-the-door journo, Katie Maguire, got Jo's mobile. 'I'm not interested,' said Jo. The journo tried harder.

Jo came home to be confronted by Maguire. Jo fled indoors. The journo hung around outside. She knew Jo arrested the church-going, bible-bashing serial killers, and the only part missing from Katie's story was a comment from the star detective.

'Come on, Jo, give us a comment,' called Katie at the well-locked front door. 'I promise I'll quote you exactly.'

Jo used her peephole. *She's lying; I can see her lips moving.*

The journo wanted confrontation. She provoked Jo hoping to draw the cop outside to abuse or arrest her. Katie's photographer was primed. Fiery footage would be the icing on the paparazzi cake.

But despite the media ratbags, Jo felt good having decided to accept DI Pierre Richelieu's invitation to fly to Paris. He needed help with his mother's funeral and financial affairs, and she needed help to escape the press. Besides, "Paris with Pierre" sounded divine.

Her phone rang. It was her favourite pathologist. 'Good evening Doctor Strange.'

'Get y'glad rags on, girlie. I'm taking you out to celebrate your magnificent serial killer success. I'll pick you up in ten.'

'I can't, Doctor.'

'Can't? There's no such word.'

'I've got the media camped on my door step.'

'What?'

'They won't leave. They're running a story on the religious serial killer saviour.'

'Jesus.'

'No, me.'

Strange would normally have laughed but knew how persistent journalists can be. 'How many?'

'Two or three. I said, "No comment" but they won't leave and if I do they'll follow me. I'm trapped, Gabrielle, and if I arrest them ...'

'Don't arrest them. They want that. Stay there. I'll ring you back. Go and top up y'lippy.' Click.

Jo had no idea what Gabrielle intended so hopped under the shower, dressed then heard voices. The paparazzi were talking to someone. Voices were raised. Then screams and curses. Jo rushed to her front door peephole. Bodies were active, and angry cries were so frightening she opened the door to be confronted by two balaclava-clad males. She panicked.

'All done, officer,' said one of the masked men.

The media representatives were spitting and coughing. The smell smacked Jo in the face.

'Hose your garden and it'll be fine,' said Hood #1. Jo sensed his friendliness. 'Enjoy your evening, Miss. Good night.'

The Beagle Boys took off with the media monsters staggering towards their car, their bodies and cameras discombobulated. Jo's phone rang. She slipped inside. 'What the hell, Gabrielle?'

'Have they gone?'

'Yes but the smell.'

'It's harmless, my version of hydrogen sulphide. Get it on your clothes or in your hair and you won't sleep with anyone for a year. Now hose your wall and garden and I'll pick you up in five.' Click.

What a night. Great success with her career, and now her colleague and friend ordered a hit on some paparazzi. Jo didn't have a hose, only a watering-can. She splashed water on her plants, front door and path. She went inside, felt powerless but made one decision. She phoned DI Pierre Richelieu. His voice asked the caller to leave a message.

'Oh Pierre, hello, it's Jo. Look I've thought about your invitation to Paris and I'd like to accept. My passport's up to date and I'll need to talk to you about tickets but please, count me in. I'll call you later. Bye.'

Her breathing became short and her pulse accelerated. She felt sick.

*What have I done? Will this damage my career? We're not sleeping together—yet. But the Homicide gossips will never believe me.*

Her mind was swirling with questions when she heard a car horn.

The pathetic pathologist sat in her Humber Super Snipe. It was her father's and Gabrielle cherished it. She went to the same mechanic, now in his 80s, who was a miracle-worker with makeshift parts and expert servicing. She recently regained her licence after being caught drink-driving. Jo opened the passenger door.

'It's all right,' anticipated Strange, 'we're both celebrating; you with your serial killers and me with my restored licence.'

'Do I smell?' asked Jo, thinking the gas attack engulfed her as well. She slid into the Humber and the gorgeous leather bench seat made it easy for Gabrielle to lean across and sniff.

'Yes but in a lovely way. Don't tell me.' She sniffed again and pondered. 'Estée Lauder, *Beautiful Eau de Parfum.*' Jo laughed for the first time in ages. The pathologist's experience in detecting perfume on corpses made her an expert. 'Now, we're going to paint the town ruby red, my girl to match your lippy.' Jo cringed. 'And here's the bad news. I'm on the wagon.' The cringe evaporated.

Gabrielle chose a small Italian eatery in her home suburb of Fitzroy where the staff greeted her like family. She introduced Jo who too got the royal service. It was a shock watching her friend drink water. The night was a brilliant success until Jo's phone rang.

She knew the number and wondered why on earth her brother-in-law was calling. They didn't get on. Jeremy loved himself and then his wife and, at a push, his children. He ignored his in-laws, Jo's parents and struggled with his sister-in-law because Jo was smart, a public figure and heroine—a challenge to Mister High 'n Mighty.

*But why is Jeremy ringing at this time and why at all?*

'Jeremy, to what do I owe the pleasure?'

Jo was prepared for his sarcasm. It didn't come. Jeremy sounded human. *What's happened?*

'It's Caitlyn.' He sounded ill, weary, distressed.

Jo blanched. Strange read her face and stopped eating. 'What's happened,' asked Jo feeling chest pain.

'She's got cancer.'

Jo froze. She couldn't speak. The word slapped her face.

Strange demanded an answer. 'What's wrong?'

Jeremy struggled. 'She's got breast cancer and they're going to operate this week.' He broke down.

'Oh Jeremy, I'm so sorry,' said Jo finding her voice.

Strange persisted. 'What's wrong, woman?'

Jo put her hand over the phone. 'It's my sister. She's got breast cancer. She's ...' Jo choked. Strange took the phone.

'Hello, I'm Doctor Gabrielle Strange, Jo's friend. Who's speaking?'

Gabrielle listened, asked questions and gave practical advice. She gave Jeremy two experts and permission to use her name. Jo watched on in shock. 'I'll get Jo to call you tomorrow. Good night.' Gabrielle ended the call and handed the phone to her friend. She signalled to the waiter. The staff sensed distress and behaved impeccably.

'Thank you,' whispered Jo. Her eyes glistened.

'Try and breathe evenly. You're in shock and not just because you've seen me drinking water.' There was a sparkle in Gabrielle's eye and Jo seized on the lighter moment drawing strength from her friend. Alas the slightly happier feeling died.

'Oh no,' groaned Jo, despairing even more. 'I told Pierre Richelieu I'll go with him to Paris this week.'

'Paris France?' gasped the pathologist, 'Champs Elysees, Paris?'

'His mother died suddenly. He asked me to help sort her affairs.'

'You mean *his* affairs.'

'I can't go now. My sister needs me.' Her phone rang. She knew the number. 'Hello Mum. Jeremy's just told me.'

Jo listened to her frightened mother. Gabrielle stood and guided Jo out of the restaurant with Jo listening to a desperate parent. Gabrielle thanked the staff with her broken Italian and signed the bill en route. The diners made it to the Strange automobile, climbed in with Jo promising to ring her mother.

'Where to?' asked Gabrielle. Jo looked at her blankly. 'Where does the randy Frenchman live?'

'Gabrielle, thank you but no. I'll call him first and then ...'

'You've got to tell him in person, girlie. He's grieving and you've given him a serious burst of happiness. Dumping a friend is done in person. Now, it's East Melbourne, right?'

En route, Jo called Pierre. He answered.

'Oh ma chérie, I 'ave discovered your message. You 'ave made me the 'appiest man in Melbourne. Merci, Joanna, merci beaucoup.'

She kept a steady tone. 'Pierre, I'm on my way to your place. I'll be there in ten minutes.'

'Merveilleux.'

'I'll see you soon.'

She hit *End* and looked at Gabrielle. Give her a peaked cap and the pathologist could have chauffeured some high-ranking politician.

'Honesty's the best policy; be cruel to be kind,' said Gabrielle.

'He sounded so happy,' moaned Jo. 'My sister could die, Pierre will be doubly hurt and, thanks to you and your rotten-egg perfume, I'm going to be front-page news in the morning.'

'You poor old thing,' moaned Gabrielle and reverted to her old self. 'There's a bottle of self-pity in the glove box. Help yourself.'

Jo let the sarcasm wash over her. The pathetic pathologist was a hard woman who never pulled a punch. Jo reckoned she was the best friend ever but boy did she tell it like it was. They drove in silence.

'I'll get a cab home, Doctor,' said Jo when they pulled up outside the former church in Powlett Street.

'No, you won't. You need to make this short. You're stressed; he's stressed and therein lies an emotional overload.' Jo looked confused. 'People under stress seek solace in sex.'

Jo sighed. *What the hell is happening?*

'I'll park over there and if you're not out in fifteen, I'm coming in. What's his apartment number?'

'I'm not telling. I've been embarrassed enough tonight. I'll see you soon.' She slid out of the Humber Super Snipe then poked her head back. 'Thank you, madam. As my Pop would say, "You're a brick".'

Pierre opened the door with his previous enthusiasm deflated somewhat after Jo's message and tone. He sensed trouble and when he saw her face he knew his dream was dead. They embraced lightly, he kissed her cheeks and they sat in his opulent sitting-room.

Jo cut to the chase. 'I've got some bad news.' She explained her sister's health. She dreaded his response. There was no need.

'Ma chérie it is terrible. Of course you must be with your family.'

Relief flooded Jo's body. For the first time tonight she cried, not buckets but generous tears keen to escape. After the paparazzi and Strange's polite thugs, after deciding to go to Paris, after Caitlyn's cancer news, and now reneging on her acceptance and then expecting Richelieu to be upset, his kindness tipped her over the edge.

He moved and placed an arm around her. She cried into his chest. He said nothing and waited. She recovered and wiped her face.

'Thank you, Pierre. You must know I genuinely wanted to go with you.' She didn't mention fleeing the press.

He looked at her and she melted. They were about to kiss when Jo saw a vision. Richelieu's face morphed into Gabrielle's face. Her voice filled Jo's head. 'People under stress seek solace in sex.'

Jo stood, surprising and disappointing the Francophile.

'Mademoiselle?' he asked rising.

'I must go, Pierre. My driver is waiting.'

'Your driver? You solve the serial killer case and you 'ave a driver?'

Jo laughed. Her amusement pushed Pierre into the romantic red zone. 'Not *that* sort of a driver. It's Dr Strange.'

'Madame Pathologist?'

'Oui. She took me for a meal and is helping me with my sister.'

'Perfect,' he smiled and followed her to the door.

She faced him. 'I will call you tomorrow, Pierre and help you in any way I can.'

'Merci,' he smiled in surrender. She paused then stood on tip-toe and kissed his lips. He struggled to restrain himself from embracing her and never letting go. 'Good night,' she said and skipped down the steps and into the night.

# 2

---

WHAT MAKES A BASTARD A BASTARD? As a child, some future psychopaths are said to be cruel to animals. What are the signs someone will treat people badly seemingly without a conscience? Were they bullies or bullied when young? Did they get away with crimes as kids? Do they ever think of the pain they cause? Who knows?

Simon Grovene, 44, gave developers a bad name. He bought old properties, demolished them and whacked up several townhouses, units or whatever. He'd sub-contract the work. Brickies, plumbers, sparkies, plasterers and glaziers were sweet talked into working for Slippery Simon who delayed payment—a nightmare for sole traders.

With work finished or nearly so, and little or no money coming in, tradies asked, begged, demanded and even threatened the evil Simon. His rotten reputation grew wings. Once when debts were so bad, Simon declared his business kaput and disappeared leaving a trail of suffering subbies broke and after blood.

Simon then got his mate to start a new business. Simon's name never appeared on the company documents yet he pulled the strings. This meant more unfinished projects, more desperate homeowners and more out-of-pocket tradesmen and women. Their families copped it big time. Marriages failed and at least one suicide was directly attributed to the misery caused by Simon.

One carpenter, unable to put food on the table for his family, arrived at Simon's abode carrying a shotgun. The police arrived before blood was spilt and the weeping, long-suffering tradie was locked up. Simon couldn't care less.

So when an estate agent entered an empty house in Kew to inspect the property, and discovered the dead body of Simon Grovene, the news was bitter sweet for many folk. Curses and toasts abounded.

DI Eleanor Rose, the recently appointed head of Homicide in Victoria Police, sat in her office. Jo Best tapped on her open door.

'Morning Jo. How is the pin-up girl and number one detective?'

Jo was after a big favour, and having lavish praise heaped on her didn't help. 'I was going to ask if I could take some leave, ma'am.'

'Oh?'

'You know about DI Richelieu's mother's death, well he's pretty cut up about it because apparently she had a stroke and couldn't raise the alarm and lay on the floor until she passed.'

'Don't say passed, she died.'

'The DI asked me to help arrange the funeral and sale of her house.'

'What, in Paris?'

'Yes ma'am.'

'I hope you're not sleeping with DI Richelieu, Senior.'

'I'm not ma'am.'

'Or planning to.' Jo hesitated and her silence sounded bad.

'No, ma'am. As corny as it sounds, we're just good friends.' She could have said "very good friends".

'You know the unofficial rule, sister. In any office romance, the woman gets screwed before and after the fact. So what's happened?'

Jo explained about Paris being off because of her sister's medical crisis, and Rose instantly changed. 'God I'm sorry, Jo. Why didn't you say? What do you need? Take leave. What else?'

'Thanks ma'am but I'd rather keep working. I may need time off to look after my sister's kids but nothing major.'

'Do whatever's necessary. And keep me informed about your sister.'

Rose's phone rang and Jo stood. Rose listened then held up a hand. Jo waited. Rose ended the call. 'Homicide in Kew. Incident room now.'

Jo joined the meeting where DI Rose gave details of the body in the empty house. 'An estate agent preparing for an inspection found the body. Uniform reckon it's interesting. With DI Richelieu on leave, Billy you're OIC with the rest of you involved. Questions?'

'Ma'am,' asked Jo, 'could I take a back seat on this one, please?'

'We can't lose our superstar detective,' chimed in DS Justin Fleming, 'not our sleuth of the year.' Others grinned and agreed.

Rose replied. 'I don't want this broadcast but Jo's sister has a serious health issue and I'm happy for her to work behind the scenes.'

The atmosphere changed. 'Sorry, Jo,' mumbled Fleming.

'Okay, let's go,' said Rose. '24 Brightwell Crescent.'

Squad members left with Billy Hughes the last to leave. She and Jo locked eyes. Both knew what the other was thinking.

'What can I do?' asked Hughes.

'I'm fine, Sarge, and thanks.'

'You could always go back to those cold cases.' She smiled and left. Jo rang her mother, grandfather and brother-in-law. No prize for guessing the topic of conversation. Gags were absent as a life-threatening disease tends to kill humour.

Then she rang Dr Jack Carr. The widower's daughter recently copped an acquired brain injury from a car accident, and Jo hadn't enquired about young Grace for a few days.

'Well, if it isn't the world's best detective. Congratulations and how are you Senior Constable Superstar?'

Jo felt warm and tingly at the sound of the GP's voice. 'I'm fine, Jack and thanks. But how is your beautiful daughter?'

'She's making slow but steady progress, Jo. We're quietly optimistic. Her speech therapist reckons she's improving every day. And if you're ever in the area, you know there's an open invitation to drop in. Harry and Rags keep asking after you, Rags in particular.'

Jo laughed. 'Actually I wanted to have a chat with you, Jack. I got some bad news. My sister's been diagnosed with breast cancer.'

There was a pause which sounded loud.

'I'm sorry, Jo. I've had a few patients go through that situation and if I can help in any way, please, any time.'

'Would tonight around 8 be convenient?'

'Perfect. I won't tell the kids because you're so busy. Till tonight.'

'Bye,' said Jo and took a deep breath. She didn't often think about Dr Carr but when she did, it made her feel nice, even warm and fuzzy.

The detectives arrived at the crime scene. Forensic officers were busy inside and out. The police gathered on the nature strip. Two uniforms stood guard, in the street and on the verandah. Rose gave instructions then remembered Billy Hughes was the OIC.

'Apologies, Detective Sergeant, after you.'

Orders given, Billy and the DI approached the verandah while DS Fleming interviewed the still shaken estate agent who discovered the body. Four detective senior constables including Baldwin and Payne door knocked in the hope someone saw or heard something—anything.

Changing into forensic outfits, Rose and Hughes entered the house. They avoided the Forensic officers but observed the body. The secateurs resting against his crotch, the chisel protruding from his chest and the coins spilling from his mouth were not there by chance.

'Not a suicide then,' said Rose without a hint of irony.

'ID ma'am,' said a technical officer handing the detectives a wallet.

'I know the name,' said Billy. 'Fraud, debts, threats from creditors, he's been in the news of late.'

'Great,' added the DI, 'dozens of suspects all with a red-hot motive.'

Their conversation was interrupted by a loud female voice.

'Kindly give me a hand, Constable. I may still be beautiful but my failure to attend Pilates means my gorgeous body is a tad knackered.'

Rose and Hughes headed to the front door. 'Good morning, Doctor Strange,' greeted DI Rose.

'If you say so, madam, and what treasure have you for me today?'

'Pathology plus a profiler may be required, madam,' said Hughes. 'There's plenty to digest.'

'Well there's a saving for your bottom line,' said Strange, struggling with her protective clothing. 'Yours truly offers both services for the one reasonable price.'

Her boasting would have been more credible had she not, when stretching into her forensic suit, lost her balance and teetered. A quick thinking uniformed constable saved the pathologist from re-arranging the hydrangeas. Her language was best described as fruity.

Inside, the forensic officers were close to completing their tasks and the pathologist got busy. Strange knelt beside the corpse and did her visual check. 'Interesting,' she mused. 'A profiler could get lost here.'

'Cause of death, please Doctor?' asked Billy.

'Obvious possibility is the stab wound to the chest but not by the implement on display.'

'Not the chisel?' asked Rose.

'When a weapon is thrust into the human body, the flexible skin wraps itself around the implement. Remove the weapon and the skin retracts. Here,' she said, pointing, 'the skin is not flush against the chisel. This poor sod was stabbed with something bigger with the chisel inserted post mortem.'

'So the coins and secateurs didn't kill him?' asked Billy.

'They appear to have nothing to do with his death. I would refer both to your profiler and, stating the bleeding obvious, the 30 pieces of silver may tell us chummy was a disciple, debtor or quisling.'

'Excuse me, ma'am,' said an officer from Forensics. He handed Rose an evidence bag containing a bullet. 'Lodged in the wall over there,' he said pointing.

The detectives looked at one another and then the pathologist. She shrugged. 'No bullet wounds front or side. Maybe he was a deserter, shot in the back. All revealed when I take him home for tea.' She struggled to rise and the detectives helped her. 'Gracias, señoras. Now my eyesight must be failing as I cannot see your star detective anywhere on the job.'

'She's taking a break, Doctor,' said the DI, 'a well-deserved break.'

Strange nodded. She understood.

Jo went back to where she worked on cold cases. She found what she wanted, made copies and popped the documents in a satchel. No evidence was missing when she left. She smiled thinking about her idea and how it would make someone happy. She sent a text to DI Rose. *Visiting family. Available on mobile.*

Rose replied. *Take whatever time you need.*

Jo headed to her sister. The siblings stopped being close years ago when Caitlyn chose boys over baby sister. Big sis found Jo an impediment to pursuits of sex, drugs and rock 'n roll.

When Caitlyn married Jeremy, the sisterly connection more or less collapsed. Jo couldn't stand her brother-in-law and saw as little of him as possible. It was only the children, Jo's niece and nephew that brought her home. Now though, the tug of family ties pulled hard.

Jeremy opened the door with none of his smarmy, smart-alec barbs, plastic smile or sincere insincerity. He became remotely human and embraced Jo who felt confusion more than anything else.

'Come in, dear Jo. Your mother's here as well.'

Jo entered the sitting-room with its imported furniture. Her sister and mother sat side by side on a settee. The embracing and kissing seemed different, was different. The women settled.

'I'll make coffee,' said Jeremy heading to the kitchen. He was never keen on domestic tasks but terrified of raw emotion.

'How are you, Caitlyn?' asked Jo.

'Fine. And thanks for those recommendations.' Jo was puzzled and Shirley more so.

'Ah,' Jo twigged. 'Dr Strange was with me when Jeremy called.'

'Who's he?' asked Shirley.

'He's a she, Mum, and a wonderful pathologist.'

'Pathologist,' shrieked Shirley. 'Your sister isn't dead or dying.'

'Mum, Gabrielle Strange has been a medico forever; she worked with Pop, and knows everyone. Her recommendations will help Caitlyn get through this and come out better and stronger and be able to go on looking after her children and you for decades.' Wow.

*Stop complaining Mother. Take heart, Sister. All will be fine.*

'So how are the kids?' asked Jo and normal service was resumed. Jeremy arrived with refreshments and Caitlyn's situation was briefly put on the back burner with Jo questioned about her serial killers' arrest. She reckoned her family were more intrusive than the media.

Shirley complained about Jo's photos being unflattering. Jeremy wanted to know when her promotion would come through and typical Caitlyn, even allowing for her major medical woes, knew little about her sister's triumph.

After promising to do various tasks, Jo endured another hug and kiss session with brother-in-law. She thought of Gabrielle Strange's advice; "People under stress seek solace in sex". She headed for Glen Iris ringing her grandfather en route.

The hug and kiss he gave Jo was the opposite to Jeremy's greeting. With Pop she copped genuine warmth built on a lifetime of love.

'Come in, Detective, said Robbo. 'I feel I should be saluting, bowing even and certainly pinning some award on your uniform.'

'Steady Pop, it's me, the chocolate-frog kid.'

They discussed Jo's dementia-ridden grandmother, Caitlyn's cancer crisis and Jo's stunning arrest results. When the conversation slowed, Jo played her trump card.

'Pop, I need your help.'

'Not boyfriend advice. I failed badly with your mother.'

Jo laughed. 'Actually I could do with some help there but not today. Right now I want detection advice. I've been looking again at the cold case you worked on before you retired.'

Robbo got serious. 'Somebody murdered Maggie,' he said, 'and we still don't know whodunit.'

'How's this for an idea? You come back to work and have another go at your last case?'

Jo sat back and said nothing. Her grandfather, for all his years of experience, shocks and surprises, was genuinely stunned. He was not expecting a job offer. Was it a job offer?

*Is my granddaughter serious? She's a lowly senior constable.*

'Your jokes are usually much funnier,' he said.

'I'm not joking, Pop. Think about it. Your brain is as sharp as ever. You know the case better than anyone. You've got the time.'

'It was 20 years ago—more'

Jo persisted. 'And you're wasted, sitting here. You visit Nan, you potter in your garden and that's fine but Victoria Police is missing out on a wealth of talent and experience.'

'You can't be serious?'

'Never more so. Look, I'm not suggesting you re-join the Force, strap on a sidearm and chase the bad guys. Why can't you be like those blokes in London on the telly, the ones in *New Tricks?*'

'That's fiction. UCOS doesn't exist.'

'Yes but you reading files and advising serving officers could solve the case. No-one else will. It's in the too-hard basket. We're waiting for the killer's death-bed confession. Here's a chance to have a red-hot crack at bringing justice to Maggie's family.' She paused and went for the killer punch. 'I know you'd love to see this case solved.'

Robbo shook his head. 'It's a terrific idea, Jo, but the powers that be would laugh it out of court.'

'They don't have to know. I give you copies of files. You decide what needs to be done. I liaise with Records and Forensics. It's me doing the case with you working undercover. Come on, think big.'

He stared at her. 'I can't believe you're serious.'

'Pop, you and other retired cops could help crack cold cases and bring justice to families. Maggie Stephens had a toddler.'

'Kaiden.'

'He'd be twenty today.'

'Twenty-four,' corrected the retired Detective Chief Inspector and Jo felt a tremor of pleasure.

'Let me run it by your former Senior Constable, Elly Rose.'

'DI Elly Rose,' corrected Robbo whose mind was buzzing. 'She was at the house in Collingwood the day we discovered Maggie's body.'

Jo handed him an envelope. 'I'll leave these files, Pop. No-one knows I've copied the originals. Have a read ... partner.'

He walked with her to the front gate. They embraced with a new energy. 'We'll talk soon, Detective Chief Inspector.'

He waited until Jo's car disappeared then walked along his garden path when a neighbour spotted him.

'G'day John. How y'goin?'

Robbo looked across and smiled. 'G'day Mary. You well?'

'Not bad for an old girl.'

He grinned en route to his front door. Anyone watching would have been surprised as the octogenarian broke into a skip.

Jo's planned visit with Jack Carr wasn't until later that evening but she took a detour and headed to Mont Albert. She knew the routine for the Carr kids. Grandpa Hugh would collect grandson Harry (and usually granddaughter Grace) and walk them home after school. Jo pulled up near the back of the school and wandered towards the gate. A few mothers and one older male were chatting, waiting for their offspring. Jo approached Hugh from behind. One mother nodded and Hugh turned. His smile was as wide as a Wimmera wheat field.

He and Jo embraced with the mothers hooked. When one realised Jo was the detective who featured on Katie Maguire's tabloid TV piece, tongues wagged. Then when Master Carr spotted his favourite ever policewoman, his greeting saw the mothers forget their own kids. The trio headed back to Jo's car with Harry asking questions and relaying news barely pausing for breath.

Grandma Peg was overwhelmed when her family and Jo entered the kitchen. Rags barked his joy. There were hugs all round and then everyone stopped because Grace, seated in her chair for feeding, banged her hands on the table.

'Look Grace, it's Jo,' said Peg who cried.

'Jo,' cried Grace and continued to slap the table. Jo moved to the girl and bent to kiss her.

'Hello Grace,' said Jo hoping like hell neither of them would cry.

Everyone stared at Grace who stopped slapping the table. She drew in a big breath. 'Hello ... Jo,' she spoke with difficulty.

To her grandparents it sounded like the winning entry in the Speech and Drama Section at Royal South Street. It was a huge breakthrough on so many grounds.

'Hey,' cried Harry. 'Grace is talking like before.'

Not quite but the boy's words summed up the heart-warming mood. Best of all was Grace's smile. She discovered how to grin. If every journey starts with a single step, Grace was away.

Jo explained her plan to drop in later and discreetly explained her sister's situation. Hugh and Peg naturally were sympathetic then invited Jo to stay for tea. Harry begged her to stay. Jo had so much on her mind—her sister, her job, DI Richelieu, her public profile—she wanted to keep moving but Harry's pleading sealed the deal.

Harry insisted on Jo taking him and Rags for a walk. When they returned, Dr Carr was there to greet them.

'Hello stranger,' he said kissing Jo's cheek. 'How lovely to see you again and not only do you solve the most complex of cases, you inspire my daughter to speak and smile and ...' He couldn't continue.

'Jo's staying for tea, Dad,' piped Harry.

'So I heard. That's great.'

'Well come on, young man,' said Hugh to Harry, 'bath time.'

Harry and Hugh disappeared and Peg helped Grace to her room. Jack and Jo sat at the kitchen table with Jo explaining sister Caitlyn's health crisis. Jack asked a question from time to time.

'She's in good hands, Jo. Those specialists have terrific reputations. Medicine's made huge strides and breast cancer patients today have something like a 90% chance of living for at least five years with many surviving well into old age.'

'It was so unexpected,' said Jo, 'and there's little history of the disease in my family.'

Jack could have said much more but wanted to get Jo back to happier thoughts. 'I'm really pleased to see you, Jo. We've all missed you. *I've* missed you.'

She hesitated and wanted to say *I've missed you too* but didn't. A silence settled in the room with both reluctant to speak. Revealing one's feelings seemed like a dangerous game.

'I'm glad you're staying. Harry will be over the moon.'

Jo's phone rang and Jack felt sick. Jo muttered, 'Excuse me,' and stood and moved away a little. 'Hello. ... Oh hello, sir. ... In the morning? ... Tonight? ... I'm not sure, sir. ...'

'Jo,' whispered Jack, 'if you have to go, go.' He hated saying it.

She half smiled and spoke again to the caller. 'What time? ... Okay. I'll see you there. Bye.'

She looked at the GP and felt terrible. She was dumping the good doctor and his family to go on a date with another man, a date date. DI Richelieu was flying to Paris first thing tomorrow. He wanted to thank Jo and say goodbye over dinner. He promised an early night.

When Harry arrived in his jim-jams and dressing-gown, the look on the face of his father and hero told all. He knew Detective Jo was a busy lady. He knew she must go when bad people did bad things.

'I'll come and see you as soon as I can, Harry, I promise,' said Jo. He hugged her then saluted. Jo kissed Hugh and Peg and walked to her car with Jack.

'If you want to talk about your sister, give me a bell.'

'Thanks Jack, I'm sure I'll have questions.'

'Anything, I'm happy to help.'

They reached her car. Jo felt pressure to tell Jack about the reason she was standing him up. Then she thought honesty may not necessarily be the best policy.

She turned to him. He was close. Without hesitating, she leant forward and kissed his lips, the first time she'd done so. He was not expecting that type of kiss, well that type of target and before he could respond or recover, she was in her car and closing the door.

Off to her dinner date with the mature Frenchman, she felt flat.

# 3

JO DROVE TO EAST MELBOURNE. She didn't want to rely on Pierre to get home. She might not make it home at all. They were to dine at *Il Duca,* a stroll from the DI's apartment. They'd been there before.

*Who else has he wined and dined in this restaurant, at this table?*

Richelieu opened up about the tasks he faced back in Paris and Jo felt envious and sad not going. He'd been given extended leave and was uncertain when he would return.

'If you feel you can leave your sister for a week or two, please ma chérie, let me know and I will 'ave your ticket arranged immediately.'

Jo smiled, whispered, 'Merci,' and continued eating.

The walk back to his apartment never eventuated as she insisted on going straight to her car. They stood beside the vehicle.

'I would be happy to feed your cat and water your pot plants, Pierre.'

He laughed. 'If only I 'ad them.'

They faced each other and stared into one another's eyes. She wanted to go to Paris with him tomorrow. She wanted to go back to his apartment tonight. She wanted to kiss him now. She did.

This was an advanced level of osculation involving body contact, arms and busy mouths. Jo faced a simple choice. Continue in a more comfortable venue or cut and run. She ran.

Pierre was miffed. He admired Jo as a brilliant detective but adored her femininity and body. He would never force himself upon any woman but knew she liked him and rejoiced as they finally expressed their feelings, not only with words but now actions.

'I must go, Pierre,' she said putting her hands on his chest. 'You have an early start and important tasks on the other side of the world. Please let me know how you go and I will think of you every day.'

Her words encouraged the former French policeman. He reckoned he'd made solid progress in wooing his colleague. He kissed her lightly on the lips, opened her door and guided her inside.

'Bon voyage, Monsieur,' she said and blew him a kiss. She drove home thinking about DI Pierre Richelieu's lips.


In the French capital, Yousef Jlassi opened a kitchen cupboard. Behind tins of soup and packets of pasta were the bomb ingredients. Nobody knew he had them or planned to wreak havoc in Paris. Nobody knew when. It depended on Yousef learning how to make a bomb.

Using the Internet would expose him. Government spies would smash him immediately if not sooner. Yousef needed bomb-making skills without being discovered. *How can I solve this problem?*


Back in Australia, retired Detective Chief Inspector Robbo Robertson poured over copies of documents his granddaughter lifted from the Cold Case files. The case was still vivid in Robbo's memory. He failed to solve it. Decades later, the killer of young mother, Maggie Stephens, remained at large. Yes, the killer might be dead but whoever he (or she) was, no criminal trial ever took place. It wasn't as if Robbo arrested a suspect and a jury returned a Not Guilty verdict. Nothing happened.

Robbo pondered the situation. *It's obvious my granddaughter is a brilliant detective but what on Earth is she thinking having me return to work? The woman is crazy.*


Gabrielle Strange studied the murder victim, Simon Grovene. Forensic pathology was her bag and bloody good she was too. The coins and secateurs didn't harm the deceased. There was a bullet in the room and powder residue from a gun on the victim's clothes.

The chisel was the weapon in the body but Dr Strange discovered a deeper wound caused by a large knife, a bayonet or sword. The chisel was placed in the chest after Sonny Jim was no more.

There were no marks or wounds on the victim's hands, arms or legs and his back was pristine. The dead man died facing his attacker. Why did he not fight? Surely he would have seen a large knife coming straight at him. And the attacker was either short or kneeling when he or she thrust the blade into Simon.

The body was arranged and the secateurs and coins placed post mortem. As to why, Strange offered no opinion. Her boast about doubling as a profiler was baloney, her little joke. She signed her report and the corpse was placed in its cubby-hole.

Richelieu travelled light. He needed a suit for his mother's funeral, and for business meetings with lawyers and estate agents. He purchased a single ticket not knowing when he would return. Money was not an issue for Pierre. He was granted compassionate leave. It's not every day your mother drops dead on the other side of the world.

He flew business class with Qantas and landed at Charles de Gaulle (CDG) airport. It was 10 months since he was last in France and as he passed through Customs, the death of his mother became especially poignant. She would not be here to greet him—ever again.

He took a train from the airport to Gare du Nord in central Paris, and then a taxi the five kilometres to Rue Crémieux in the 12th arrondissement. He paid the driver and stood at the end of the now famous street. The houses were painted in different pastel colours. On the footpaths, terracotta pots with their blooming mini gardens smiled at him. Even an independent cat sitting on the cobbles gave him a look. *I know you,* mused the feline. Pierre felt he was home.

Outside the house, he hesitated. He knew what his mother looked like, her perfume, her hair. He knew exactly what she would say.

'Oh Pierre, où étais-tu?' (Oh Pierre, where have you been?)

He looked up at a first floor window. The window box was perfect. He waited. *Will she open the window, wave and call to me?* No.

Opening the door caused chest pain. All the tears he shed in Melbourne, the restless nights, the unbelievable sorrow knowing his mother could and should be still alive if she'd been able to summon help, crowded in on him. He closed the door, sat on the stairs and wept.

The thought kept coming back to him. If he rang and got no answer, he could have called her best friend. He knew blaming himself was pointless but having no belief in God, who else could he blame?

Only a few kilometres away, Émile Bastien was making love. He had a list of lovers and today being Tuesday, Monique was the designated concubine. They may have been making love but feelings of love were nowhere to be enjoyed. This was lust, impure and simple.

Bastien's phone rang. He was a walk-and-chew-gum simultaneously kinda guy so kept thrusting as he answered the mobile.

'Yeah?'

'Monsieur, this is Claude from Customs at the airport.'

'Who?'

'You told me to call if certain people came into the country.'

'What people?'

'You want me to say the name?'

'Yes. Yes. Yes. Yeeeesss!'

Claude was confused. It sounded like the man who worked for Laris of Paris was doing something or someone. He was—Monique. Bastien, having reached the smoke-a-cigarette-time, paid attention to the caller.

Bastien remembered Claude from Customs was on his payroll and would earn his wedge if he informed the former cop about the whereabouts of certain individuals. One of the names on Claude's list was Pierre Grégory Richelieu. Bastien lost interest in Tuesday's lover.

Richelieu showered, changed then searched. On a recent trip to Paris, his mother discussed her will. Richelieu laughed not wanting to discuss her demise. She showed him the file with her personal and legal documents. She insisted he take her solicitor's details back to Australia.

He entered her bedroom and felt awful. She died on the bathroom floor unable to raise the alarm. He refused to enter her bathroom. He found the file with her will. It made a modest provision for her charities—cats and an order of nuns to which her cousin belonged. The remainder, the bulk of her estate was left to her only child, her son.

Pierre was wealthy thanks to maternal grandparents but his wealth expanded. His mother had a powerful share portfolio and her house would have buyers super keen to buy. Mother had cash as well.

A friend of Pierre's mother rang him in Australia with the heartbreaking news of her sudden death. Later he rang his mother's law firm asking them to choose a quality funeral director.

Once in Paris, Pierre made an appointment to see the solicitor. Examining his mother's papers, he found his father's Florida address and phone number. Did this stranger know his first wife was dead? As Richelieu had no contact with his father, he did nothing.

Jet lag kicked in but the detective shunned sleep. He went for a walk heading towards Rue de Lyon not knowing he was being followed.

# 4

JO FELT LOUSY. Her sister could die. The media kept chasing Jo for interviews. She missed a trip to Paris and she walked out on the Carr family, so to help lighten her misery, she went to work and sat in as the Simon Grovene homicide was discussed.

Simon developed an army of enemies. He owed money all over town and his ability to close companies, declare bankruptcy then continue trading under another name using others as a front, sent already furious creditors into apoplexy. The homicide detectives quickly saw their problem. DS Billy Hughes ran the meeting.

'Sarge, I've got 19 people with motive, means and opportunity to kill this bastard, sorry, victim,' said Charlie Baldwin.

'I've got 23,' said DS Fleming, 'with more to come.'

'Yes, all right,' replied Hughes. 'We must eliminate the impossible.'

Jo smiled as Hughes copies Dr Strange and her Sherlockian quotes.

DI Rose observed and, unlike her predecessor, chipped in with ideas. 'The pathology report should help eliminate suspects. The weapon was a long knife or sword. The killer is short or was kneeling when striking the fatal blow. The blade was thrust deep requiring considerable force. The bullet recovered in the wall was from a Browning 9 MM pistol. Who amongst the suspects has a firearm? Who is short and strong or fit and able to kneel? We need a plan, Sergeant.'

'Thank you, ma'am,' replied Billy being told the bleeding obvious.

'Now Forensics,' said Billy. 'We need whatever they've got on the secateurs, chisel and coins.'

'We've lost our key contact, Sarge,' smiled Baldwin. Others looked at him. He looked at Jo. They remembered how Jo was misled by a forensics officer who had the hots for her.

'Congratulations, Charlie, you're the new gofer for Forensics.'

Lots of laughter as Jo grinned and Baldwin suffered.

Jo had a thought. 'Is it possible we're looking in the wrong direction, Sarge?' Silence. Here was the least experienced detective, who outshone everyone to solve the serial killer murders. Her arrest record was impressive and her thoughts were certainly respected.

'How so?' asked Billy.

'Well his creditors may produce the killer but could someone not a creditor have killed him under the cover of his financial crimes.'

'What, a jilted lover?' asked Rose.

'Or the husband of said lover,' added Fleming.

'Or the real estate agent who was there to show him the house but was paid to assassinate the deceased,' added Stephen Payne who surprised everyone with his thinking.

'Thanks for nothing, Jo,' said Hughes dreading the growing list of suspects. 'And I thought you were on leave.'

'She can't keep away,' joked Baldwin winking at Jo.

'Right,' said Hughes wanting to make progress and wishing DIs Richelieu or Rose were the OIC. 'Let's work on the following areas.'

She gave directions, the detectives went to work and Jo approached DI Rose. 'May I have a word, ma'am?'

'Sure. My office in five.'


Robbo Robertson didn't sleep well. Nothing unusual there since his wife of 55 years went into care, her dementia causing him ongoing grief. But now he acquired a new concern. One of his granddaughters was seriously ill and her sister, Detective Senior Constable Joanna Best, recently offered him a job. Well not exactly a *Dixon of Dock Green* type job but he was to help solve his last case when head of Homicide.

He regarded it as a well-meaning idea, an attempt to help him think less of his ailing wife. But the more he thought about it, the more excited he became. Why couldn't he be a sort of PI, an unofficial detective? After all, this was his case all those years ago and it was still unsolved. He thought of an idea and decided to test the waters.


The Belgrave station hummed; it was the HQ for the narrow-gauge tourist railway known as Puffing Billy. Robbo joined the crowd. Tourists, kids, retirees and train lovers climbed aboard the latest "express" with its top speed of about 15 mph. The stationmaster, resplendent in his uniform, watched as the guard blew a whistle and waved a flag. The engine whistle shrieked and the loco strained as it set off into the beautiful Dandenong Ranges.

'G'day Tucky,' said a voice and the stationmaster turned. His face became a mix of surprise and delight.

'Boss, is that you?' Robbo moved towards the former Homicide detective, DS Raymond Tuck, and the men enjoyed an energetic handshake. 'What the hell are you doing here?'

'I could ask the same bloody question.' They laughed.

'You're looking well. How are ya?'

'Good but look, this isn't a social visit. Do you fancy a cuppa?'

'Sure. Me shift is almost done.'

'I know.'

Tuck shook his head. 'Why am I not surprised?'

They sat and enjoyed their tea. Tuck was quietly excited. *If this was bad news, Robbo would not be grinning. What the hell is going on?*

Robbo explained his granddaughter's suggestion. Tucky remained silent. Robbo began his sales pitch.

'So I've decided. I'm in but I can't do this without my best sergeant. We'd naturally have to work around your Puffing Billy shifts but it shouldn't be a problem. So, Detective Sergeant Tuck, are you in?'

Silence from the SM. 'The wife'll kill me but, hey, let's do it.'

They clinked tea cups and grinned.


'Come in, Jo,' said DI Rose. 'What's the latest with your sister?' Jo gave a redacted version thinking too much information to anyone not close to the family was probably unwise. 'So what can I do?' asked the boss.

'I have a suggestion that might solve a case you once worked on.' Boy did that get Rose's attention.

'*I* worked on?'

Jo explained her idea about having her grandfather, Rose's former boss, unofficially work on solving the murder of Maggie Stephens in Collingwood in 1996. Rose didn't interrupt until Jo finished.

'I can see you're serious.' Jo didn't reply. 'You make a good case, Jo, but there are red flags everywhere. The media would have a field Day. *Dad's Army joins the police. New Tricks Down Under.* Then there's insurance, union and workplace regs, costs, legals, blah, blah, blah.'

Jo let her boss point out why this shouldn't, couldn't and wouldn't work. When Rose finished, Jo went for the jugular.

'I think you need to understand, ma'am, this will go ahead whether the powers agree or not.' Rose glared. 'If an experienced ex-copper wants to think about solving a cold case, there's nothing anybody can do to stop him. And if he chooses to walk along a public street in which a murder took place, what are you going to do, arrest him?'

Rose liked Jo and admired her sleuthing skills but hated a junior officer telling her how to behave. She chose her response with care.

'To quote the Yanks, Senior, "You can't fight City Hall". I know your grandfather and am getting to know you. I'd hate to see either of you get hurt. My friendly advice is "hasten slowly". Out of respect for your grandfather, I'll give the idea some thought but I'll be surprised if HQ don't kill it stone dead. Now go and help DS Hughes find a killer.'

'Ma'am,' said Jo and left feeling she'd been dismissed from the principal's office with her tail between her legs. She had.

The car crept along the dirt track. This was bushfire country deep in the Yarra Valley, 50 kilometres from Melbourne.

'Bugger me, would you look at that,' said the passenger.

'Friend of yours?' asked the driver.

They stopped and a man with masses of hair approached. The travellers alighted. 'Can I help you, gents?' he asked.

'Colin?' queried the passenger.

'Sarge?' spluttered the bewhiskered homeowner.

'Stand to attention for a senior officer,' snapped the driver.

'Bloody hell, as I live and breathe—DCI Robbo Robertson and DS Raymond Tucky Tuck. How the heck are ya?'

The former Detective Senior Constable Colin Melk headed straight for his former colleagues and they shook hands and laughed.

'So you lost your razor then?' goaded Tuck.

Melk ruffled his long hair and beard. 'Guilty as charged.' More laughter. They went inside and Melk boiled the billy. They sat and let Melk tell his life story, well, the last 15 years of it.

'My marriage went south. I didn't wanna stay policing and looked for something completely different. I bought this place, built some cabins out the back and became an alpaca farmer. I rent the cabins, shear the alpacas, get a couple of expert knitters to make all sorts of woollen knick-knacks and sell 'em here and in gift shops around the Valley.' He held out his hands. 'Life is just a bowl of cherries.' He grinned. 'But I'm dead-set bewildered as to why the hell you're here.'

'We're alpaca lovers,' said Tuck telling the biggest lie of his life.

Robbo told Melk the plan to try and crack the Maggie Stephens cold case. The more he said, the more Melk looked gobsmacked.

Tuck took over. 'So wotcha reckon, Colin. Are you in or are you in?'

'You're mad, both of you, nutcases.' He paused and shook his head then shouted. 'But it's the best bloody idea I've ever heard.'

The kitchen cum lounge cum office filled with laughter. They all spoke over the top of one another until Tuck interrupted.

'Hey, hey, we haven't got a name. What are we gunna be called?'

'*The Three Amigos*,' said Melk.

'Or *The Three Musketeers*,' added Tuck.

'Or WATTI,' said Robbo. Confusion reigned. Robbo explained. '*We Are The Three Idiots*.' Even more laughter.

DI Rose went to her regular meeting with John Crowley, the Assistant Commissioner (Crime), and her boss. The AC took a risk supporting Rose as head of Homicide and wanted to keep on top of all she did.

Rose explained the latest homicide and its many suspects. They discussed staffing levels and budgets.

Crowley asked about his favourite Senior Constable, giving Rose the opportunity to raise the loopy idea about Jo's grandfather becoming an unofficial cop. Rose finished poo-pooing the idea and waited for the AC's affirmation. Then she nearly died.

'Brilliant, Elly. I knew you'd get the squad firing. DI Steele had everyone afraid to suggest anything. Jo Best's been inspired by your terrific people skills.'

Rose felt sick. 'I'm glad you like the idea, sir,' she said, lying.

'There has to be a way to make this happen. Create a report on the pros and cons of Robbo Robertson becoming a consultant. I knew you were the right person for the job.'

*Oh shit* thought Rose. He held out his hand. Rose shook it and left feeling she'd been dismissed from the principal's office with her tail between her legs. She had.

# 5

RICHELIEU WANDERED THE STREETS, feeling good in his beloved Paris. He grew up here. He worked here. And it was autumn, his favourite time. Couples with sweaters and scarves held hands for added warmth. Their language drove him to eavesdrop. He stopped at a curb side café and watched the world go by. He wandered again and sat on a park bench. His mother loved walking, loved seeing and being seen. Her style rubbed off on her son. They would walk arm in arm on a crisp winter's afternoon. Luxurious scarves, coats, gloves and quality boots. Now, never again would he tease and delight in her company.

He arrived home and something caught his eye. He looked at the mail on the hall table. A letter from his mother's cousin was the envelope he placed at the top of the pile. Now another envelope sat there. It was a bill from a local florist. His mother loved fresh flowers.

*I'm certain cousin Eva's letter was the one on top.*

He shrugged and headed upstairs. He was sad and hungry and bloody tired. He didn't bother to wash, clean his teeth or even undress. He kicked off his shoes, flopped face down on the bed and slept.

He woke and hunger kicked in. Seven hours sleep killed his jet lag. A long shower washed away his grime but made no inroads on his sadness. He boiled two eggs, devoured chunky toast and honey, and drank a lot of his mother' coffee. He shaved and shoe-shined and set off for the unpleasant task of arranging his mother's funeral.

He took a taxi to his mother's solicitor. The firm had long handled her affairs and an old secretary remembered Pierre as a child.

He was greeted with respect and affection and settled in the office of a senior partner. After the usual condolences, the business began.

'Everything in your mother's will is in order, Monsieur. If you wish for this company to administer your mother's estate, we would be honoured to do so.'

'That is my wish.'

'Very well, Monsieur. I will prepare a report showing how you can access your mother's bank accounts and share portfolio, and do what you will with your charming house in Rue Crémieux.'

'Merci,' replied Pierre not wanting to raise the other matter.

'Following your instructions from Australia, we have engaged one of the finest funeral directors in Paris and they await your orders. If you wish, we can handle these matters for you.'

'Merci but no,' replied Pierre.

The solicitor hesitated. 'Have you been able to visit your mother?'

Pierre's face spoke. He shook his head. Before the solicitor could reply, there was a door knock and a man's head appeared. He spoke with an upper-class English accent.

'So sorry to interrupt, Maurice, but I'm rather keen on that file.'

'Of course,' said Maurice hopping up. 'Come in, Antony.' The visitor was introduced. 'Detective Inspector Pierre Richelieu meet the Honourable Antony Heron-Royhay.'

They shook hands. 'My condolences on your recent loss, Monsieur,' said the Englishman.

'Merci,' said Pierre not interested in small talk or any talk.

The senior partner gave the wanted file to his colleague. 'You two may well have met had the detective remained in Paris.' Both men were curious. 'Mr Heron-Royhay is our criminal expert helping set free those who have been arrested, and Detective Richelieu was once an officer with the French National Police here in Paris.'

The men smiled again and the barrister departed.

'Here are some documents for your signature, Monsieur.'

Pierre signed then left for the funeral parlour. He felt terrible and would have felt worse if he knew he was being followed. The person observing rang her employer and described Pierre's movements.

The funeral parlour was in a magnificent Parisian building—solid, regal and befitting the care of the deceased. Staff members were respectful. The funeral details were straightforward. Pierre wanted what his mother wanted—a lack of fuss. He signed the contract then dreaded the next activity.

His mother lay in an expensive casket in a small, air-conditioned room. Pierre waited outside. The attendant avoided Pierre's personal space then opened the door and stood back.

'Please take your time, Monsieur.'

Pierre paused then entered. He approached the open coffin. This was a first. Dead bodies were part of a homicide detective's job, a regular occurrence. But this was different. He had a huge emotional investment in this body. He stood beside the coffin and closed his eyes.

The attendant spoke. 'When you are ready to leave, Monsieur, please press the buzzer.' The attendant closed the door.

Pierre paused with eyes shut tight. How long he stood there he didn't know. He opened his eyes. His mother looked peaceful which only made his heart ache more. His pain was a combination of losing his mother and the possibility she could still be alive if she'd been able to summon help. Her dying, alone and in pain on the bathroom floor with help close at hand was a vision he could not forget.

He spoke as if his mother were alive. He told her about his life in Australia, his cases, his favourite colleague. Oh he dwelt on her. 'You would like Joanna, Maman. She is beautiful, brave, clever and loyal. And she would like you. She would make you laugh.'

As he spoke he paid no attention to the tears decorating his cheeks. Finally he blew his nose. He felt better and relieved.

He wiped his face, bent over his mother and kissed her forehead.

'Goodbye my darling. I have always loved you and I always will.' He placed a hand on her clasped hands and squeezed gently.

He forgot the buzzer and opened the door. The attendant was surprised and hurried towards him.

Pierre stepped into the fresh air and walked. He was several kilometres from Rue Crémieux but in honour of his dear mother, he walked.

When it rained, he kept walking. He lifted the collar of his coat, tugged his cap tighter, shoved his hands in his pockets and walked. By the time he reached home, he was soaked. He didn't care. He would change then make a phone call to Australia. He wanted to hear the voice on a certain Senior Constable.

Jo Best snored. Not sharing a bed, there was no-one to advise her of these nocturnal mutterings. It was midnight in Melbourne and Jo was well into dreamland when her phone trilled.

Phone calls at odd times are common for homicide detectives. People are murdered at all hours and sleuths are sometimes in the Land of Nod when called into action. Jo reached for her phone not bothering to check caller ID.

She spoke with a husky voice. 'Jo Best speaking'.

'Bonjour Mademoiselle and 'ow are you?'

Jo sat up. 'Pierre?'

'Oui, it is Pierre your favourite Franco Aussie.'

Jo worried. 'Are you all right?'

'Much better now I 'ave 'eard your sweet voice.'

'You do know what time it is?'

'What is time when your 'eart commands you to sing?'

'Are you drunk, Pierre?'

'Oui, drunk on love, ma chérie. So please, 'ow are you? Make me 'appy and tell me you miss me.'

'Pierre it's nearly midnight here and I was asleep.'

He changed. 'Oh, pardon, Mademoiselle.' He felt guilty and the sadness of the visit to see his mother crowded in. He cried softly, enough for Jo to tell. She sensed his mood and spoke with sympathy.

'What has happened, Pierre? Have you arranged the funeral?'

'Oui.' He paused. 'I saw 'er and she looked peaceful and beautiful.'

There were pauses in their conversation. Jo said, 'I've been thinking about you, Pierre.'

'I told my mother about you, 'ow enchanting and clever and beautiful you are, and 'ow she would like you very much.'

Jo thought grief, alcohol and distance made him speak like this. She changed the subject hoping to change the mood.

'We have a new and tricky homicide with any number of suspects. And without you, Inspector, we're in a mess. You are missed, Pierre. We need you.'

'Ah, but the real question, Mademoiselle remains. Do *you* miss me?'

She hesitated, which only heightened the tension. 'I do, Pierre but now I must get some sleep. Take care, Inspector. Au revoir.'

She hung up not hearing him say, 'I love you, Joanna Best.'

# 6

DI ROSE WAS MISERABLE. Her brightest detective came up with a crazy idea involving her retired grandfather returning to active police service. *God help us, he's gotta be 80 if he's a day*, thought the DI.

Rose politely told Jo it was a dumb idea and to forget it. Cheekily, the young detective hinted Robbo would investigate a particular cold case regardless. *The nerve of the girl.*

But when Rose told the Assistant Commissioner (Crime) about the preposterous suggestion expecting him to agree with her, she crashed. Not only did the AC like the idea, he ordered Rose to come up with a proposal to make sure it happened.

*Shit! I have to write a detailed proposal, and tell my underling her madcap suggestion is brilliant. Shit again!*

To create a plan to enable her former boss to investigate a crime they worked on 22 years ago, Rose began by watching *New Tricks*.

Robbo double-checked his supper supplies, and plumped cushions. He told his granddaughter nothing about his visits to Ray Tuck and Colin Melk. He wanted to be sure they were fair dinkum before he made any announcement about WATTI - *We Are The Three Idiots*.

His visitors arrived together, Colin having picked up Ray.

Handshakes all round, visits to the loo—not surprising as these three scored a cumulative age of about 200—before they began.

Robbo doled out Jo's documents. The men flicked through them. Then Robbo handed out screeds he'd produced over the last few days. He took this seriously.

'These are people we interviewed, or didn't but should have.'

Tuck and Melk shook their heads at the amount of information. 'We can't do this on our own, Robbo,' said Tuck. 'Finding let alone interviewing this lot will take forever.'

'I've got me alpacas, boss. I'm keen to help but this is big. And what happens about pay and expenses?'

'Look,' replied Robbo. 'My granddaughter reckons I can help her solve the Maggie Stephens murder. It's too big for me but with you two, we might get somewhere. If it's too hard, just say.' Tuck and Melk kept quiet. 'I told Jo she was crazy but she took it to her boss.'

'Fancy little Elly Rose running Homicide,' said Melk.

'I wouldn't call her little if I were you,' said Robbo.

'And?' asked Tuck.

'Haven't heard. I'm sure Jo would tell me if the idea was canned.'

'So how do we do this?' asked Melk.

'We draw up a plan. I give it to Jo, she gives it to Elly and then we wait. If it gets the all clear, and you still want to be involved, we move forward. If they say no or if you two want to pull out, we go back to the alpacas, Puffing Billy and runner beans. Okay?' The others nodded. 'Right, you lot start reading and I'll get the coffee.'

'Tea,' said both guests simultaneously.

Robbo pottered in the kitchen when his phone rang. 'Robertson.'

'Hi Pop, it's Jo.'

'Hello Senior Constable. How did the DI react to your crazy idea?'

'She seemed interested,' Jo lied. 'Listen Pop, I'm on my way to see Caitlyn and have more cold case material. I'll drop it in.'

'Okay, when?'

'Five minutes. Bye.'

Robbo entered the lounge looking worried. 'Bad news?' asked Tuck.

'It's Jo. She's got more material for me to read.'

'For *us* to read,' corrected Melk.

'Of course,' replied Robbo. There was a break for think music.

'You haven't told her about us,' said Tuck looking at Robbo.

'I was going to come up with a plan first.'

'Should we hide under the bed or in the wardrobe?' asked Tuck.

'Don't be daft,' said Robbo.

Melk joked. 'My ex used to say I was buried so deep in the wardrobe, my best friends were the Lion and the Witch.'

Robbo barked. 'Knock it off. She'll be thrilled to meet you and to have you on the team.'

The others looked at an unsure Robbo. Then the doorbell rang and he left. Tuck looked at Melk.

'I've never met the wonder cop. You?' Melk shook his head.

Robbo's voice was heard in the hallway. 'I've got a couple of former colleagues over for a chat. Come and say hello.'

Jo entered smiling. Both visitors stood for introductions. Everyone stared at the elephant in the room—a vast array of documents on tables, spare chairs, the floor, arm rests and even the mantelpiece.

'Well I guess this is not a book club,' said Jo. Everyone laughed.

Robbo explained. 'I've kinda made an early start on our cold case.'

'I see. And are these your filing clerks?' The males laughed.

'I thought retired cops who worked with me on the Maggie Stephens murder might help. Many hands make light work.'

'I'm impressed,' said Jo. 'Brilliant idea, Pop.'

Looking at Jo's bundle of papers, Melk asked, 'Have you brought some more paperwork, Detective?'

'Ah yes, it's the path reports.'

'Medicals over there,' said Tuck pointing. Jo hesitated, grinned and placed the new material on a pile by the fireplace.

'How's your sister?' asked Melk. 'Your grandfather told us about her situation.'

'She's not too bad, considering. I'm on my way to see her now.'

Robbo wanted a direct answer in front of his team. 'So Senior, what did DI Rose say about your plan to involve Dad's Army?'

Jo's face answered first. 'To be honest, gentlemen, she thought it was crazy. But,' she added raising a pointed finger, 'when she learns that three officers with whom she once worked are raring to go, I reckon she'll hightail it to the AC and get his blessing.'

The others didn't believe her. Jo didn't believe herself. But brave faces appeared.

'We've even got a name,' said Melk, and Robbo and Tuck inwardly groaned. 'It's WATTI.' Naturally Jo looked confused. *We Are The Three Idiots.*

Jo shook her head. 'You're mad and I love what you're doing but I have to go. It's been lovely to meet you gentlemen.'

They reciprocated and Robbo followed his granddaughter.

'Give my love to your sister,' said Robbo.

'Will do.' She looked at him. 'I'm not sure where this'll lead, Pop, but I reckon the journey could be pretty damn interesting.'

She leant in and kissed him then walked to her car.

Next morning Jo pestered Billy Hughes for something to do re the homicide in Kew. 'Come on, Sarge, there's gotta be something.'

'Ask DS Fleming. He'll have witness statements to check.'

'Thanks Sarge,' said Jo and went looking for Fleming. She heard her name and turned.

'My office, Senior,' called DI Rose who turned and walked away. Jo followed dreading the tone of voice her boss used. 'Sit,' said Rose.

Jo thought she'd strike the first blow. 'DS Hughes has asked me to work on collating witness statements for the Kew homicide ma'am.'

'Forget it.'

Jo was confused. 'Ma'am?'

'I want you to concentrate on the Collingwood cold case from 1996.'

Jo's mouth mimicked a fish. 'Do I work alone, ma'am?'

'No, you'll work with your grandfather.'

Jo's goldfish routine continued. 'I thought, ma'am ...'

'Don't think, Senior. I'm working on a plan where you'll investigate a cold case with help from a retired officer. I want you to ask DCI Robertson if he's interested. Do you understand?'

'Yes ma'am?'

'Do you think he might consider the idea?'

Jo worried. *Should I tell the truth?* She did. 'I'm afraid DCI Robertson's a little ahead of us, ma'am.'

Rose was hooked. She made serious eye contact. 'Meaning?'

'He's made contact with other retired officers and all three have made a start on that particular cold case.'

Rose mixed her surprise with anger. 'Other retired officers? Who?'

Jo trembled. 'DS Tuck and Detective Senior Constable Melk.'

Flames metaphorically spurted from Rose's beehive hairstyle. 'Tucky and Colin Melk? Are you winding me up?'

'No ma'am.'

'Robbo Robertson's dragged in two former officers, both of whom worked with me on that murder, and set up some sort of *New Tricks* operation without anyone knowing or approving it?'

'Well, if you didn't know about it, ma'am, it would be impossible to approve it.'

Rose leant back. She knew her brilliant senior constable wasn't being a smartarse. 'How the hell did you find Tuck and Melk?'

'Nothing to do with me, ma'am.'

Rose was stunned. 'Robbo found them?'

'He did.'

'What are those two reprobates doing these days?'

'DS Tuck's a stationmaster on Puffing Billy and Colin Melk runs a B and B on his alpaca farm.'

Rose blew air. 'Bloody hell,' she expelled, then decided to come clean. 'Look, I'll be honest, Jo. I thought your idea was dumb and a waste of time. I told AC Crowley who thought it was the best thing since sliced bread and asked me to prepare a case for your grandfather to become some sort of consultant to Victoria Police.' Jo's heartbeat jumped. 'And now Robbo's jumped in at the deep end, the AC will be over the moon.' She looked at Jo. 'Looks like you've landed a new job, Senior, working with your grandfather and a couple of retirees.'

'Is that with or for, ma'am?'

'You're in charge and those ratbags will be working for you.'

Jo smiled.

# 7

YOUSEF DESPAIRED. He was a lone wolf terrorist planning a devastating blast in a busy Parisian venue with a suicide bomb to follow but didn't know how to make the devices.

As a potential terrorist, he behaved impeccably. He told no-one and flew under the radar of police and security agencies. But he was stymied. He had the ingredients but not the knowledge. Seeking help could kill his project. Being discovered would end it. For Yousef to get this far and be stopped would, for him, be a catastrophe.

*How can I learn to make a bomb and not be found? Help!*

He became a pretend tourist looking for the best spot to detonate a bomb. He would place it amongst a large crowd. Then, wearing a suicide vest, he would set off another weapon of mass destruction taking martyr Yousef straight to Paradise.

But the longer he delayed, the greater the risk. What if there was a fire or gas leak in his apartment building? The authorities might accidentally discover his material. It was time to take the big risk.

At the local mosque, Yousef sat on the floor and listened to the words of indoctrination. The meeting ended and a young man beside Yousef turned to him. 'I haven't seen you before. I'm Javed.'

'Yousef,' he said wishing he'd used a false name.

They chatted about the inspirational leader with neither giving any personal details. Loose lips sink terrorists. Javed suggested coffee.

They sat in a café and Yousef kept thinking of ways he could ask for information without revealing his plans. There didn't seem to be a right way. Javed acted the same. They talked about "the struggle" in general but when Javed mentioned football they discovered they both supported Paris Saint-Germain and the conversation went to a new level. The men spoke about a second meeting, not at the mosque but at the Parc des Princes, the home of PSG.

They parted and Yousef, despite his relaxed demeanour, still wasn't sure about his new friend. He trusted nobody. They walked in opposite directions and Yousef, crossing the road, looked back. There was Javed heading away without looking back. Yousef relaxed and headed home.

He didn't know Javed was an undercover police officer working with two colleagues who waited for a signal. Javed, not his real name, was in deep cover mixing with potential terrorists. Javed and his colleagues belonged to RAID, an elite French counter-terrorism unit.

Javed's signal was simple. He would stand still for a moment, hitch his rucksack and then head off away from the target. Javed gave the signal and two highly-trained operatives followed Yousef. Without trying to attract attention, Yousef did just that. Worse, he didn't know.

One surprising aspect of human trafficking is how many of the criminals in this vile practice are female. In fact being a woman can give the criminal an advantage.

Adamma was 15 and lived with her family in Nigeria. Dirt poor was accurate and the family struggled to survive. When a charming black woman ingratiated herself into their home, Adamma's fate was sealed.

The visitor offered Adamma a wonderful job in Europe working for a kind and wealthy family. Adamma would send money to her parents and could return to Nigeria at any time. The fake NGO the woman claimed to represent would provide Adamma with a passport, visa and ticket. And better still, Adamma's parents would be paid, what to them was a small fortune, for allowing their daughter to leave home.

This scam, this pernicious crime thrives today. The innocents are transported to Europe and exploited in modern-day sex-slavery. Some are in domestic servitude in private homes where they are rarely paid and suffer beatings and sexual abuse. Some work on farms for peanuts with no rights. Some, like Adamma, are forced into prostitution. They engage with sex partners who are animals, which of course is a slur on the animal kingdom. The women are degraded.

Adamma turned 16 when she started her horrendous life. When not being with the bastards who raped her, Adamma found her pimp to be as bad as the clients. Every day was a gruesome Groundhog Day.

But for the criminals, this was big money and one such criminal was Yousef's brother, Laris. He was the brains of the business. He paid the black woman to go to Nigeria and recruit Adamma. He gave Adamma to one of his pimps who gave Laris cash every week. There were no tax problems for Laris as his bagman, former policeman, Émile Bastien, a money launderer par excellence, washed the dirty money.

And Laris was evil. If anyone crossed him, he killed first and ignored questions. No wonder Yousef steered well clear of big brother.

Émile Bastien was a creep. As a cop in Paris he pressured women for sex. At break-ins he helped himself to cash and worse, he tipped off villains when the police were closing in, all for a generous cash tip.

But such corruption came to an end thanks to brilliant sleuthing by a colleague, Lieutenant Intern Pierre Richelieu. Bastien was jailed.

Prison is never pleasant for a corrupt cop. Bastien seethed for years and, like an elephant, a slighted criminal never forgets. Richelieu's name was implanted in Bastien's brain, and if Pierre had remained in France, he would have been murdered. Going to Oz saved his life.

Bastien tried to contact criminals Down Under and pay them to do what he couldn't. He failed. Aussie crims had never heard of Bastien and killing a cop guaranteed a massive police response.

Richelieu was safe in Oz but now back in France, life was different. Bastien called on his employer and fellow criminal, Laris of Paris.

'I need a favour, Laris. The bastard who shafted me all those years ago is back in Paris.'

'What, permanently?'

'Not sure. I heard his old girl died.'

'Well give me his photo and address and he can join her.'

'I don't want him dead.'

'No problem. For the same price we can fuck his kneecaps, chop off his hands, and tattoo his forehead. I know a bloody good tatt artist,' he said rolling up a sleeve, 'look.'

'Not necessary,' replied Bastien feeling queasy at the thought of even his worst enemy having his kneecaps and hands butchered.

'I thought you hated the prick.'

'I do, which is why I've got a plan and I need a favour.' Bastien explained his plan and Laris laughed.

'No way, no fucking way.'

# 8

BILLY HUGHES WAS UP FOR A WHINGE. She landed in DI Rose's office. 'Ma'am, we have four possible candidates for the Kew murder.'

'I heard it was forty-four.'

'It was until we cut all those with a cast-iron alibi.'

'But any of the creditors could have paid for a hit.'

'True, ma'am, but we have to start somewhere.'

'Go on.'

'We're waiting on Forensics for the bullet, chisel, secateurs and coins and we've got second interviews with the four possibles.'

'Not forgetting a robbery gone wrong or an angry lover.'

'And with DI Richelieu away for possibly weeks, Jo Best now tells me she's on some cold case. What the hell is that all about?'

'The AC asked me to produce a plan on how we might use retired detectives to work on cold cases.'

'Retired detectives?'

'It's a small trial with a murder back in 1996. Because Jo Best came up with the idea, the AC wants her to liaise with the retirees.'

'Ma'am, there's a killer on the loose; DI Richelieu's on indefinite leave and our best detective is entertaining pensioners. We need help.'

'I'm working on it. Until then, make do with what you've got.'

'Ma'am,' said Hughes who wanted to leave.

'And Billy, keep the retired detectives thing under your hat.'

'Ma'am.'

Billy entered the incident room. 'What's happening, Sarge?' asked Charlie Baldwin.

'I've no idea when DI Richelieu is coming home, and now Jo Best is on some special assignment.' The others complained. 'Don't start; it's nothing to do with me. Now, these four interviews, Stephen, you're with me and we'll take Shoreham and Devlin. Charlie you're with DS Fleming and you've got Ward and Bello. The rest of you chase up Forensics, and all those phone responses.'

There was movement at the station and as the quartet headed along the corridor, Fleming sang. 'A hunting we will go, a-hunting we will go.' Baldwin joined in. 'Hey ho the dairy-o, a hunting we will go.'

They were happy but in her office, DI Rose grimaced.

Not far away, Detective Senior Constable Jo Best waited outside the office of AC (Crime) John Crowley who appeared smiling.

'Come in, Detective' He held out his hand. 'And again, many congratulations on your splendid work with those serial killers.'

'Thank you, sir.'

'Now DI Rose has produced a brilliant proposal on how we can take advantage of former officers working on unsolved cold cases.' He paused. 'Is that tautologous? By definition, a cold case *is* unsolved. Anyway, I digress. How are you?'

'Well, thank you, sir.'

'I've run the proposal past the legal eagles, the association, and Commissioner who, apart from a few queries, has given his blessing.'

'Thank you, sir.'

'No, thank *you*, Detective. So what's happened with recruitment?'

Jo explained how DCI Robertson persuaded two of his retired colleagues to join and how all three officers were involved in the original investigation.

'Excellent. Now I've asked DI Rose to release you from normal duties and you will be OIC reporting directly to her. Clear?'

'Yes sir, thank you.'

'And stop all this "thank you" business. We're the ones thanking you.'

'Yes sir.'

'Now, questions, problems, requests?'

'Not immediately, sir, but if there are issues, I'll consult DI Rose.'

Crowley stood and moved to the door. 'You've come up with another brilliant idea, Jo. Good luck.'

They shook hands and Jo left wondering if her so-called brilliant idea would cause her grief.

Hughes and Payne arrived at the building site of a new home. Inside was Gareth Shoreham, one angry tiler.

'Hello, police,' called Hughes at the open front door.

'In here,' came the reply.

The police found him. 'Gareth Shoreham?' asked Billy.

'That's me.'

The police introduced themselves. 'We have some more questions, Mr Shoreham, about the death of Simon Grovene.'

'Still not caught the bastard then? I told the other cops I promised to buy the killer a beer.'

'On the day Mr Grovene died, have you remembered where you were between 10 am and 2 pm?'

'No idea. A few mates said I was with them but they're lying.'

'I'd get serious, Gareth. Murder isn't funny,' snapped Hughes.

'Am I laughing?' He resumed affixing tiles to a bathroom wall.

'You told my colleagues you have a firearm licence and own a Glock pistol. You were asked to take both to your nearest police station. Why haven't you?'

'I've lost it.'

The detectives bristled. 'You've lost your weapon?' fumed Billy.

'No, the licence. If I brought in the gun without the licence, you'd fine me and thanks to the delightful Simon Grovene ...' He spat the next words, 'I haven't got any fucking money.'

'Where is your weapon now?'

'Under lock and key at the gun club. And I haven't been there for weeks as I can't afford the fees because ...' His voice went up as he mocked himself. 'I haven't got any fucking money.'

The police took the gun club details. Hughes told Shoreham he'd be arrested if the weapon was not at the gun club. They left.

'We should arrest him, ma'am. No alibi, refusal to surrender licence and gun, massive motive to kill Grovene—he's a prime suspect.'

They checked the gun club. Gareth's gun was where he said it was. The manager confirmed Shoreham was behind in his membership and hadn't been to the club for months. The detectives left.

'His gun didn't fire the bullet at the crime scene,' said Hughes.

'Yeah but the man has expertise and experience with weapons.'

'Thanks for the bleeding obvious, Senior. Now, who's next?'

Fleming and Baldwin found Peter Ward renovating an old house. There were three men and one woman working on site. Fleming held up his ID and the young female pointed to the back of the house.

Ward looked up and groaned. 'Not again.'

'More questions, Mr Ward,' smiled Fleming.

'And if I refuse, you arrest me and stop me earning money to pay off the debts I owe because prick Grovene ripped me off. Some choice.'

'Well the sooner you answer, the sooner we're gone.' Ward glared at them. 'Alibi, again. Where were you when Mr Grovene was killed?'

'I told you. I went for a drive on me own to get away from my darling partner who'd just told me we were through.'

'And nobody saw you for what, the whole four hours you were away?'

'Of course people saw me. I walked around the shops in Eltham but I never asked people to remember me—silly me.'

'Did you stop for petrol, or buy food? Anything?'

Ward shook his head. 'Can't remember. I had misery on me mind.'

Baldwin took over. 'You have a police record, Mr Ward, affray, threatening a police officer and resisting arrest.'

Ward scoffed. 'That was a hundred years ago. I was a spotty kid.'

'Can we see your tool box, Mr Ward?' asked Fleming.

'What for?' The cops stared at him so he led them to an old wooden chest with many well-used tools.

'Happy?' was the sarcastic question from Ward.

'Anything missing?' asked Fleming.

'Yes, a plane, a bloody good plane, an old pair of pliers and a chisel.'

'What size chisel?' asked Baldwin.

Ward took out two chisels. 'Bigger than this, smaller than this.'

'When and where did you lose it?' asked Fleming.

Ward was growing increasingly upset. 'I don't know,' he snarled.

'When?' snarled Fleming in reply.

'A couple of weeks ago, I think. Okay? Now you pricks are preventing me earning my living.'

Fleming understood. 'Tell us if the chisel turns up.'

'Why?' asked the builder. Then he twigged. 'Oh don't tell me Slippery Simon was stabbed with a chisel?' The police said nothing. The builder laughed and his laughter followed them to the front door.

Hughes and Payne arrived at the home of Bradley and Donna Devlin. Billy interviewed Bradley earlier, and when he opened the door, he turned and walked inside. The cops followed. Devlin sat in front of a telly watching a race meeting, his form guide beside him.

'Mr Devlin,' said Hughes, this is Detective Senior Constable Payne.' Devlin ignored them. His wife entered.

'Hello Donna,' said Billy.

The housewife folded her arms. 'What now? You gunna arrest us?'

'Look, we know Grovene screwed you. We know you were upset.'

'*Were* upset? We're still upset,' yelled Donna. 'And if I see his mail-order bride again, I'll tell her exactly what I think.'

'You were lucky to avoid being charged, Donna. Go near his wife again and you'll be inside.'

'Why should she be walking around spending money when her husband owes us thousands? How is that justice?'

'Twelve grand,' said Bradley not taking his eyes off the screen.

It was obvious they hated Grovene with a passion.

'And I'm sorry he's dead,' said Bradley. 'I wanted the pleasure of killing the bastard meself.'

'And both of you, your alibi for that day is what?' asked Billy.

Bradley finally looked at the police. 'Listen. My old man's 82. He's a Vietnam Vet now in a wheelchair. I built him a flat in the backyard to keep an eye on him. When Grovene ripped me off, I spent a fortune on lawyers for nothing but more debt. I asked my crippled old man for a loan knowing I'd be taking all his money, knowing I can't pay him back.' He shouted. 'Do you know how that feels?' He paused. 'Well?'

Before the police could answer Bradley's rhetorical answer, a wheelchair and two feet appeared. Then the person in the wheelchair pushed himself into the room.

'Have we visitors?' asked the returned ex-serviceman.

The mood changed. 'It's the useless coppers, Dad,' said Donna.

'G'day,' said the war veteran, holding out a hand. 'I'm Ed, the proud father of the son with the big mouth and the bigger debts.'

Both detectives moved to the old man and shook his hand.

'We're sorry to hear you're doing it tough,' said Hughes.

'Oh I'm fine,' replied Ed, 'never better. So who killed Mr Scumbag?'

'We're still looking, Mr Devlin,' offered Billy wondering how she could get more information from the father.

'Good luck,' smiled the war veteran.

'I don't suppose you can remember where you were on the day of the murder, sir?'

'I'm a suspect?' asked Ed, indicating his wheelchair-bound body.

'No sir, we're trying to establish an alibi for your son and daughter-in-law. If you can remember what you were doing at the time, maybe you can help your family.'

'What day was it again?'

'Last Thursday between 10 and 2.'

'Well if it was a Thursday, I'd be bowling.'

Payne saw a weakness. 'Do they allow wheelchairs on the green?'

'Carpet bowls, sonny.' He mimed how he bowled. 'I've had able-bodied bowlers rave about my backhand.'

'And you were away from the house for how long?' asked Billy.

Ed sniffed. 'I get picked up about ten, and after lunch, depending who's in the mini-bus, I get home between three and four.'

'And when you came home, who was here?'

Ed thought. More sniffing then he remembered. 'Donna was unpacking the shopping.'

'And your son?'

Ed thought again. 'No idea; probably out assassinating Grovene.'

'Not funny, Dad,' snapped Bradley.

Ed reflected. 'Only wish my old body wasn't so knackered otherwise I would've cheerfully cut Grovene's throat.'

Hughes had heard enough. She headed to the door. 'Thank you. If anyone remembers anything about an alibi, please let us know.'

She left with Payne in tow. 'We have plenty of motive there, Sarge.'

'There's something about Donna.'

'Donna?' exclaimed Payne.

'She's short meaning the right height for the entry wound. She's wiry meaning she'd have the strength to thrust a blade, and did you see the collection of knives in her kitchen?'

'Ah no,' replied an embarrassed Payne.

'Observe, Senior, it separates the detectives from the dickheads.'

Fleming and Baldwin had one more name on their list—Luigi Bello. Middle-aged, from strong Italian roots, Bello lived up to the meaning of his name—beautiful. Despite decades of smoking and red wine consumption, Luigi still had the looks. For a living, he was Mr Concrete and could pour and level a load before it even thought about going hard. The detectives found him creating a driveway.

'Signor Bello,' called Fleming. Baldwin wasn't sure about his colleague's Italian accent. *Does that offend the suspect?*

'Not now,' bellowed Luigi, in the middle of a concrete pour.

The police watched the skill displayed by the men spreading and levelling the concrete over the wire mesh. When the job was done, Luigi beckoned to the police.

'We're police officers, Signor Bello.' He knew.

'You can cut the Signor business. I'm Luigi and you're too late.'

'Sorry?' asked Fleming.

'I've just buried the thieving bastard under this concrete.'

'Not funny, Luigi. Now my notes tell me you weren't able to provide an alibi for the day Simon Grovene was murdered.'

'And I still can't so what, you arrest me for not having a note?'

Baldwin spoke. 'We know you've been handy delivering concrete to people who haven't ordered it.'

Luigi shrugged. 'The guy was married. I warned him to stay away from my daughter. He didn't so I gave him a free load of concrete.'

'At 2 am in his driveway?'

Luigi shrugged again. 'He never complained.'

'Do you often take revenge, Luigi?' asked Fleming.

More shrugging. 'I don't like people who do the wrong thing. Grovene conned me into providing a lot of concrete knowing he was never gunna pay me. In my opinion he got what he deserved.'

'Did you kill him, Luigi?' asked Fleming.

'Now officer, please, where are my rights? No warning, no offer of a solicitor, just incriminating questions. Not good enough. Now, you can arrest me or you can piss off. Capisci?'

Fleming left using a throwaway he hated and which Baldwin thought laughable. 'Don't leave town, Luigi.'

The first official meeting of WATTI took place in Robbo's lounge. All three former homicide detectives were buzzing.

'And this whole thing has official approval?' asked Ray Tuck.

'From the AC Crime himself,' replied Robbo passing a bowl of nuts. 'And would you believe, my granddaughter is the OIC.'

'Bloody hell,' said Melk. 'They're sending a girl to supervise three delinquent pensioners.'

'Did you blokes ever see the UK cop series *New Tricks?*' asked Tuck. They all knew the show. 'That could be us.'

'Yeah and I bags be Dennis Waterman,' said Melk.

'Oh great,' retorted Robbo, 'so I'm Arfur Daley.'

'Wrong show, boss,' quipped Tuck.

Their laughter stopped when the doorbell rang. Robbo departed. Tuck and Melk looked at one another. Neither knew what would happen but both thought this was better than steam locos or alpacas.

Jo entered and smiles were out on show. They settled and looked at their "senior officer". She was about half the age of Colin Melk, the youngest ex-cop in the room. The retirees were working for a child.

'Gentlemen, welcome and congratulations.'

'We haven't done anything yet,' said Tuck.

'We have official approval for this activity but there are strict rules and you need to sign this document.' She produced screeds. They read as Jo explained. She was in charge and nothing was to be done without her prior approval.

'As you can see you are not police officers. You have no authority and are employed as consultants on a casual-employee contract. The pay won't make you rich and any future for you and this type of activity depends solely on results and your ability to *not* be noticed. Clear?'

They muttered and wondered if this might become one almighty cock-up. Paperwork over, they started work.

A huge advantage was that all three former detectives worked on the original case with intimate knowledge of the murder and, having failed before, were motivated to solve it now.

'Can I start by asking how each of you would like to be addressed?'

They hesitated. Melk went first. 'I was a Senior Constable and DCI Robertson used to call me Senior.'

Tuck chimed in. 'I used to call you Useless.' Jo didn't laugh trying to set a professional tone. Tuck understood. 'I used to get Sarge or Tucky.'

'Thank you,' said Jo and looked at her grandfather.

He was embarrassed. 'Well you can't call me Pop.'

'What about Boss?' suggested Melk.

Tuck interrupted. 'But *she's* the boss.'

'How about sir?' asked Jo.

'Fine,' replied Robbo, 'but there's no need to salute.' He winked.

'Excuse me, Detective,' said Melk, 'but how do we address you, and please don't say ma'am.'

Jo looked at all three faces. They were keen on her reply.

'I'll settle for Senior or Jo.' They smiled. 'Now I know two of you have got other jobs so to start with, Officers Tuck and Melk will review files, while DCI Robertson and I tackle the field work. But I don't want anyone stuck in an office. Okay?' Nods all round. 'Right, let's start by you telling me who you think murdered Maggie.'

Melk began. 'Unless we find a better candidate, it's the last boyfriend. He confessed albeit in a suicide note.'

'I never liked the pimp,' said Tucky. 'I reckon those young uni girls were terrified their families would find out they were on the game and so gave what's-his-name an alibi.'

'Karl Benedek and he's still around,' said Jo.

Everyone looked at Robbo. 'I think the killer was never interviewed. It's someone we never discovered and unless we're lucky, never will.'

'Interesting,' said Jo. She handed out another screed. 'Here is a list of interviewees which the DCI and I will tackle.'

'That's a long list, Senior,' said Tucky.

Jo kept going. 'You two, Sarge and Senior, will review previous interviews, pathologist's and coroner's reports and list flaws, unanswered questions, evidence issues and the like. Agreed?'

'Agreed,' said the three amigos/musketeers/idiots. They liked being referred to by their old ranks. They liked this "girl".

# 9

THE MORNING OF THE FUNERAL dawned overcast and chilly; a sombre atmosphere for a sombre occasion. In the Richelieu abode, its sole occupant remained in bed. Today, Pierre would bury his mother. She dominated his thinking.

Wherever he looked in her house, now his house, memories called to him. Her knick-knacks, her paintings, her bowls of fruit and vases of flowers, even her choice of towels in the bathrooms reminded him of his mother. He never felt more alone.

His work and friends were some 10,000 miles away and the detective didn't want to get out of bed.

The funeral was at 11 with a light buffet in the antechamber at the funeral parlour to follow the short service in the chapel. His mother wanted to be buried and owned a plot she bought ages ago.

Lying in bed, his mother's words flooded back. 'Do not set me on fire, Pierre,' she said.

'No Maman, you will rest in the most comfortable coffin in Paris.' She loved his gentle humour. 'I will 'ave your favourite champagne and perfume by your side and photos of all your cats.'

'If any outlive me, make sure you find them a good home.'

On the morning of her funeral, her presence was never more real.

Eventually he fell out of bed, and washed more thoroughly than ever before. He shaved so not a single hair dared appear. His black suit, tie, socks and shoes, and white shirt were immaculate. He wanted his mother to be proud of him. He sensed her watching to ensure his appearance was perfect. His black overcoat was pure wool.

The funeral attracted a small crowd; his mother's cousin, three neighbours, her best friend, seven members of the church she went to twice a year, and two employees from her solicitor's office. An unknown woman arrived late.

At the light luncheon, people approached Pierre, shared their memories of his mother then made their excuses. Staff fussed over the plates and cups as a well-dressed woman approached Pierre. She was about 30, attractive and a complete stranger.

'This may come as a shock to you, Monsieur,' she said in English with an accent hard to pick. 'I am your step-sister, Michelle Richelieu.' Pierre froze. 'I am the daughter of your father and his third wife.'

Pierre stared at her in astonishment. 'My sister?'

'Oui.'

'But did you know my mother?'

'No. One of my cousins is obsessed with family history. You and your mother are listed on our family tree. My cousin studies death notices and saw your mother's passing. Please accept my condolences.'

'Merci,' mumbled Pierre, still struggling with this revelation.

*I have another family!*

'You may be surprised to know you have several half-siblings. Your father with his many wives has two daughters apart from me and two sons apart from you.'

Pierre swore under his breath.

'Apart from me,' continued Michelle, 'all our siblings live in the United States. I live in Paris which is why I was able to come today.'

'Well to say I am shocked is an understatement.'

'Forgive me intruding on your grief but I was not sure exactly where you live or even if you are a Parisian.'

'Ah,' said a shocked Pierre. 'Yes, I'm living in Paris but only until I can finalise my mother's affairs.' He struggled. 'Could we meet? I would love to learn about this family I 'ave never 'eard of.'

'Of course,' said Michelle but I am flying to the States tomorrow to see my parents—my mother and our father.'

*Our father.* The words boomed inside Pierre's head.

'Then tonight. May I take you to dinner?'

'How kind. Merci.'

'Can I call for you or could we meet somewhere?'

'Tonight I am staying next to the airport for my early flight. I am happy to come to your home and we can go from there.'

'That will be wonderful.' Pierre found himself shaking as he wrote his Paris address on a card and handed it to his half-sister.

'Oh, you are a policeman, a detective inspector no less.'

'Oui,' said Pierre smiling for the first time.

'I will leave you in peace,' she said, and kissed his cheeks. 'Till tonight, brother,' she said, smiled and left.

Pierre stood rooted to the spot.

*She called me brother. I 'ave five siblings? 'ow can it be? Do they 'ave children? Am I an uncle? Who are these siblings? Do they know I exist? Did my father tell them about me? What a day. I lose one family member and gain five. Mon dieu!*

The burial took place in soft but persistent rain. Pierre wept and the rain mingled with his tears. He hated watching his mother's coffin lowered into the grave. But his grief became less painful as he thought about his step-sister Michelle and his half siblings.

As he stood there with the priest and the handful of mourners, all he could think about was his new family. He apologised to his mother. She had no connection to her former husband's offspring.

The coffin disappeared and the priest whispered to the chief mourner. Pierre snapped out of his reverie, picked up some soggy earth, and gently tossed it into the grave.

'Goodbye Maman,' he choked. 'Thank you, my darling. Thank you for your endless love. Thank ...' He couldn't speak. He wept with the rain getting heavier and seeping into his black woollen coat.

The funeral director approached Pierre. 'Monsieur,' he said. Pierre didn't react. A hand gripped his arm. 'Monsieur, your mother needs to find shelter from this rain.'

Pierre was guided away. The gravediggers worked quickly to prevent the grave flooding and the funeral director drove Pierre home.

After removing his wet clothes, bathing and dressing for his dinner date, he wanted to make a phone call. Late afternoon in Paris was around midnight in Melbourne but such was Pierre's emotional state, he didn't think about time zones.

Jo Best was dead to the world when her phone woke her. 'Jo Best.'

'Bonjour my favourite detective and 'ow are you?'

'Pierre, are you all right?' She'd been thinking about him a lot knowing the funeral must have been soon.

'Oui but oh ma chérie, I 'ave some news.'

Jo tensed. 'I hope it's good news, Pierre.'

'But first I must say what is the most important thing.' He paused. Her heart beat faster. 'I miss you, Joanna Best. My 'eart it aches to be close to yours.'

Jo felt her blood racing. To be woken from a sound sleep by a handsome, wealthy and caring man on the other side of the world and have him whisper sweet nothings down the line was exciting.

'How was the funeral, Pierre?'

'Ah, my mother would 'ave enjoyed it. But Joanna, I 'ave received news which 'as made me confused.' Jo held her breath. 'Today I 'ave found my step-sister.'

'You have a sister?'

'Not one but three, and two step-brothers.'

'Pierre, that's wonderful.'

'Michelle came to the funeral and introduced 'erself. This morning I 'ad only my mother. Now I 'ave a new family.'

'How exciting. Are you going to meet them?'

'I 'ope so. Tonight I will 'ave dinner with Michelle and learn about the other four siblings who live in America. On the day when I 'ave buried my darling mother, I 'ave discovered I am not alone.'

Jo was confused about her response. 'I'm so happy for you, Pierre. Have you any idea when you'll come home?'

'After tonight I will know. But whenever, I will be thinking of you ma chérie. I am always thinking of my darling detective.'

Jo went weak in the knees which was tricky because she was lying in bed. 'Thank you, Pierre. I miss you too.'

'Au revoir, Joanna Best. I cannot wait to see you again. Au revoir.'

The call ended and Jo lay there thinking. Forget sleep. There was so much going on in her life, with work, family and friends requiring her attention. And through it all, a man she felt seriously attracted to was making love to her over the phone.

Pierre opened his door to step-sister Michelle. Both smiled in unison. She pushed a small suitcase on wheels. They kissed.

'Bonsoir, sister dear. There is a wonderful restaurant a short walk from 'ere and I insist on you being my guest.'

'Merci Monsieur, merci beaucoup.'

'Please put your case 'ere and we can collect it later.'

He offered his arm and they set off for a meal with a difference. It's not every day you dine with a close relative you didn't know existed.

Pierre kept observing Michelle. *Do we look alike? In some ways, yes but per'aps not in others.* The food was secondary. Their life stories and their father were far more important.

Pierre knew next to nothing about his father who left when Pierre was a toddler. As he grew, he asked his mother for details. She was honest and open. Christmas presents would arrive but then stopped. His mother's older brother was a constant caller until he died. As a young teen, Pierre lost interest in his father. Now life changed. Did it ever? Pierre wanted to know everything about his father.

Michelle gave Pierre her number and he promised to make contact once he sorted his domestic affairs. She would return to Paris in three weeks. For Pierre, there were so many unanswered questions.

Over coffee, Michelle reminded Pierre of her early morning flight. He apologised, paid and escorted her outside. He looked to hail a taxi having forgotten about her suitcase.

They stood looking for a cab when the world went mad.

# 10

THE HOMICIDE SQUAD was short of detectives. DI Richelieu was on leave and Detective Senior Constable Best on special assignment. Those present discussed the four most likely to have killed crooked developer, Simon Grovene. Five photos (one was Grovene) were stuck on the display board.

'Of course,' said Billy, 'it might be none of our fab four. All have motive, means and opportunity, and none has an alibi.'

Fleming had news from Forensics. 'There's DNA on the chisel which is the one Peter Ward had stolen two weeks ago.'

'So he says,' added Baldwin.

Billy continued. 'What about the bullet? If it wasn't part of the murder, who fires a gun indoors? If it was part of the murder, who misses from such a short distance?'

DI Rose added her thoughts. 'Ballistics say it's an older handgun and the bullet might even be homemade and if so, that tells us what?'

Silence from the squad. 'Someone from a gun club or gun collector,' said Billy. 'It points to Gareth Shoreham but his gun isn't old and the bullet in the wall doesn't match.'

'We need a profiler, ma'am,' said Fleming. 'The killer has a gun but stabs the victim. Why? There's a pair of garden clippers on the victim's crotch and his mouth is full of coins.'

'Exactly thirty coins,' added Baldwin.

'It's probably religious,' said Payne.

'It *is* religious,' said Baldwin.

Billy Hughes grew restless. 'I want all four interviewed again. Let's shake them and see what falls out.'

'I agree,' said Rose. 'But we need a bigger net. Let's talk again to the widow Grovene and Grovene's parents and in-laws. Push hard. We can't let this drift.' She looked around. 'So, who else?'

Silence before Baldwin took the plunge. 'Get Jo Best back in here.'

His comment provoked a reaction. 'And DI Richelieu,' said Payne.

Rose was unhappy. Two of her best detectives were off the case. New ideas and clever insights were needed and Richelieu and Best were perfect in that area. 'Yes, all right, I've asked for back-up. Just don't ask me when.' She walked out. 'Carry on.'

Jo rang her sister and her mother answered. 'Hello Mum, it's Jo. How's the patient?'

'She's complaining which I think is good,' said Shirley.

'And I heard the surgeon was pleased with the op?'

'He was. With any luck she'll be home soon.'

'So how are you surviving at Camp Jeremy?'

'I'm not. When are you coming to do some babysitting? The children keep asking for you.'

'I'm working tonight but I'll give you a ring in the morning? Give my love to Jeremy.'

'Ha ha.'

Jo told nobody about her new cold case role. Telling Shirley her octogenarian father was back working with the police would be a massive issue. Jo imagined her mother going crazy.

She thought about ringing Jack Carr and checking on his daughter, Grace. Something stopped her. She wasn't sure what. Instead she headed to Pop's place. The cold case investigation of who murdered Maggie Stephens was about to begin in earnest.

Paris Saint-Germain were at home and Yousef and his new mate, Javed agreed to meet outside the main gate. Javed's work colleagues at RAID followed Yousef to his apartment block the other night and his personal details were now in RAID's computers. Yousef's email and phone and social media posts were monitored.

One problem for anti-terrorist officers is timing. If they arrest a suspect too early, they possibly miss catching other terrorists. If they delay making the arrest, the bomb may do its evil work.

Yousef and Javed enjoyed each other's company and especially when their team won 3—0.

For Javed, it revealed nothing of any plans Yousef may have. But slowly slowly catchee monkey was the routine from RAID.

Jo called for her grandfather. They'd drawn up a list of interviewees and first was the former toddler, Kaiden. Thankfully he slept as his mother was murdered. Pop and Jo wondered if he carried any scars.

Kaiden, now 24, turned out all right. He was placed with elderly foster parents who showered him with love. He studied catering and today worked as a chef in a popular Carlton restaurant.

Jo and her octogenarian partner entered before the busy lunch hour and were led to the kitchen. The owner grumbled.

'As quick as you can, please.'

Kaiden was intrigued. Jo and Robbo took him to the backyard.

'I was told my mother's boyfriend was responsible.' said Kaiden

'And so he might be,' replied Jo. 'But we wondered if there is anything you can remember from your early years.'

The young chef shook his head. 'My only memories are of my foster parents; nothing of my mother. I guess that's the saddest part.'

'What about your Mum's family?' asked Jo. 'Did you ever meet your great Uncle Harold or his mother, your great-grandmother?'

Kaiden shook his head. 'If I did, I can't remember. When I was 16, I was told about Mum's family but none of them came to see me and I've never been interested. Is that wrong?'

Jo shook her head. 'Of course not.'

Robbo addressed the young man. 'So, Kaiden, if we discover the truth, would you like to know?'

Kaiden thought. 'I'm not sure. Ask me if you learn anything new.'

# 11

PIERRE AND HIS NEW FOUND SISTER stood on the curb looking for a taxi. Pedestrians and cars were everywhere when pandemonium arrived. Five men and a woman in uniform rushed from different directions, screaming and brandishing guns. Pedestrians screamed and scattered. Michelle screamed. Pierre saw several weapons pointed at him.

He recognised the uniforms—he used to wear one when he worked for the French Police. They shouted as one.

'Get down! Get down!'

For a moment Pierre thought it was a terrorist attack with a bomb about to explode. He squatted. Guns kept pointing at him as two officers pushed him from behind yelling, 'Get down!' He tumbled over then looked up at Michelle who was in shock.

Before Pierre could protest or ask a question, he was handcuffed then dragged to his feet. Guns were placed in holsters as police officers surrounded him.

'Pierre Grégory Richelieu, you are under arrest for possession of Class A drugs with intent to supply.'

'What? This is crazy,' shouted Richelieu.

The officer ignored him and ordered the prisoner removed. As Richelieu was hustled to a police van, he looked at his sister and yelled.

'Please 'elp me, Michelle. Tell my solicitor, my colleagues in Australia, 'elp me.' She looked stunned and helpless.

'Mind your head,' shouted an officer as Pierre disappeared into the back of the van. The doors slammed and the vehicle raced away with siren blaring and lights flashing.

What a day. He buried his mother, discovered his family, and was arrested for dealing in Class A drugs.

The Honourable Antony Heron-Royhay enjoyed unusual sexual interests with S & M being a favourite. As a young boy, his nanny used to smack him, all with parental permission of course, and Antony reckons that gave him his taste for pain. "Fair crack of the whip" was his masochism motto as Madame Lash gave him what for.

Madame Lash was in fact Lorraine Morton from Birkenhead in The Wirral, Merseyside. Most of her clients were aging Parisians but her current client was a potential goldmine. She discovered the real name and pedigree of the Honourable Englishman and pondered a sale of secrets to a UK tabloid as part of her future pension fund.

Antony dressed down for the tickler sessions wearing only a leather thong giving his buttocks the chance to throb with pleasure as each welt appeared. His mistress always had the whip hand.

Antony endured a hard day at the office and needed a solid slapping before a slap-up supper. Mid whipping, his phone rang.

'Leave it,' cried the dominatrix. Antony reached a compromise whereby his phone was allowed to be on speaker so any important call could be monitored as the punishment progressed.

After the recorded message ended, the desperate caller spoke.

'Monsieur, this is Pierre Richelieu. We met in your colleague's office two days ago. I 'ave been arrested on some crazy drug charge. I beg you, come to my aid. I am at the 36 in Batignolles. Please 'urry.'

The message ended and Antony looked at his tormentor.

'Sounds important, Monsieur' said the woman, wondering if the incident might make a chapter in her unpublished tacky memoir.

'It is important because the gentleman is a police detective.'

Antony and Lorraine both tingled but for different reasons.

Antony arrived at Police HQ with a throbbing bottom—covered of course. The staff knew the minor aristocrat and lawyer from previous visits. Antony was advised of the charges then shown to an interview room. He entered and Pierre came alive.

'Bonsoir Monsieur,' said the lawyer.

Richelieu stood and grasped the barrister's hand with both hands.

'Oh Monsieur, merci, merci beaucoup.'

'Sit, Monsieur, s'il vous plaît.' They sat. 'I did not expect to see you again and certainly not under these circumstances.'

Pierre couldn't settle. He'd been stewing for hours. The shock and appalling injustice smashed his nerves. With his mother's funeral and newly-discovered family vivid in his mind, this latest episode proved overwhelming.

'There 'as been a terrible mistake, Monsieur. Please inform the authorities they 'ave the wrong man.'

Antony held up a hand. 'Monsieur, I have only just been advised of the charges and ...'

'Charges? There is more than one?'

'Shhhh. Monsieur, please, try and stay calm.'

'Calm? Are you serious? I 'ave been arrested in public for a shocking crime and for which I am absolutely not guilty.'

Richelieu stressed. Being shot at in the line of duty or facing the prospect of same didn't match the strain he felt right now.

'Let me outline the charges, Monsieur,' said the lawyer, shifting to stimulate some lingering pleasure from his posterior-patting. 'The police claim a tip-off directed them to an address in Rue Crémieux, where they found significant quantities of cocaine and heroin.'

Richelieu's face roared. His eyes bulged, his cheeks reddened and his mouth fell open. 'Impossible!' he whispered.

'I assume, Monsieur, you wish to engage my company's services.'

'Oui,' was all he could say as tears welled in his eyes.

'Do you have an explanation for the police claims, Monsieur?'

His suspicions were confirmed. 'Oui. It is, 'ow you say, a stitch-up.'

'You claim to have been framed, Monsieur?'

'Of course. Why on Earth would a law-abiding citizen and a police officer with an unblemished record, 'ere and in Australia, return for a family funeral and become a drug dealer overnight? It is nonsense.'

'It may be nonsense, Monsieur but with significant incriminating evidence. The police found a commercial quantity of Class A drugs in the ceiling of your mother's bedroom.' Antony paused. 'I assume we can rule out your late mother as being responsible?'

Richelieu's face gave a crystal-clear answer. He fell silent. He knew how this worked. Evidence wins. Someone planted drugs in his mother's home. He knew that someone. But could he prove it?

The fact the drugs were in his mother' bedroom twisted the knife. *They have invaded my darling mother's room. Salauds!*

It got worse. 'The police claim, Monsieur, your fingerprints are on at least one plastic bag containing the packets of drugs.' Richelieu shook his head. 'Getting you bail, Monsieur, is our first task.'

'Remember, sir, I was once a police officer based 'ere in Paris.'

'I know, Inspector. Now, did anyone witness your arrest?'

Richelieu brightened. 'Oui, my sister. She was with me.'

Antony took notes looking confused. 'I was told you were an only child, Monsieur.'

'I was until today.'

'Today, Monsieur? It is only 1 am.'

Richelieu realised. He'd been in custody for several hours. 'I mean yesterday. A woman came to my mother's funeral and introduced herself as my half-sibling. Her father is my father.'

'I see. And your sister's name and address, Monsieur.'

'Ah, Michelle Richelieu and … I do not know her Parisian address. She is flying to the United States this morning to see our father.'

'Her contact details please, Monsieur.'

Richelieu patted his jacket. 'Her phone number is in my wallet.'

'I will enquire. Now what is the explanation for your arrest?'

'Eight years ago, I arrested some fellow police officers here in Paris. They were charged with corruption, dismissed and sent to prison.'

'And how is this related to your arrest?'

'I fear Monsieur if you 'aven't worked it out by now, I may need to engage another lawyer.'

Antony gave a forced smile then asked for details which Pierre supplied. 'Merci,' said the lawyer who stood and closed his briefcase. 'Try and get some sleep, Monsieur. You will have a court appearance soon and there we will apply for bail. I will see you later today.'

'One more thing, Monsieur, if you please. Could you ring my colleague in Australia and advise 'er of my predicament?'

'Of course.'

Richelieu gave the lawyer Jo Best's details. 'She will advise my commanding officer and my leave may need to be extended.'

'I think *may* should be replaced by *will*, Monsieur.'

Richelieu understood. This matter would not be resolved in five minutes. He looked into the lawyer's eyes. Pierre's eyes were begging, pleading for help. Antony half smiled.

'Au revoir, Monsieur,' said Antony. Bonne nuit.'

Jo and Robbo discussed the other interviewees. Their interview with Kaiden meant Robbo missed his lunchtime visit with wife, Ida. Her severe dementia meant she would be none the wiser but Jo knew the importance Robbo placed on daily visits. She drove him to the home.

As they walked to her room, Jo's phone rang. 'I'll catch you up, Pop.'. A number she didn't recognise showed on her phone. 'Jo Best.'

'Good afternoon, madam,' said a superior-sounding English voice. 'I'm ringing from France on behalf of Inspector Pierre Richelieu.'

'What's happened?' Jo's nerves jangled.

'My name is Antony Heron-Royhay and I am Monsieur Richelieu's lawyer here in Paris. He asked me to advise you of his arrest.'

Jo shouted and staff looked at her. 'Arrest? Is this a joke?'

'Alas, no, madam.'

'On what charge?' Antony explained and she spoke even louder. 'This is a joke.' She saw people looking and moved to the garden.

'Monsieur Richelieu wishes you to inform his commanding officer his return to Australia may be delayed.'

Jo struggled. 'Look a charge of handling Class A drugs is absurd.'

'Of course, madam, and we shall mount a rigourous defence.'

'And you're in Paris?'

'Indeed.'

'You don't sound French, sir.'

'Perhaps because I'm English.'

Jo fought to stay calm and think with a clear mind. 'Would you please give me your name again and the details of your legal firm.'

'Certainly.' My name is the Honourable Antony Heron-Royhay.' He listed his employer's details. Jo struggled with "the Honourable".

*Could Pierre be a criminal? Is this caller who he says he is? Is this one stupid practical joke?*

'Thank you, sir,' said Jo checking her notes. Please keep me informed of any developments and give my regards to Detective Inspector Richelieu. I will be in touch. And again, thank you.'

'It's a pleasure to be of service, madam. Goodbye.'

*This can't be right. What's his name? Antony Heron-Royhay? And he's an Honourable. He can't be honourable; he's a lawyer.*

Jo found her grandparents. Robbo chatted about Jo to Ida. She gave little indication of understanding. Jo dived in.

'I have some bad news, Gran.' Robbo looked shocked. 'Caitlyn's got breast cancer. Did you tell me Great Auntie Hilda had the disease?'

Ida froze. For a second the words "Auntie Hilda" pinged inside her head. Her eyes seemed to shine and she spoke. 'Auntie Hilda.'

Robbo and Jo looked at one another. They took it in turns to engage in any form of discussion about Auntie Hilda with some success.

As Ida tired, Robbo kissed his wife, Jo gave her a strong hug, and the visitors left. As they walked down the corridor, they did so in silence. Robbo felt pain seeing his wife with an incurable condition, and Jo was still stunned by the news of her colleague's arrest.

Driving Robbo home, Jo held back. She wanted to talk to someone about Richelieu but her grandfather didn't seem the right person. They made a time to meet tomorrow for more cold case interviews and Jo headed home. En route she made a call.

'Michael Chan speaking.'

'Jo Best speaking.'

'Who?'

'It's your favourite detective.'

'I'm sorry, I missed a word. Did you say *least* favourite?'

'Long time no see or speak, Dr Chan.'

'Thank goodness.'

'I'm in the neighbourhood, sir. Are you receiving?'

'I'll need to check my life insurance first.'

Jo laughed. 'I'll see you soon.'

In Paris, Pierre appeared before a magistrate. Monsieur le président was relatively young but a tartar. He hated criminals and threw the book at them at every opportunity. But when an alleged criminal had a day job as a police officer, the judge lit up the night sky with his rage.

When the charges were read and Pierre was asked to plead, Antony spoke with Rumpolian vigour. 'Not guilty, Monsieur le président.'

Bail was sought and refused. The case was adjourned enabling police to make further enquiries. At least the judge agreed to hear another bail application. Hope was a scarce commodity. Pierre Richelieu, looking older, returned to his cell.

# 12

MICHAEL OPENED HIS DOOR. Both he and Jo thought about her first visit to this former warehouse and their subsequent adventures. Both pretended their relationship was rocky yet both had huge respect for the other. Jo added admiration to her feelings. Michael added love.

Jo entered and Michael made a show of stepping outside and looking towards the street. 'What, no paparazzi?'

'Ha, ha.' As they approached his wall of computing equipment, Michael's cat appeared.

'Alan,' cried Jo and bent to greet the feline. 'You're looking great; you and your sidekick.'

'Coffee?' asked Michael entering his open-plan kitchen, bigger than Jo's entire flat. It was a rhetorical question. In some ways they were like an old married couple.

'So what have you been up to, Michael?'

'Absolutely nothing to do with criminals and crime.'

'Oh?'

'And loving it.'

Jo laughed. 'You make a terrible liar, Michael.'

'But a brilliant barista,' he replied preparing the brew.

Jo paused. She wanted to tell someone about Richelieu's situation. *Michael is wise and clever. He'll have sensible suggestions.*

The coffee arrived and Michael spoke first. 'I may be a terrible liar, Detective, but you are a terrible actor.'

'How dare you,' said Jo with mock indignation.

'You don't do social visits. You have something to tell me, yet you make small talk avoiding the real reason you're here.' He handed her a coffee which smelt divine. 'As always.'

'Thanks. And you're right—as always.'

She told Michael everything she knew about DI Richelieu in Paris.

'Is it true?' he asked.

Jo shrugged. 'I'll make some more enquiries but I can't believe the man's a criminal. Can you check a French law firm, please?'

'Sure.'

'And cases listed in Parisian courts?'

'Can do.'

He put his IT skills to work and Jo discovered all about the law firm which employed the Honourable Antony Heron-Royhay. Listings in Parisian criminal court proceedings revealed the case of the Melbourne-based DI and his alleged crimes involving Class A drugs.

Jo felt chest pain. The shock lingered and her misery grew. After a pause where the silence was loud, Michael asked the obvious question.

'So what will you do?'

'Go to France and have the charges thrown out.'

'Just like that?'

'Just like that.'

'What, scale the Bastille and release the aristocrats?'

'Michael, Pierre is my colleague and friend. You know him. On a scale of 1 to 10, how preposterous do you rate these charges with 1 being guilty and 10 being ridiculous?'

'I'd say 11.' Another pause and silence. 'So when do you plan to go?'

Jo was planning as she spoke. 'As soon as possible.' She looked at him. 'Is your passport up to date?' Ever so slightly, he trembled.

Jo's biggest hurdle was getting leave from DI Rose. Jo wrote her speech. She tightened it and read it aloud. She made a list of objections her DI might raise. She read aloud each point then spoke off the cuff in her answer. It was a late night.

Next morning, she knocked on Rose's door. 'Come in, Senior. Tell me you've cracked the cold case and those three ratbags now want to rejoin the force.'

'Not exactly, ma'am but we've made some progress.'

'Great.' Pause. 'Well come on, explain.'

'Before I do, ma'am, I want to put in a request.'

Rose frowned. She, like most of the Homicide Squad admired the brilliant young detective but Jo could be a right royal pain at times.

'What request?'

'I'd like some leave, ma'am.'

Rose reacted with power. Her voice, body language and choice of words left Jo in no doubt. The boss was unhappy.

'Leave? Now? I've stuck my neck out for your cold case adventure and now you want to quit?'

'Not quit, ma'am.'

Jo used her script, the one she rehearsed last night. Once she explained the Richelieu arrest saga on drug charges in Paris, Rose lost her resistance. Her head shook in disbelief. She listened, uttering the odd swear word or three.

'And you're sure it's true?'

'I'm afraid so, ma'am.'

'Unbelievable.'

'Which is why I'm asking for leave.'

Rose came back down to Earth. 'There's nothing you can do. We can contact the Police Association, have the Australian Embassy in Paris provide support, and his lawyers, we hope, will do the rest.'

'Ma'am, he's been set up.'

'Then the police will sort it out. It's what they do.'

'What if the police set him up?'

They hit a roadblock and Rose froze. 'You don't know that.'

'Please ma'am, he's my colleague and needs help. At the very least I can offer moral support.'

Rose stared at Jo. Her tone was blunt. 'Are you sleeping with him?'

'You asked me before, ma'am.'

'And I'm asking you again.'

'No ma'am, I am not sleeping with DI Richelieu.'

'You've just started a new job, a job you practically demanded I create for you. You've persuaded three former officers to help, the AC has given his backing, and now you want to dump the job and your fellow workers one of whom is your grandfather.'

'I don't wish to dump anyone or the job, ma'am, but delay things for an emergency.'

Rose could see Jo had planned this discussion. Her answers used logic coupled with a powerful emotion—respect for a colleague. Jo played her dangerous trump card.

'The cold case investigation can continue ma'am. There is a perfect replacement for me.'

66

'Oh yes, who?'

'You, ma'am.' Rose seethed. Jo pushed her dangerous point. 'You worked on the original case *and* with the three consultants. And it need only be till I return having helped DI Richelieu, someone we all need, return to Homicide, ma'am.'

'Oh, so now you're Wonder Woman?'

'You need all your officers, ma'am.'

Jo Best was right. And secretly Rose liked working on cold cases and the thought of being the OIC working with three men who were once her superiors gave her a buzz.

'I think you're over-reacting,' Rose said not meaning it.

Jo went for the sucker punch. 'If you were in trouble overseas, ma'am, would you want a colleague to try and save your skin?'

Rose bit her bottom lip. 'Let me think about it.'

'Thank you, ma'am. But could you please think quickly? I'm hoping to book my ticket today.'

Rose's face meant she wouldn't want the wind to change direction.


The Assistant Commissioner took the call from DI Rose. He pushed for her appointment but worried she lacked toughness. A DI must make tough calls, decisions that would impact even upset other officers.

'DI Rose, what can I do for you?'

'Sir, I have a situation and would like your input.'

'Certainly.'

He didn't like this behaviour. Running to the boss for every problem didn't inspire confidence. "Make the hard calls yourself, Elly", is what he wanted to say. But when she finished explaining the DI Richelieu saga, Crowley understood DI Rose's predicament.

'It sounds incredible,' said Crowley.

'It *is* incredible, sir, but do you object to Senior Constable Best heading off to a foreign land with no authority in said jurisdiction?'

'And she suggested you head up Robbo Robertson and his mates investigating the cold case?'

'She did, sir.'

'Bloody hell, she's a forward planner all right.'

'Yes sir.'

Crowley hesitated. This time he was glad Rose contacted him. 'It's your call, Inspector. If Best wants to go, it must have no official recognition. She's on holiday. Understood?'

'Sir.'

'And what did the pensioners say when you met them again?'

'I haven't met them yet, sir. I'll tell them I'm taking over tonight.'

'God, I'd like to be a fly on the wall.'

The three ex-coppers met at Robbo's. Jo was given two weeks' leave to go overseas to report to the Australian Embassy in Paris with no authority to intervene in the case. She was there to provide moral support for a colleague and liaise between the Embassy and Richelieu's lawyer. She was to say nothing about her leave to the cold case officers, and arrive at their next meeting, half an hour late.

To date, Tuck and Melk worked on witness statements, and reports from the pathologist and coroner. Jo emailed them her notes from the latest interview with Kaiden. At the meeting, the banter flowed.

'I'm not sure I fancy only doing paperwork,' said Tuck.

'Same here,' said Melk. 'I wanna chase crims on me Harley.'

'Tell the boss when she gets here,' added Robbo. The doorbell sounded. 'Speak of the devil.' He went to the front door.

Melk kept moaning. 'I wasn't expecting car chases and shootouts with deranged killers, but paperwork ain't what I signed up for.'

'You're bigger than she is,' replied Tuck. 'Stand up to her.'

'Stand up to who?' asked the female who entered the room.

Melk spun round and gasped. Tuck looked perplexed. Robbo followed and shrugged.

'Gentlemen,' said Robbo and indicated they rise. They did.

'Be seated,' said DI Rose. She pointed to an empty chair. 'This okay?' Robbo nodded. Rose sat and the others took their places. She felt good inside. 'Well, firstly my apologies for not having been to see you sooner; better late than never.' She looked from one to another then dropped the officialdom approach and smiled. They remembered her grin. 'It's lovely to see you "boys" again. How are you?'

They grinned, offering congratulations. Then it turned serious.

'I have news,' she said and paused. Every male in the room sat transfixed. 'We're putting the band back together.'

Silence. No response. Melk had watched *The Blues Brothers* many times and spoke without thinking. 'We're on a mission from God.'

Robbo and Tuck looked confused. Rose grinned and Melk thought his former colleague was definitely cool.

Tuck wanted answers. 'What's going on?'

'A lot, DS Tuck,' said Rose. She told them about DI Richelieu in a French jail, about Jo taking leave in Paris, and that the current head of Homicide was now their OIC. It was a lot to take in. Robbo spoke.

'I need to speak to my granddaughter.'

'She'll be here soon, sir,' said Rose treating Robbo as if he were still a DCI and her boss.

'So what do we call you?' asked Tuck struggling to absorb the news.

'How about what you used to call me? How about Elly—Tucky?' He grinned. *She's all right, this lady.*

'I used to call you names,' confessed Melk.

'I know, *Steve* or do you prefer *For Sale?*'

Tuck laughed. He remembered. 'We called you Steve as in McQueen because of your motorbike.'

Melk understood. 'I knew about Steve but what's this *For Sale?*'

'You were handcuffed to the *For Sale* sign,' added Rose.

Everyone laughed. Then it got serious. Rose asked for reports. She made notes then gave instructions.

'I'd like to get Tucky and Steve out doing more investigating.' Both men were keen. Rose suggested places where the two ex-detectives could go snooping. Then the doorbell rang and Robbo fetched his granddaughter.

She entered and spoke. 'Ma'am,' she said to Rose. 'Gentlemen,' she said to the others. They all sat and Rose took over.

'Jo, I've explained the situation and we're good to go. You can help the DCI make tea while I chat with my assistants.'

Tuck and Melk grinned at their description, and Robbo and Jo went to the kitchen where Jo was given a "Please explain".

'Please, Pop, don't tell anyone about my trip till I've spoken to Mum and Caitlyn?' He agreed. There was a lot going on.

Next morning, the Homicide squad resumed their investigation into the murder of Simon Grovene. None of the four main suspects had been eliminated. Each had motive, opportunity and no alibi.

DS Billy Hughes discussed follow-up tasks but stopped when DI Rose entered with a dapper looking gent wearing a bespoke suit and sporting a hairstyle which was sculptured rather than cut.

'Good morning,' said Rose and the detectives responded. 'I'd like to introduce DI Callum Blunt who is joining us today and will be working with DS Hughes on the Grovene homicide. That's the good news.'

Everyone, apart from Blunt, sat spellbound as their boss told them of DI Richelieu's predicament, Jo Best's proposed overseas venture, and Rose's move to manage the cold case investigation. When she finished, squad members looked at one another. Shock was in.

'Any questions?' asked Rose.

'Only a hundred,' said Fleming speaking for the squad.

'If I knew any more, Justin, I'd tell you.'

'But why is Jo Best going to Paris, ma'am?' asked Billy. 'Surely it's nothing to do with us?'

Rose grimaced. 'I think it's to give moral support. Certainly she has no official status.' More silence. 'Right, DS Hughes, please introduce DI Blunt to the team and let's crack this homicide.'

She left and while the new arrival was greeted with courtesy, the team members buzzed with the news about DI Richelieu being a drug baron, and if there was any sexual element to the Richelieu Best relationship.

# 13

YOUSEF SWEATED a lot of late. If having the bomb ingredients but no instructions was a worry, he would have died knowing he was under surveillance by RAID, the elite anti-terrorist unit. He had to become a martyr but without bomb-making skills, he stared at failure.

Then he thought of a possible solution. By visiting a library, he might learn about explosives without being discovered.

He entered a large public library, asked about encyclopedias and was directed upstairs. He didn't expect a section on *How to Make a Bomb* or *Tips for Terrorists* but there should be something about the history of explosives. Anything would help.

In case his notebook fell into enemy hands, he buried his bomb-making notes in scribble about weaving.

After a solid hour of research, he wasn't much closer to making a bomb but at least knew some basics. He needed a pee and headed for the toilets. He passed tall thin windows en route and glanced out of the last one. He stopped and went back. He pressed his cheek against the glass because who he saw, was in line with the side of the library. Yousef stared. It was Javed.

*I'm sure it's him.*

He was in the park surrounding the library, facing the building, and talking to someone wearing a hoodie with their back to Yousef. The lining of the hoodie was bright red.

With bladder demands increasing, Yousef went to relieve himself. He hurried back to his observation post to find no-one. Javed and Hoodie were gone.

Yousef kept telling himself it was nothing; Javed was there by chance and the man in the hoodie was waiting for a friend or asking for directions or a light.

With notes buried inside his clothing, Yousef headed home. He took an unusual route and from time to time would surreptitiously look behind to see if he was being followed. Yousef would make a lousy spy.

Back in his street, he looked for anyone out of place. He knew the locals. Then outside a cafe he saw unemployed youths smoking, killing time. One of the young men wore a hoodie with red lining.

*I'm being followed by the man I saw at the library with Javed.*

Yousef's heart exploded.

*If I go inside he'll call the cops. If I don't go inside he'll report me. Maybe the cops are already inside and he'll tell them I'm here.*

What Yousef lacked in intelligence he made up for in rat cunning. He strolled into the café as if to order a coffee. He grabbed the phone on the counter and dialled 18, the emergency number for the fire brigade, the Sapeurs Pompiers.

Turning from a couple of drinkers, he pretended to panic, and reported a fire at his apartment block. He hung up, placed coins on the counter and headed to the toilets.

His heart pounded as time dragged. Then he heard sirens and went outside. Firemen raced into his apartment block. People gathered to watch. Yousef joined the crowd and saw the man with the hoodie walk away. Eventually a false alarm was declared and the fire brigade left. Yousef quietly entered his flat.

He checked everywhere. His ingredients were safe. He looked for other signs. Was there a camera with a peephole in a wall? Did his TV or radio have some recording device inside them? He found nothing.

Then he decided. It was now or never. He would go online and seek bomb-making information. Then he would construct and detonate his bombs. He ate a meal, collected what he needed and waited till dark.

'You owe me my drugs or the cash, Bastien,' said Laris.

'Aw c'mon, Laris. You know I'm good for the gear or the money.'

'No I don't and I can't believe I let you talk me into this. Cash, coke or cripple—it's your choice, arsehole.'

Bastien acted tough and nonchalant. In reality, he shat himself. 'If you nobble me, Laris, you'll lose the best money launderer in Paris.'

Laris knew it but couldn't believe he'd given away his finest cocaine and heroin to set up a sting on a former cop. Laris fumed.

'What really hurts is my drugs are gunna be fucking incinerated.'

'I told you,' moaned Bastien. 'My mate will swap your gear for some rubbish and if not, I'll pay you out. So give it a rest, will ya?'

'Or what?' asked Laris sounding evil.

Bastien didn't answer and wanted to leave. He'd seen Laris deal with people who crossed him. Bastien could inflict torture but Laris enjoyed it. Torture excited him.

Bastien got his perverted thrills from degrading women and the younger the better. He changed the subject. 'What happened to that piece of young, black arse you promised?'

Laris went along with Bastien's perverted desires only because the ex-cop made Laris so much money. Washing dirty money is an art and Bastien was the best.

Laris rang one of his pimps and ordered his latest black chick. The pimp obliged. Why wouldn't he? Laris provided him with the bitches from Africa and Eastern Europe in the first place.

'No problem, boss,' said the pimp.

'What's her name?'

'Adamma.'

Yousef used to work as a kitchen hand in a busy restaurant. The owner was a wealthy businessman who exploited young people desperate for work. Yousef earned slave wages.

The owner's son, Hakan, came into the kitchen, took food, and chatted with the workers. He was disliked but enjoyed using the lowly staff as sycophantic "friends". To refuse his offer of drugs and alcohol was tantamount to being sacked. One night, Hakan invited Yousef and two other poorly paid workers to his home.

Yousef trod carefully. Telling the obnoxious son to get lost would cost him his job. Hakan's parents owned a substantial home with their son having his own kingdom on the top floor. The other two workers, unused to taking drugs, passed out.

Hakan looked at weird porn until his computer crashed. He swore. Yousef, who knew some programming, offered to help. He fixed Hakan's computer even improving the download speed. Hakan was impressed. He gave Yousef some cash and promised more if he'd help the next time his digital devices went haywire.

Yousef agreed and was pleased to escape. He feared for his semi-conscious co-workers.

Weeks later, Yousef returned to Hakan's house uninvited. It was 2100 hours and the family restaurant was busy. No-one was home. Yousef crept along the lane at the rear of the house. Being a wealthy part of Paris, the area was well lit. Yousef scrambled up the rear wall and looked into the garden. It was dark. He dropped into the garden and immediately it filled with light.

'Shit,' whispered the terrorist-in-training and ran through the garden. Last time he came to this house, he saw Hakan turn off the alarm and hoped gaining entry on the top level would not trigger it.

Using a combination of downpipe, windowsills and trellis with ivy, Yousef made it to the top floor and Hakan's "suite". There was a balcony outside Hakan's bedroom. Yousef crouched on it and caught his breath. He picked the lock. He paused then opened the door. He froze waiting for the alarm. Nothing.

*But is it a silent alarm sounding in the office of some security firm?*

Yousef scrambled inside to Hakan's computer and used the same password. Bingo. Lazy Hakan used the same one. Yousef tingled and searched for *How to Make a Bomb* and *How to Make a Suicide Vest*.

Whacky and dangerous web sites popped up. There may not have been a house alarm but other alarms screamed. Spooks came alive.

Yousef was thrilled with his success as he copied information to a USB stick. Of course such information was useless if he were arrested.

He buried the USB stick deep on his person and going down the pipe and trellis was easy. He sprinted through the brightly lit back garden, went up and over the back wall and ran.

He didn't stop running till he reached a Metro station, got out at his run-down suburb and walked home. With pounding heart he ran upstairs. He closed and double-locked his door, and leant against it gulping air. He wanted to shout for joy.

He guzzled water, splashed his face, dried his hands and produced his USB stick. He squeezed it. He was in metaphorical paradise and reckoned with his new information, would soon be in literal paradise.

Bomb-maker Yousef Jlassis was up and running.

# 14

DI CALLUM BLUNT lived up to his name. He was blunt in his opinions, reasoning and ambitions. His greatest strength lay in rubbing people up the wrong way. He was 38, good-looking and knew it, married into money, and planned to win promotion by any means, fair or foul. Whatever psychological testing was used to weed out the wrong people, failed. He was the exception to the rule that everyone who joined the police did so for all the right reasons.

Billy Hughes took an immediate dislike to him. He figured as the senior officer working on the Grovene homicide, he should be OIC. Never mind the fact he'd just arrived, had never worked on a homicide and was up against DS Billy Hughes with her solid experience solving murders all over the state, as well as being liked and respected by her fellow officers. Without trying, Blunt quickly lost any goodwill he might have been given as a newbie. He blew his Homicide honeymoon.

'So what part of the investigation do you want me to manage, Sergeant?' he asked without a trace of humility.

'Arse licking,' whispered Fleming, and Baldwin and Payne smiled.

Hughes politely put Blunt back in his box but was interrupted when DI Rose entered with the youngest member of the squad. Immediately officers stirred Jo about her forthcoming overseas trip.

'Hello, it's Fifi from French France,' said Baldwin.

Rose glared at him. 'Sorry to interrupt, DS Hughes,' said Rose. 'As you all know, DI Richelieu has been arrested on a serious charge. Detective Senior Constable Best has been given leave to see if she can help either the Australian Embassy or DI Richelieu's legal team. If any of you wish Jo to take a message to DI Richelieu, now is the time.'

Billy jumped in. 'I'm sure we all want his speedy release, ma'am. Tell him, Jo, we're all thinking of him and want him back here a.s.a.p.'

'Hear hear,' was the immediate response.

Jo thanked the squad and left with Rose to cries of 'Bon voyage' and 'Don't do anything I wouldn't do'. DI Blunt remained statuesque.

Rose's speech to Jo was a cross between a pep talk and hellfire sermon. The women shook hands and Jo left wondering when or if she would ever see her fellow detectives again. She drove to see Michael Chan.

'Are you *sure* you want me to come?' he asked.

Jo ignored his question. 'Through his lawyer, DI Richelieu has provided the tickets and put ten grand in my account to cover expenses.' Michael gasped. 'His lawyer has the key to Pierre's home in Paris. And we leave on Sunday.'

'Hang on,' protested Michael. 'Are you sure the DI wants me there?'

'He wants you, I want you. Now what's happening about Alan?'

'My brother-in-law's coming to stay but only for two weeks. He's completing a thesis and I've told Alan to let him work in peace. But he and my sister have a holiday planned for the first of next month.'

'Perfect,' said Jo. 'I suggest we travel light but make sure you're carrying.' He looked at her. 'You know, mobile, laptop, hacking gear.'

He shook his head and thought. *This woman is crazy. She'll be the death of me.* She smiled at him. *And I can't wait to go.*

Jo needed to tell four people about her trip—her mother, her sister and doctors Strange and Carr. She was able to kill two birds with one stone with family. Shirley was at Caitlyn's as the cancer patient recuperated.

'And about time,' said Shirley opening the door.

'Hello Mum. How's the patient?'

Caitlyn was in bed looking a lot less superior. Copping a potentially fatal illness tends to humble people. Jo sat on the bed.

'Thanks for coming, Jo,' said big sis. Jo cringed. Love and goodwill between the sisters was not the norm.

'We could really do with some help, Joanna,' said her mother.

Jo delayed revealing her news. They discussed the patient, Jeremy, Malcolm X (Jo's father), and Caitlyn's kids. Finally Jo took the plunge.

'Ladies, I have to tell you something and it's not good news.'

'You're pregnant,' stated Caitlyn resorting to type.

Jo ignored her sister. 'I have to go away for a couple of weeks.'

Shirley protested. 'But we need you here.'

'I'm sorry, Caitlyn, and you too, Mum. Something serious has happened overseas and I'm needed to rescue a colleague.'

'Overseas?' asked Shirley, thinking Tasmania.

'In Paris.'

Shirley and Caitlyn exploded. 'Paris?'

'A fellow officer's been arrested and faces a long prison sentence. With an expert, I'm going to help the lawyers have the charge thrown out. But I'll be back in a fortnight, maybe less.'

The flak was not too bad. Jo felt relieved and wanted to escape. She was about to when activity downstairs killed her plan.

'It's Jeremy and the kids,' said Grandma Shirley.

'Shit,' said Jo under her breath as the sound of footsteps soon saw the children and dreaded brother-in-law arrive.

'Auntie Jo,' they cried hugging their favourite cop and grown-up while ignoring their recovering mother and misery-guts Gran.

After fun times for Jo and the children, Shirley took the kids downstairs. Jeremy made a cursory enquiry about his wife's health then asked about Jo's latest adventures.

'She's running away,' said Caitlyn with a serious serve of jealousy.

'Wow,' exclaimed a fascinated husband. 'From whom?'

'No I'm not,' protested Jo.

'To Paris,' spat her sister.

Jeremy admired people with wealth and prestige. Having his talented sister-in-law swanning around Europe grabbed his attention.

'It's work and I'll be back in two weeks,' explained Jo.

'International murder,' oozed Jeremy. 'You're in the big time, Miss.'

Jo kissed her sister and promised to keep in touch. Jeremy escorted her downstairs. She waved goodbye to her nephew, niece and mother. The kids were sad to see her go. Shirley was angry.

Jeremy attempted his brotherly hug routine but Jo was too quick. He waved as she escaped to her car.

Her next port of call was the Carr residence. Little Harry would be home and obviously his sister Grace and their grandparents. Jo wasn't keen on facing Jack Carr. Telling him she was off to try and rescue a man he knew was keen on her might upset the GP.

*Why am I thinking that? Do I care if I upset him?*

She walked down the drive and was spotted. Rags saw her and barked. Harry yelled with delight. 'Detective Jo!' he cried and he and Rags took off. Jack appeared as this was his one free weekday.

'Hello, hello,' he said catching up with the welcome party.

'I was in the area,' lied Jo.

'Come in. It's lovely to see you.' They entered the kitchen 'Look who's here,' said Jack and the grandparents' faces shone. Greetings all round until everyone turned to the young girl seated, waiting to be fed. Jo smiled and went to greet Grace but was too late.

'Hello Jo,' said the child and the shock was palpable.

Jo recovered. 'Hello Grace,' she said and moved to her.

From the lips of the child with the acquired brain injury, and in emphatic terms came the words, 'How are you?'

Her family stared in shock. Yes, the speech was hesitant with a slight slur but the logic used was normal. Jo bent and kissed Grace's forehead. The child placed her hands on Jo's cheeks then stroked Jo's face. Tears appeared in the eyes of both grandparents. Jack's tears were already heading south. Harry stated the bleeding obvious yet proved that wisdom does come from the mouth of babes and sucklings.

'Grace is talking like she used to,' he declared.

What excitement. What joy. When they settled and grandparents and grandchildren exited stage left, Jo didn't mince words.

'I'm going overseas, Jack. A colleague's in trouble in Paris and Michael Chan and I are going to try and help.'

'Why am I not surprised?' said Jack smiling to cover his sadness. 'You rescued Rags so of course you'll rescue your colleague.'

Jack had questions. *Who is the colleague?* His mind raced. *Is it the man you kissed in the school grounds?* They walked to her car.

'Say goodbye to your folks and the kids. I'll be back in a fortnight.'

He became serious. 'I know about medicine and sometimes I see cases which defy logic and the opinions of doctors. Grace is going well and has all manner of medical support. But one visit from you, and she makes progress like never before.'

Jo felt good. 'I'm so glad.'

'You inspire my kids. They adore you.' They reached her car. Jo felt something serious was about to happen. He put in a request.

'I don't suppose I could hire you to visit my kids on a regular basis?' Jo laughed. Jack was serious. 'I'm even tempted to kidnap you and have you here permanently to entertain and educate my children.'

His face gave away nothing. *Is he joking?*

She looked at him. 'You wouldn't need to kidnap me, Jack.' They paused. Something romantic was about to happen when a woman walking her dogs passed by on the other side of the road.

'Hello Dr Carr,' she called and waved.

Jo slipped behind the wheel and lowered her window. 'I'll send you a postcard from Gay Paree.' He stepped back, blew her a kiss and she set off thinking about life and especially her love life.

Her final port of call found Gabrielle Strange examining a body. Jo stood at her door. 'Knock, knock.' Gabrielle left the corpse to talk to itself and went to embrace her favourite detective. Jo pulled back.

'Is it something I'm wearing?' asked Strange, grinning.

They enjoyed the joke and then Jo told the pathologist her news.

'Lucky you,' said Gabrielle. They chatted then Jo left with Strange calling after her. 'Keep yourself nice, girlie.'

DI Rose loved being boss of the cold case team. Her former Homicide colleagues, now retired, paid attention. 'I've divided the persons of interest into two groups—those we interviewed and those we didn't. She distributed screeds. 'I'll work with DCI Robertson and ...'

'You can drop the DCI,' said Robbo. 'Call me Robbo.'

Rose looked at him. 'So I'm with Robbo, and you two are Team B.'

'B for Best,' said Melk and was ignored.

'Team B has no authority to make an arrest. If you two try any heroics, you're back on the farm and choo-choo never to return. Clear?'

'Clear,' said Tuck and Melk as one.

'We do exactly as discussed. Get statements and bring same to our next meeting. I want this cold case solved so I can get a gold star.'

The others thought as one. *A gold star? Is she serious?* She was.

'Trust me, gentlemen, being a female senior officer is tough. I have to work faster and smarter, and produce better results than my colleagues who stand up to pee, so a result here would be rather nice, thank you linesmen, thank you ball-boys. Now, questions?'

Silence. She continued.

'Robbo and I tackle the pimp, Karl Benedek and those two uni students who gave him an alibi. Tucky and Colin, you take the former boyfriend, Danny Farr and his motor mechanic mate Ricky Towns.'

'We tackled them years ago,' said Melk.

'Which is why you'll tackle them again,' smiled Rose.

'The mechanic was smart,' said Tuck.

Rose buzzed. 'After that lot we tackle those we didn't interview. Call me if there's a problem, otherwise meeting tomorrow with reports.'

She drove Robbo as in the old days but struggled to call him Robbo. 'What's your thinking here, boss?'

'Those teenagers are middle-aged mums who may have a different take on life. If even one of them withdraws Benedek's alibi, he's back in the frame. What do we know about the women?'

'Blythe Jordan is 42, a single mum, has a teenage daughter and works for the Dunkley council as an Arts officer.'

At the council HQ, they told the CEO little and were shown to a vacant room. Soon a surprised Blythe arrived. Rose explained who they were and their mission. Blythe remembered and felt sick.

'But that's 20 years ago,' she protested, 'more.'

Rose struggled to break down the woman, and Robbo took over.

'Blythe, all those years ago, you and Gabby were struggling students. You came from respectable families and were terrified they'd discover your private income activities.'

Blythe despaired. 'We only did pictures. Please don't tell anyone.'

Robbo used his avuncular charm. 'We won't but we do want the truth. If something awful happened to your daughter—how old is she?'

'Seventeen.'

'You'd want the person responsible before a court.' He paused. 'Well?'

Blythe nodded and Rose admired the technique and care used by her old boss. He popped the question. 'Did you lie when you gave Karl Benedek an alibi for the day Maggie Stephens was murdered?'

Blythe dropped her head and whispered. 'Yes.'

Mission accomplished, it was time for the heavy questions. 'Have you had any contact with Karl Benedek?' *No.* 'Have you discussed your testimony with Gabby?' *No.* 'Will you sign a new statement?' *Yes.*

Blythe pleaded for anonymity and Rose promised she would try to keep Blythe and Gabby out of any future police action. They left with Blythe in no fit shape to work. She went home.

Rose and Robbo found Gabby Wendall at home. With four kids aged 6 to 14 and a husband, having this event appear now scared her to death. When told they'd spoken to Blythe, Gabby suffered serious stress.

'What did she say?' asked a now shaking Gabby.

Rose and Robbo gave Gabby the same spiel. They refused to reveal anything. Gabby sensed Blythe's response and wanted the matter over.

'I've thought about that poor woman. If it *was* that Karl guy, he was never charged because of me—I gave him an alibi.'

'You *and* Blythe,' said Rose.

Gabby broke down. She cried, confessed, and signed a new statement. The detectives left and sat in Rose's car.

'Good start, sir,' said the DI.

He looked at her. 'But it doesn't prove Benedek murdered Maggie. When can we have a go at him?'

'He's away, back in Melbourne tomorrow.'

'And what about the suicide?'

Rose looked at Robbo. 'Sir?'

'Just because the boyfriend confessed proves nothing. We should talk to his family to rule him out.'

'But if we find someone else, we *can* rule him out.'

Robbo smiled. 'Just testing, Inspector.'

Ricky Cable was a motor mechanic and mate of Danny Farr, a former boyfriend of Maggie Stephens and prime suspect in her murder. Danny assaulted Maggie when they were an item, and his DNA was found in the house where she was killed. But Danny was never charged because his mate Ricky gave him an alibi.

Tuck and Melk interviewed Danny and Ricky 22 years ago. Fast forward and Ricky now owned his own garage and was under a hoist when the two former cops arrived.

'G'day Ricky,' said Tuck. 'How's it goin'?'

Ricky studied his visitors, feigning ignorance. 'Do I know you?'

'Danny Farr,' said Melk.

'What about him?' asked the now worried mechanic.

'You gave him an alibi in 96 when his girl was murdered.' Ricky remembered everything. *How come these cops are still working?*

'We've reopened the case, Ricky,' said Tuck moving closer.

'We're looking at new evidence, Ricky,' oozed Melk moving closer.

'Accessory to murder won't appeal to customers, mate,' added Tuck.

'How are y'books, Ricky? GST up to date?' asked Melk.

Ricky hated cops and these in particular. He hadn't seen Danny for years and now the favour he did for him last millennium roared back to bite his arse. Ricky folded. He signed a new statement leaving Danny Farr high and dry.

# 15

IN HIS MODEST PARIS FLAT, Yousef made his bomb. The data he downloaded in the posh house of his former employer's son was gold. He hastened slowly and one idea excited him.

*I could make a mini version of my bomb, do everything according to the instructions but only use 10% of the recommended amounts. I can test it first to make sure it works.*

As Yousef made his bomb, police officers from RAID, wearing full protective gear, crept towards a house in which a computer recently downloaded terrorist material. It was a raid by RAID.

Hakan's father only opened the door to someone he knew and could trust. In this case he didn't have a choice. The door was demolished with the gun-carrying men storming the citadel. Wearing headphones and snorting coke, Hakan knew nothing until the police burst into his room. His computer was seized, Hakan was seized, his outraged parents were seized, and their son found himself in a world of pain.

Good.

Jo collected Michael using Uber. The computer expert was ready. He'd given Alan a lecture on manners and promised to send the moggie regular emails and texts. Like Jo, Michael travelled light. They were dressed by Kathmandu and Patagonia, and each carried a rucksack—unusual for international business-class travellers.

In the car they said little. When they did it was small talk. Both copped racing heartbeats and queasy stomachs.

They arrived at Tullamarine (Melbourne Airport) and Jo was unhappy with their tickets. 'I think we should downgrade,' she said. Michael's jaw dropped.

'You *up*grade, Detective. And why? We're not paying for them.'

'I know but it feels like a junket and I don't like it.'

'I do.'

She held out her hand. 'Let's try, please.' Reluctantly he gave her his ticket and they approached the Qantas desk. The woman behind the counter sported red lipstick some of which adorned her teeth.

'Hi,' she said.

Jo placed the business-class tickets on the counter. 'We'd like to exchange our tickets for Economy, please,' said Jo.

'Premium Economy,' said Michael.

'I'm sorry, I can't,' said the woman.

Jo went for the honest explanation, how a friend gave them the tickets and they didn't want him to spend so much money.

'I can't exchange them or give a refund because these tickets were bought with frequent flyer points.'

'Oh,' was all Jo could say. Michael took her arm.

'Let's go,' he said and to the woman, 'Thanks.'

Michael steered Jo around but turned back to the woman and pointed to his teeth. She was confused before grabbing a compact and discovering her red streaked pearly whites.

They checked in as business-class passengers and, with time to spare, Michael announced he would go for a walk.

'Don't get lost,' said Jo.

She studied a street map of Paris then switched to a French language audio lesson. She wore headphones and spoke aloud. She heard a cough and looked at the coughee. She lifted her headphones.

'You do know,' said Michael, 'your French phrases can be heard on the Champs Elysees?' She winced. 'And the correct pronunciation is Répétez s'il vous plaît?'

She looked at him and said, 'Repeat, please.' He half smiled.

The PA made the first call for their flight. They were not required. Those in cattle class went first but eventually they were called and off to Gay Paree they went.

Detective Inspector Callum Blunt was easy to dislike. He was the wrong person to join the police. It was all about him, his career, and joining Homicide when he did was perfect timing—for Blunt.

His boss, DI Rose, chose to go on special assignment, and the only other senior officer, DI Richelieu, was residing in a Parisian police cell.

The current homicide case was being run by DS Billy Hughes. *A DS* thought Blunt. *Surely as senior officer I should be running the show.*

Rose told Billy to treat Blunt with respect but he was *not* to run the investigation. 'I'm only a phone call away, Billy,' she said. 'Call me.'

'Ma'am,' smiled Billy appreciating her boss's instruction and trust.

Billy assigned DS Fleming and Senior Constable Baldwin to work with the new DI. Blunt liked having a team to command not realising the experienced Fleming and Baldwin were there to prevent him making dumb decisions. At least that was the plan.

Billy spoke. 'I hope a fresh pair of eyes from DI Blunt will find a chink in anyone's armour. Justin and Charlie, you've both dealt with the suspects, so you can background DI Blunt. Any questions?'

Baldwin wanted to ask when *background* became a verb, and the new team sallied forth. They visited Dr Gabrielle Strange. Her bullshit meter was the best in town and it crackled even before Blunt entered her domain. She nodded to Fleming and Baldwin, and stared at Blunt.

He introduced himself. 'DI Blunt, madam. I'm in charge of the homicide in Kew. Fleming and Baldwin exchanged glances. Really?

'Congratulations,' replied Strange with barely disguised sarcasm. 'And how can I help?'

'All material from the crime scene will do for starters,' said Blunt.

'All material from the crime scene was delivered to Homicide last Friday. You could have saved yourself a trip, Inspector.'

'That's Detective Inspector, madam.'

'Well whatever the nomenclature, squire, it doesn't change the fact you've wasted your time. And while I may look like a madam, I'm really a medico so that's *Doctor* Strange to you. Now, I have a rather smelly stiff to explore so you can all piss off.'

Blunt hated being mocked and especially in front of colleagues. He glared at Strange, thought, *I'll fix you, you fat bitch*, and stormed out.

Fleming and Baldwin looked at Strange who winked. 'Smart move by young Ms Best, slipping off to Paris.' The detectives smiled and left.

Blunt was a tad less bombastic when the trio arrived at Forensics. He buttonholed a female technical officer. She gave in to the DI's request and provided him with photos of the items found on the body.

'I think you'll find copies of this material were sent to Homicide.'

'But I've been assigned to this case and need my own copies.' His colleagues again exchanged glances. 'Is this the lot?'

'As far as I know, sir.'

'I don't want to come back because you forgot something.'

Other technical officers looked across to see what Detective Rude looked like. They made mental notes to avoid him in the future or, where possible, to make his life as difficult as possible.

In the car with Fleming ready to drive and Baldwin in the back, Blunt studied the photos and reports.

'So this chisel is the murder weapon.'

'Yes and no,' said Fleming. 'Dr Strange reckons it was placed in a larger wound made by a larger weapon.'

Blunt persisted. 'What do we know about the chisel?'

Fleming explained how a suspect admitted to having lost a chisel.

'Name?'

'Peter Ward, sir,' replied Baldwin.

'Right, let's have a chat with Mr Ward.'

Finding the carpenter was easy—same job, same location. Blunt led the way into the house. A female apprentice watched the cops. Baldwin gave her a forced smile and pointed towards the rear. She nodded. Blunt entered the kitchen where three men were working.

'Peter Ward?'

The chippie groaned. 'Oh not again. What is it with you bastards?'

'DI Blunt from Homicide,' said the bulldozer flashing his ID. He didn't bother to introduce his colleagues. 'I'd like a word.'

'We're in the middle of a delicate operation?'

'I'm investigating a murder. Co-operate or I'll arrest you.'

Fleming and Baldwin wished they were anywhere else as Ward looked like he might get arrested for assaulting a police officer. Reluctantly he stopped work and approached the detective.

'I understand you've lost a chisel.'

'I've already told you that.'

Blunt produced a photo. 'Is this your chisel?' Ward looked closer. 'Could be.'

Blunt spoke louder and with emphasis. 'Is this your chisel?'

'All right, yes. Where did you find it?'

'In the chest of the man who allegedly owed you a lot of money.'

'Allegedly?' sneered Ward. 'What's this fucking allegedly? I don't care if you accuse me of murdering the prick—I'd be proud to have done it—but I get seriously pissed when you call me a liar.'

The other detectives worried. Winding up a tough tradie who was ripped off was dumb. Suggesting he invented the story of being defrauded was red ragging a bull. Tempers frayed.

'You need to come to the station for fingerprint and DNA analysis.'

Ward reluctantly agreed. 'All right, I'll drop in on me way home.'

'No, now,' said Blunt. He indicated. 'Come on.'

Ward's blood boiled, his face contorted. 'I said I'll drop in today.'

Blunt was defied. He moved. 'Peter Ward I'm arresting you on suspicion of murder.' He went to grab the suspect and copped a right cross to the side of his head. Blunt went down taking a workhorse and planks with him. Fleming and Baldwin leapt to intervene. Ward ran.

'Get him,' screamed Blunt desperate for revenge.

Ward fled down the corridor and dived into the front bedroom. The cops scrambled after him. A terrifying scream exploded. Ward held his female apprentice in a headlock with a Stanley knife at her throat.

'Come any closer and I'll cut her.'

'Easy, easy,' said Fleming. 'There's no need for this, Peter.'

'Get out, now, all of you.'

Nursing his sore head, Blunt arrived. 'What's happened?' He acted tough. 'Put it down, Ward, or you'll be in serious trouble.'

'Get out,' screamed Ward. 'Get out and leave me alone or you'll be responsible for what happens.'

The young woman whimpered, begging with her eyes.

Baldwin showed leadership. 'I think we should leave, sir.'

'Leave? He's threatening a member of the public.'

Fleming backed Baldwin. 'He means it's a job for the Soggies, sir. We back off and let them sort it.' Blunt hated the situation. He wanted to arrest the murderer on his first homicide. Now it went pear-shaped and worse, he might be responsible *for* a homicide.

He yelled. 'We're leaving but if you hurt her, you'll regret it.'

Outside, Blunt gave orders. 'DS Fleming, report this to the SOG.' To Baldwin, he snapped. 'Report our situation to Homicide.' It was now "our" situation as Blunt sought to spread the blame.

As he fumed in the street, his colleagues were on their phones. Baldwin rang DI Rose as per her private instructions. When he explained the situation, she swore and told him to stay put. *What else are we going to do?* thought Baldwin.

Soon the elite SOG officers arrived, were briefed by an annoyed DI Blunt then went inside. They came out almost immediately.

'He's gone,' said the SOG officer. Blunt fumed. 'His van was in the lane at the back of the property. Did you have anyone watching it?'

Blunt's day went from bad to worse. DI Rose arrived with retired DCI Robertson as her chauffeur.

'What about the girl?' asked Blunt with a vision of his homicide career becoming the shortest ever.

'The guys inside said he took her.'

'Jesus,' whispered Rose seeing her role as head of Homicide being wiped out by one cowboy officer.

'Home address?' asked the SOG leader.

Blunt was clueless and Baldwin saved his bacon. The Soggies headed to Ward's home while Rose took Blunt to one side. She called back to Fleming and Baldwin. 'Interview the other workers.' They did.

Rose was blunt with Blunt. He stood there and took it. He had no choice. When he tried to interrupt, her curt, 'Shut up and listen' worked. At least it wasn't in front of the team; little comfort to the new DI with a throbbing head and a smashed ego. She lashed him.

'If we get out of this without another homicide, no thanks to you DI Blunt, you'll have nothing to do with Peter Ward. Understood?'

'He assaulted me, ma'am.'

'Good. Did you hear what I said?'

He forced out the word, 'Ma'am.'

'Rendezvous with Fleming and Baldwin, follow and support the Soggies. Return to Homicide where I will expect an unexpurgated report of this complete fuck-up on my desk before close of play. Clear?'

His nod was equally as hard as any spoken word.


Blunt was lucky. Ward felt terrible having threatened his young apprentice. He broke down and cried. Grovene owed him thousands and he would never see that money. He was a good boss and the woman was rapt to have the job. She suffered more from his pathetic apologies than his brief maniacal threats. He drove her home and told her he would hand himself in. She recovered enough to tell him she knew he would never have harmed her.

The SOG arrived at his home. He opened the door with his hands held out. Blunt was unsure about arresting Ward and having him charged with assault. The words of DI Rose rang in his ears.

In the end Homicide took him but Blunt asked his colleagues to process the prisoner while he became a reluctant essay writer.

The female apprentice wasn't the only young woman being threatened that day. Adamma, the now 16 year-old girl from Nigeria, a victim of human trafficking, was degraded in Paris working for a pimp. He obtained his girls thanks to Laris Jlassi, organized crime lord, drug dealer and big brother of would-be terrorist, Yousef.

Laris' mate, crim and former cop Émile Bastien, fancied young flesh and persuaded Laris to let him borrow anything black. Adamma was it.

Bastien collected his entertainment and chatted to her in a creepy way as they drove to his place. She was "on loan" for 48 hours and he taunted her with lecherous questions.

What could she say? Her body ached, her mind was a mess and her soul broken. Her new "career" in France had ruined her life. She dreamt of escape but how? With no money, passport, friends or family, the wretched girl was a candidate for self-harm.

Snorting cocaine and swallowing uppers meant Bastien was good for hours of "fun". He recruited one of his on-call girlfriends who performed with Adamma for Bastien's perverted pleasure. He gave orders and watched. What a man.

Adamma thought about her family and how glad her parents were to see their oldest child get a break in life. Their tears and fears as they waved goodbye kept invading her thoughts. How would they react if they could see her now? Bastien moved from spectator to participant.

Yousef caught the Metro late at night. With a trial bomb in his rucksack, he was doubly careful about not being followed but the anti-terrorist professionals outsmarted him. Yousef headed for the largest park in Paris, the Bois de Vincennes with its 1000 hectares of woodland, streams, lakes, zoo, buildings and more. His parents took Yousef and Laris there when the boys were young and innocent.

Yousef wanted to test a mini version of his bomb. In the deserted woodland, his terrorism dress rehearsal would help him perfect the deadly device designed to slaughter dozens.

Into the woodland he went. No moon, no lights and only his small torch to light the way. His RAID tail cursed. It was easy to follow the suspect on the Metro and in the streets, but once in the giant park, life turned tricky. The spy radioed his position and problem.

Yousef knew his destination. He followed a path until the woodland became thick. He walked into the wood, undid his rucksack and carefully removed the mini bomb.

The small torch in his mouth gave enough light. The wind picked up and tree branches swayed. Fallen leaves danced in the dark.

A sound scared the nervous Yousef. Was he being followed? Was he about to be arrested? An animal scurried away and Yousef sighed.

He had memorized the instructions. Once exploded, nothing would remain to identify Yousef as a lone wolf terrorist.

Back on the pathway, the RAID officer peered in the dark. He listened. Nothing. Then he saw a light. It moved. It disappeared.

The officer headed into the wood. Moving quietly was impossible but if Yousef Jlassi was a terrorist, he must be stopped.

Yousef placed his mini bomb against a tree. He checked the wiring, checked his phone and decided. Test time arrived. He felt his phone, prepared to back away then heard a sound. He froze.

In the silence of the park came the soft crunch of footsteps. Yousef panicked. He wouldn't even get to test his bomb. He'd be arrested or killed without going to Paradise. He started to run.

The cop heard him. A powerful torch picked out the fleeing figure.

'Hey! Stop!'

The wannabe terrorist stumbled and fell. The footsteps became loud. A brilliant light lit the trees around him. He died inside. Then, lying on the ground, he faced his pursuer. The bright light exposed Yousef. He held his phone, felt for the button and pushed. His mini bomb worked. The man from RAID became a number of body parts.

It was dawn when the authorities located the missing RAID officer; at least the bigger pieces of him. Yousef's fame as a terrorist grew and he moved up the wanted list. He fled.

At Charles de Galle airport, two Australian tourists cleared French customs. Joanna Best and her travelling companion, Michael Chan, caught the airport train to Gare du Nord in Paris.

# 16

COLIN MELK'S MARRIAGE produced a son. Josh, 20, lived with his Mum but saw his old man often. Now an adult, Josh would call Colin for a chat and the two caught up for birthdays and at Christmas.

Colin's life changed when he became a police consultant working on a cold case. There was a spring in his step but that disappeared when his son arrived with an arm in a sling.

'G'day Dad,' he called walking along the drive.

Colin stopped feeding his alpacas. 'What are you doing here? And what's with the arm in a sling?'

'Good to see you too,' said Josh. Colin was pleased to see his boy but concerned about the broken arm. 'Skateboard accident,' lied Josh.

'Skateboard? How old are you?'

The chat continued with Colin's concern growing. He once listened to lies for a living, and his boy's tale rang alarm bells. The truth came out and Colin despaired when his son dropped his act and cried.

'I've been stupid, Dad. I've been dealing drugs.'

Colin felt sick. 'Dealing drugs?' gasped Colin.

'It's nothing big time; only weed and uppers.'

'Are you insane? What the hell for?'

Christopher shrugged. 'Money.'

'I told you if you needed dough to ask me. You know I'll help.'

Josh explained. He wanted to quit dealing and the boss didn't want anyone leaving his empire. When Josh told the boss he was out, he copped a beating which included a broken arm.

'He said it'll be a broken leg next. Should I go to the cops, Dad?'

Colin despaired 'No, absolutely not. Tell me about this guy.'

Josh did and moved in with his old man. When Colin picked up Tucky for their latest cold case meeting, he told his former sergeant the sorry tale. The two men hooked up with Robbo and before DI Rose arrived all three discussed the young drug dealer's dilemma.

Tucky suggested a solution. The other two men looked at him.

'Ridiculous,' said Robbo.

'Agreed,' said Colin. 'Dad's Army wouldn't stand a chance.'

Even so, the seed was planted and the members of WATTI thought about adding *vigilantes* to their revised CV.


Jo and Michael stepped from the train at Gare de Nord in Paris. They took a taxi to Pierre's lawyer's office where the receptionist wasn't used to clients in casual gear with rucksacks. A 30ish gent wearing a bespoke suit with waistcoat spotted the travellers.

'Hello, I'm Antony Heron-Royhay,' he spoke with an old Etonian accent. 'You must be Miss Best and Mr Chan.' They shook hands. 'Come this way,' he said leading them to his office which was so big the visitors wondered if shouting was required. 'Pleasant journey I trust?'

'It was thanks to your client sending us business-class,' replied Jo.

Antony smiled never having endured steerage. He handed Jo a large envelope. 'This has the key to your Parisian home, a copy of the charges against your colleague, and details of his current location.'

'Thank you. What's the situation with bail?' asked Jo.

'There's another hearing next week although with Monsieur Richelieu being a serving police officer and considering the quantity of drugs in question, I think we'll have our work cut out.'

Jo despaired. 'But you must see Pierre's been framed. We have a highly respected policeman in both France and Australia who returns to Paris to bury his mother and immediately sets up as a major drug dealer. It's absurd.'

Antony opened his palms to express hopelessness. 'I agree.'

Michael joined the conversation. 'Does Inspector Richelieu have enemies from his time in Paris?'

'Alas I know very little,' replied the lawyer. 'I have the feeling your colleague is waiting to speak to you.' He paused. 'Unless Monsieur Richelieu is completely frank with me, he may not see the sights of Paris for a very long time.'

The room fell silent. A ticking clock seemed loud.

'What do you suggest?' asked Jo.

'Visit your colleague as soon as possible. Tell him I'm not so much his best hope as his only hope. Unless I'm told everything relevant to the case, he is wasting his money engaging my services.'

Jo understood. 'Thank you, sir.' She paused. 'I'm sorry, I don't know how to address you.'

'My friends call me Antony,' he smiled—not at Michael. 'My father is the Earl of Eynesbury but being the younger son, it's my big brother who snaffles the moniker of Lord. I'm plain old The Honourable.'

Jo stood and Michael followed. 'Well thank you, Antony. We'll let you know how we get on with Pierre.'

He handed her a card. 'This has my mobile. Once you've seen my client, I'd be happy to talk tactics over dinner tonight.'

Whoa. Where did that come from? Jo was surprised; Michael suspicious.

'How kind. Perhaps we'll find our lodgings and visit Pierre first.'

'Super,' he said guiding them back to the foyer and out to the lift. He waved them goodbye and Michael hummed *Freres Jacques*.

'What?' asked Jo, frustrated.

He mimicked Antony with an over-the-top old Etonian accent. 'I'd be happy to talk tactics over dinner tonight.'

'He's trying to get something happening.'

'He certainly is.'

Jo despaired. 'Oh Michael, don't be a pain. We need to work together if we're going to help Pierre.'

He grimaced and they looked for a cab.


Robbo asked Rose if they could take a break for a day. With the fiasco caused by DI Blunt, Rose was happy to agree. She needed to rescue the Grovene homicide investigation.

Robbo, Tuck and Melk devised a plan. What they now lacked in muscle, they could make up for in smarts. They knew how to find a criminal and threaten him with the full weight of the law, even if they no longer had any police powers.

All three ex-detectives wanted to help young Josh Melk and have him out of the drug scene once and for all.

They pulled in a few favours from local police and gathered information about the ratbag who threatened young Melk and broke his arm. The plan was to trap the crim alone and use all their years of experience to intimidate him, warning him off Josh Melk. No arrest, no fisticuffs, just some old-fashioned police bravado. No problems. The three amigos felt a rush of adrenalin as they launched their raid.

The drug boss, hardly Pablo Escobar, ran a panel beating business as a front for his drug empire which covered all of three suburbs. He bought the gear from heavy hitters and ran a small army of low-level operatives of whom Josh Melk was one.

The trio parked in a side street just before closing. As the roller door descended, the ex-cops slipped under surprising Dwayne, the Mr Big of Preston.

'Hey,' he yelled thinking the group were cops or worse, rival drug dealers. Looking closely at the visitors, he relaxed. Here were two pensioners and a middle-aged hippie. They must be lost.

'G'day Dwayne,' said Tucky, sounding friendly but threatening at the same time.

Dwayne went back to worrying. *They're not lost. They know my name.* 'Wadda y'want?'

'A little chat,' smiled Melk invading Dwayne's personal space.

'Who are you?' he asked with a mix of anger and fear.

'We have a proposition for you, Dwayne,' said Robbo as arthritis pinged in his dicky knee.

'I don't do pensioner discounts. Now piss off.' He reckoned he could beat them although Melk looked a bit tasty. But all three at once might prove tricky and the old guy's walking stick could do some mischief.

Tucky moved closer. 'It's a small request, Dwayne. We want you to back off one of your drug mules.'

'Dunno what you're talkin' about.'

Melk came at him from another direction. 'It's more of a demand than a request.'

'Fuck off,' said the panel beater quietly shitting himself. His fear came from the unknown. *These geriatrics know the lingo.* They oozed experience. Robbo rested his walking stick on his shoulder, holding it by the ferrule. It was poised to strike.

Dwayne sniffed then turned and sprinted across the concrete floor. The trio gave chase. Melk ran, Tucky jogged and Robbo stepped carefully. Dwayne dived inside his office, a small hut in the corner of the factory. He snibbed the lock. A drunken weakling could have kicked it in but Dwayne was, for the moment, safe.

Three faces peered in at him.

'Come on Dwayne, we just want a chat,' urged Tuck.

Dwayne was having none of it. 'Piss of or I'll call the cops.'

'We *are* the cops,' said Melk with immediate regret.

'We know about your drug dealing, Dwayne,' said Robbo. 'We can have the Drug Squad here in five.' He paused. 'Fancy a raid?'

Dwayne hesitated. Calling the cops was never an option. He resorted to what he knew best. 'All right, I'll come out but first you've gotta move away from the door.' The trio remained still. 'Move back or I ain't coming out.' The trio shared glances then retreated a couple of metres. 'Further back,' shouted Dwayne. The trio moved.

The Yale was unlocked. Dwayne paused then pulled open the door and stepped out brandishing a pistol.

'Shit,' said Tuck.

'Move and I shoot,' snapped Dwayne. He looked scarily believable, moved to one side and waved his gun. 'Now get inside.' The trio froze. 'Move!' screamed the unbalanced crim. The trio moved single file towards the office. 'In!' screamed Dwayne standing well out of reach.

With the trio inside, Dwayne followed pointing the gun. He pulled the door, used a key to deadlock it and stepped back.

Tuck yelled. 'This is crazy, Dwayne. Drugs are bad enough but stolen guns are fucking stupid.'

'Shut up,' snapped a rattled Dwayne. He would have been fine with other druggies but old age crims in suits were tricky. He grabbed his phone and made a call.

'Well,' said Tuck to the others and imitating Oliver Hardy. 'Here's another nice mess you've got me into.'

Melk panicked. 'What'll we do?'

'Call Elly,' said Robbo.

'Forget Dwayne,' replied Tuck, '*she'll* shoot us.'

Robbo took out his phone and made a call. 'It's either Dwayne or the boss. You choose.' The phone was answered. 'Hello Elly, it's your favourite DCI.' The others looked worried.

Robbo explained then held the phone from his ear and hit *Speaker*. The trio cringed as DI Rose turned the air blue. They were told to sit tight and do nothing. 'Including breathing,' she spat and hung up.

'I think this is the end of *We Are The Three Idiots*, lads,' said Robbo genuinely disappointed. Tuck and Melk said nothing. In their misery, a back door to the panel beaters opened and two blokes arrived.

'Dwayne's goons are here,' said Melk peering through the unwashed window. 'The odds have shortened.'

All three ex-cops worried. They knew this could go horribly wrong.

'What'll they do, boss?' asked Tuck.

'No idea but we'll do nothing. If we're lucky, Elly will have the local uniforms pop in and Dwayne and his pals will quietly surrender. The drug squad will buy us a beer and you two can go back to alpacas and Puffing Billy.'

That seemed wishful thinking as the three drug dealers approached the office. 'Here's trouble,' said Melk. 'They're all carrying.'

'Stay calm,' urged Robbo. 'Don't do anything to upset them.'

'They're already upset,' whispered Melk.

'Oi,' shouted Dwayne. 'You're gunna come out, one at a time. Any tricks and we've got three shooters.' He moved in and unlocked the door. 'Now, Grandpa, you're first.'

'*I'm* a grandfather,' muttered Tuck.

'Yeah but I'm a *great*-grandfather,' said Robbo moving to the door.

'Slowly,' shouted Dwayne and stood back. Robbo opened the door and walked out leaning heavily on his stick, trying for the sympathy vote. He'd faced many an armed criminal over the years but still his heart moved through the gears.

He was made to kneel which was super cruel. Getting down was bad but if they didn't shoot him, he'd have bugger all chance of getting up.

'Next,' yelled Dwayne and Tuck appeared and made to kneel. What a way to end a life and a wonderful career in policing. Melk was called and joined the party. This whole "adventure" was his idea.

He whispered. 'Sorry Sarge, sorry Boss.'

'Shut it,' spat Dwayne and moved behind the trio. The sound of a gun being cocked bounced around the concrete and tin building. 'Say goodbye, Pop,' said Dwayne and none of them heard the gun discharge because of the racket as the back door was smashed. The cavalry came through the roller door too.

The same SOG officers who were called out to arrest Peter Ward, burst in and caused three middle-level drug dealers to fold like a short-sighted night-watchman on a green top. DI Rose entered and the trio then felt real fear. She walked them outside and if looks could kill, the entire membership of WATTI were dead and buried. At least young Josh Melk's tormentors were off his back.

Jo and Michael caught a cab to their Paris home. They walked along the Rue Crémieux cobbles admiring the pot plants and brightly coloured houses.

'This is stunning,' said Jo.

'True,' agreed Michael, 'and you've walked past our house.'

Jo produced the key, they entered and both reckoned it was the best Airbnb in Paris. They explored the ground floor then upstairs.

'This is Pierre's mother's room. We can't sleep in here,' said Jo.

*We?* thought Michael. *We?*

They found a bedroom each, dumped their luggage and headed downstairs. Michael made coffee while Jo re-read the charges against Richelieu. She muttered and swore.

'So what's the plan?' asked Michael.

'We visit Pierre, trust nobody and especially not the police.'

'What about the Honourable Antony?'

'We have to trust him and hope he knows his onions.'

They went to the police station where Antony interviewed Pierre. He was on remand in La Santé Prison, in the 14th arrondissement, only 10 minutes by cab across the Seine from Rue Crémieux. They waited in the visitors' room. Michael subtly indicated the CCTV cameras and Jo appreciated having her own IT expert.

Pierre appeared looking terrible. For an immaculate dresser, and a man for whom haircuts and shaving were a ritual, Richelieu failed. At least his smile remained in reasonable working order.

Prison officials explained the rules about contact. Jo and Richelieu longed to embrace and kiss. Michael's jealousy stocks soared.

The trio talked. Guards observed. CCTV cameras operated. Richelieu gave them the story about how, years ago, he arrested corrupt officers, and how these ex-cops have always wanted revenge.

'But why not kill you, Pierre?' asked Jo.

'Too easy, ma chérie, too quick.'

'And you're sure about this, Monsieur?' asked Michael.

'Naturellement. They know I am in Paris, my mother's 'ouse, and they 'ad access to a commercial quantity of Class A drugs. Only criminals and corrupt police officers could know and do all that.'

'Criminals *and* corrupt police?' asked Jo.

'It 'as to be.'

They paused. If true, this was a terrible situation. Pierre was fitted up with no help in his own city.

Jo needed facts. 'Who should we see?'

'Commandant Erec Bonnaire. We worked together and 'e is your best contact. Only you must never let 'im know you are investigating my case. Tell 'im you are working for my lawyer.'

'What about the Honourable lawyer? Do you trust him?'

Pierre shrugged. 'I 'ave no choice.'

There was a time limit to the prison visit. Michael said little. When he spoke he did so in a quiet voice with his hand across his mouth.

'I am going to place a mini recorder on the table.' The others worried. 'It's a test to see what they do. We'll talk about your lawyer and his approach. Give away nothing of value. Okay?'

The others gave tiny nods. Michael placed a small voice recorder on the table and hit *Record*. He spoke first.

'But we need to let Mr Heron-Royhay know what we think. If you speak honestly, we can play him your thoughts. So, are you happy with his services and if not, why not?'

Richelieu understood. 'Yes, I like 'is experience and attention to detail. But I am not 'appy 'e even thinks about making a deal and 'ave me plead guilty.'

'You mustn't do that,' said Jo.

They continued before a guard came for the prisoner. Richelieu was overcome that the woman he loved and a brilliant IT expert came from Australia to help win his freedom.

'We'll return soon, Pierre,' called Jo. 'Stay strong.'

He blew Jo a kiss, gave Michael a thumbs-up, and left. The visitors went to Reception and signed out. A guard spoke.

'Pardon Monsieur, empty your pockets, s'il vous plaît.'

Michael hesitated then placed everything including his mini recorder on the table. The guard examined it.

'What is this?'

Michael explained. The guard told them to wait and took the recorder. The visitors looked at one another and waited. Eventually the guard returned and handed Michael the item. He collected his bits and bobs and the couple left.

They went looking for a café. Once seated, they ordered and Michael discretely opened the recorder. They chatted with their eyes.

'Is anything missing?' asked Jo.

'No but they've given us a free tracking device.'

The coffee arrived and Jo worried. 'What does it all mean?'

'Pierre may well be correct. A gendarme or three is corrupt.'

'What do we do?'

He shrugged. Ring your toffy chum and go on a dinner date.'

'You're coming too, Michael.'

He smiled. 'Ah no, you're on your own there, Detective.'

After coffee they went cab hunting. Passing a homeless chap, Michael dropped two euros in his container. The man's few and filthy teeth appeared. 'Merci, Monsieur,' he muttered.

'Sell this for ten euros,' said Michael, surreptitiously handing the man the voice recorder. 'Ten euros,' he repeated and walked away.

'Was that wise?' asked Jo.

'With any luck the cops will follow the tracker all over Paris.'

She looked at him then slipped her arm into his as they walked the streets of Gay Paree. Michael beamed inside.

# 17

OUTSIDE THE PRESTON DRUG HQ, the look on DI Rose's face was scary. She confronted the three cold case detectives in tongue-lashing mode. The fact it came from a person who was once their junior, made it worse.

'I've bent over backwards to get you reprobates a chance to do some more policing and this is how you repay me.'

'It was my fault, Elly,' interrupted Melk.

Using her name made her anger worse. 'Shut up, For Sale. You're supposed to crack a cold case not join the French foreign fucking legion.'

She regretted her language and more so when she saw Robbo's face. She pulled back. 'Look the AC went out on a limb to appoint me as Homicide boss and there are plenty of people keen to see me fail. If we can't solve this cold case, so be it, but please don't think you're back in Homicide. You're not. Clear?'

The elderly schoolboys muttered agreement and more apologies.

'What did the drug squad boys say, *ma'am*?' asked Tuck. He knew.

'Don't be a smartarse, Tucky. You know they were rapt to grab those bastards. But you were deadset lucky. If one of you had been shot, my career would've been over.'

'Wow,' said Melk, 'you're sacked while we're only dead.'

Rose winced. She worried more about herself than her team.

'So it's all's well that ends well,' added Robbo smiling.

It took a while for Rose to smile. 'Touché, but gentlemen, can we please stick to the cold case.'

It took a moment but soon smiles appeared all round.

'I've got this idea,' said Melk.

'No,' said the others as one.

'Meeting tonight at Robbo's,' she said walking away. 'Don't be late.'

Once home from the park, Yousef worked fast. In amongst his fear was joy. He knew how to make a bomb. His test run worked but would bring the cops to his door. He killed his first infidel but his goal was to kill many more. To be successful, he must flee.

Every ingredient for his bomb was carefully packed in his holdall. Emergency rations stockpiled for weeks were in his rucksack. He needed a safe place to prepare the proper bomb. He could never return to this flat. He slipped away and spent the night under a bridge.

Next morning he needed sanctuary. Not his parents or the mosque. *Where else?*

He decided and approached the building. He'd been here before and vowed never to return. But these were desperate times. He rang the bell in the street.

'Yes?' The voice sounded like a threat to kill or bash.

'It's Yousef.'

'Who?'

'Yousef Jlassi.'

He could hear the person in the building talking to someone else. Then the voice boomed again. 'Waddya want?'

'To see my brother.'

'Why?'

'Could I come in and see him, please?'

More voices sounded inside and then the gate pinged. Yousef pushed it, stepped inside and the gate crashed back. He climbed the steps to the front door. It opened and a man who was once a finalist in *Thug of the Year* filled the frame.

'Are you carrying?'

'Just the rucksack and holdall.'

'Have you got any knives or guns?'

'No, of course not,' said Yousef. He didn't mention his bomb-making material. To add weight to his claim, he opened the bags.

The thug knew about his boss's little brother being a wimp, possibly gay and religious, and who wouldn't say boo to a goose. The thug saw the food packages and the laundry type packets and assumed his boss's beliefs were true. No guns or knives on board.

'In,' said the thug. Yousef felt relief and entered big brother's office.

'Little brother,' said the normal criminal.

'Hello Laris,' said the abnormal criminal. 'I've come to beg a favour.'

Yousef turned on a sob story how he was bashed and robbed, lost his money and job and is leaving Paris for work in Lyon. All Yousef wanted was a place to stay until his friend brought money and clothes.

'Clothes?' asked Laris.

'I'll be a chef in a hotel so have to dress neatly. My friend'll be here in two days, three at the most.' Yousef indicated his rucksack. 'I even have my own food. Please Laris.'

Laris ordered. 'Put him downstairs, anywhere.'

'Thank you, brother. You won't even know I'm here.'

Laris felt nothing for his brother and little for his parents but the request was so piddling he agreed.

'Three days and you're gone.'

Yousef wanted to cry. 'Thank you, brother. One day I hope you will be proud of me.'

'The cellar next to the garage,' said Laris to his muscle and Yousef left praising his sibling.

The cellar was perfect. It was out of the way, solid, freezing and primitive—perfect for undisturbed bomb-making.

Jo rang Antony and explained the meeting with Pierre. 'Excellent,' said the Englishman. 'We have much to discuss over dinner.' He confirmed her address. 'I'll collect you in half an hour. Oh, and wear your glad rags.'

Jo hung up. Michael wanted news. 'What did he say?'

'Wear your glad rags.'

'Should you ring your mother?'

Jo worried, went to change and wished her wardrobe had more than one half-decent outfit. She went black. Slacks, roll neck sweater, Versace jacket, gold belt, gold necklace and earrings, and stylish black boots with her hair in a French bun. She entered the room and did a twirl for Michael.

'Will I pass?'

He wanted to say, "Wow" but held himself in check. 'Not bad.'

'Not bad?'

'Remember we have two weeks to save Pierre from the guillotine.'

Jo grimaced. What a thought.

The doorbell rang. Antony was on time. Jo grabbed her black quilted shoulder bag. 'Wish me luck,' she said and left.

Michael raised his voice. 'Call me if you ....' He wanted to say "need me" but the words stuck in his mouth. He thought about Jo Best.

*Will the aristocrat pass me in the queue? Am I even in the queue?*

Jo was glad she left her jeans, trainers and puff parka behind. The restaurant reeked of class, and staff fawned over Antony with the lascivious maitre d' assessing his female guest as quality eye candy.

The food was slightly better than sensational and Jo worried the evening concentrated on flattery and not business.

'What is your background, Joanna? I am curious.'

She explained her training as a lawyer and work as a homicide detective. He seemed genuinely impressed, and such information only intensified his desire to seduce the lovely lady from Down Under. For Antony, a beautiful woman with brains was the ultimate challenge.

'So tell me, Joanna, what news from my client?' She told him. He listened than opined. 'I agree with Pierre. You should visit his former colleague—what's his name?'

'Commandant Erec Bonnaire.'

'I would not mention your lawyer status. Simply reveal you are a fellow police officer shocked at your friend's situation, and wanting to help his legal team help their client.' Jo agreed but wanted more.

'Can you recommend anyone outside the police who might know the type of people who framed Pierre?'

Antony opened his phone. 'When I worked in London, we used a former police officer with experience at Interpol.' He handed his phone to Jo who added the details to her contacts.

'Thank you,' she said.

'He lives in London, is eccentric but knows about crims in France.'

Jo felt better having even one contact. Without outside help, she and Michael would struggle. Antony continued to do most of the talking and Jo grew tired.

'Antony, I'm sorry but I'm rather tired. It's jetlag.'

He signalled to the waiter. 'Of course, forgive me.

She stood with a hovering waiter on hand to assist. 'I'll pay a visit.' She headed for the *Mesdames* not used to rich French food, English manners and corrupt police officers, 17,000 kilometres from home.

They took a cab to Rue Crémieux. He made the driver wait then escorted her to the front door, flicking the charm switch.

'I'm going home on the weekend, Joanna. You should come. We could plan Pierre's defence en route. Do you ride?'

Jo was tired, wined and dined, and now being offered a weekend in the English countryside. 'Oh, I'm not sure.'

'You'll love it. I'll arrange your Eurostar tix and you can choose from half a dozen suites in the Eastern wing. Good luck tomorrow with Commandant Bonnaire. I'll call you.' He lifted her hand, kissed it, then turned and headed back to his waiting cab.

'Bugger me,' she whispered and opened her front door.

'Evening officer,' said Michael trying hard not to disguise his curiosity re her night out. Then mimicking Dick Van Dyke mimicking a cockney, he said, 'Cuppa tea, darling?'

She told the IT expert everything. He was quietly jealous but such emotion took flight when Jo described her weekend in the country.

'Six bedrooms?' he asked.

'In the Eastern wing.'

Michael opened his laptop. 'I found the Heron-Royhay family seat. It's a bit of a lean-to.'

'What?' gasped Jo. She gawped at Bulwer Hall, a stately home in a measley 3,000 acres. 'Oh my god! Is that his house?'

'It's where his folks hang out—The Earl of Eynesbury and his missus, Countess Jonquil.'

'Jonquil? Don't tell me her sister's Daffodil.'

'There's a photo of Mumsie here somewhere.'

Jo lost interest. 'Michael, how is my swanning off to England going to help Pierre? This rescue mission is turning into a junket.'

They looked at one another. Luxury travel, superb accommodation and no progress in sorting Pierre's drug charges.

'First thing tomorrow, Michael, we're off to see Commandant Erec Bonnaire. But right now I'm pooped. Sleep well. Goodnight.'

'Goodnight,' he called and watched her from behind or rather, he watched her behind.

# 18

BILLY CALLED THE SQUAD TOGETHER. Everyone was aware of the fiasco caused when new boy, DI Blunt, did his bull-in-a-china-shop interview. He was read the riot act by DI Rose in private meaning Blunt spewed and now worked dressed in sackcloth while seated in ashes. Billy addressed the squad.

'Peter Ward has been arrested and charged with assault. Thanks to DI Blunt we now know it was Ward's chisel found in the victim's chest.'

Wrong. Blunt didn't identify the chisel but Billy was trying to make Blunt look slightly less of a goose. She challenged the squad.

'If Ward is our killer, and remember he's got a massive incentive being owed mega-bucks by the deceased, plus no alibi for the day of the murder, then why would he leave his own chisel at the scene?'

Various answers were offered.

'He didn't care his rage was so great.'

'He panicked and forgot.'

'The real killer pinched the chisel hoping to incriminate Ward.'

'It's a double bluff,' said Payne. 'No-one would think he'd leave his own chisel at the scene and thus we look at everyone else.'

'But the chisel wasn't what killed him. It was added later,' said Blunt, desperate to get back into the game. This was old news.

Billy exhaled. 'Right, Justin and I will interview Ward. What else?'

'We're looking at the victim's and estate agent's phone records, Sarge,' said Baldwin. 'There are two unknown calls on the day Grovene was killed coming from a lawn bowling club in Hawthorn.

'What?' exclaimed Billy. 'The victim and the bloke who found him were both called from the same number on the day of the murder? We'll have the killer on CCTV. Why wasn't I told?'

'Only just received the records, Sarge.'

'Bloody hell, Charlie, make it a priority. Trace the caller.'

'Or callers, Sarge,' he cheekily added. She glared at him.

DI Rose observed. 'What's happening with the grieving widow?'

'She's next on the list, ma'am,' replied Billy.

'I can interview her,' piped up DI Blunt hoping, begging more like, to get back in the game. Billy flattened him.

'There's something else for you, Callum. Forensics have photos of a bicycle tyre impression in the yard of the murder scene. Can you find a cycle expert and ID the tyre and then hopefully the bike? If someone on a bike, even a kid, was there on the day, he or she may have seen something. Take Detective Senior Constable Payne.'

*Great,* thought Blunt, *I'm on school crossing duty with a dork.*

Payne experienced an identical thought.

'Right,' said Billy, 'let's go.' She looked at DI Rose. 'Unless you want to say something, ma'am.'

Rose did. 'Only that Jo Best has arrived in Paris and is doing it tough working day and night to get DI Richelieu out of his bloody awful mess. Carry on.'

'Oh ma'am,' interrupted Blunt. 'Any news on the cold case team?'

*What a bastard* thought Rose. *He cocked up and had the Soggies arrive to save his bacon. Now he wants to rub my nose in it for the same thing. Those rumours about Blunt are true.*

'All under control, thank you, Inspector.'


Hughes and Fleming interviewed Ward with his solicitor who spoke. 'I want it on record that my client believes he was bullied by your officers, and placed under duress causing him to panic. And furthermore, the young apprentice employed by my client refuses to press charges.'

Billy paused. 'Finished, sir?'

'For now,' he said and sat back.

'Thank you,' said Billy and her polite words and friendly body language calmed the confrontational atmosphere. 'I've spoken with senior officers, Peter, and we are still considering what charges you'll face. A lot depends on our talk about the death of Simon Grovene.'

'My client will be making no comment,' said the solicitor.

'It's all right,' said Ward raising a hand for the solicitor. 'Ask me.'

Billy was pleased and Fleming impressed. 'When did you notice your chisel was missing?' she asked.

'Not sure. Things disappear and you don't know till you need them.'

'So the chisel was in your tool box in the back of your ute?' Ward nodded. 'Do you leave the ute where someone has easy access?'

'It's secure at home but if I go out at night, it could be forced.'

'When were you and the ute last out at night?'

'I went to a meeting of Grovene's creditors a couple of weeks back.'

'And the ute?'

'It was parked next to the school hall.'

'And the tool box was secure?'

He hesitated. 'I think so.'

Billy looked at him. 'Now I need to establish your alibi.'

'I told you, I haven't got one. The only time I left me ute was in Eltham but I never went in a shop.'

'Service station?' asked Fleming, 'public loo?'

Ward shook his head and the detectives let him go.


Blunt and Payne arrived at Forensics. The scientists remembered the prat they dealt with before. Blunt had yet to grasp how treating people with respect was the best way to get what you wanted. He never learnt how *please* and *thank you* paid dividends.

Payne saved the day and the bicycle tyre photos were handed over. 'There's a bloke been selling bikes for 40 years in Fairfield, sir' said Payne and that's where they went.


Charlie Baldwin entered the Riversdale bowling club in Hawthorn. Immaculate greens surrounded the clubhouse. A few keen bowlers were playing but the members who lunched were yet to arrive.

'Good morning,' said the manager. 'Members only, I'm afraid.'

Baldwin held up his ID. 'This phone number,' he said showing the manager a piece of paper, 'it's here, yes?'

'Indeed.'

Baldwin explained the situation. 'Do you have CCTV?'

'We do, sadly it's required in today's society.'

'I'm interested in last Thursday between 10 am and noon.'

The manager left then returned with a disc. 'I'll need a signature.'

'Of course,' said Baldwin. 'Anything unusual happen that day?'

The manager shook his head. 'Don't think so.'

'Could someone who wasn't a member come in and use the phone?'

'Unlikely, especially when we're busy and were made by a stranger.'

'Thanks,' said Charlie and left hoping the footage he carried would identify the person who murdered Simon Grovene.

Blunt and Payne arrived at the bike shop. It was dusty, higgledy-piggledy and smelly—nice smelly. They found the owner, Gordon "Dolly" Mount in the back repairing a bike.

'Today's bikes are either state-of-the-art and expensive or cheap and ripe for repair. Now, how can I help you gents?'

The police identified themselves and showed Dolly the tyre photos. He studied them being up for a challenge. 'I think it's a Schwalbe Marathon Plus or a Schwalbe Marathon Racer. I'd have to check.'

'Right, will you do that,' fired Blunt.

'Say please,' said Dolly.

Blunt froze. The word refused to trip off his tongue. Payne saved the day. 'Please, sir,' he said and Dolly smiled. Blunt couldn't.

Dolly disappeared then returned. 'I think I'm right,' he said and confirmed the tyre's make and model. Payne took notes.

'Who would ride this bike?" asked Blunt. 'A kid, a middle-aged bloke looking ridiculous in lycra? Who?'

Dolly laughed. 'No idea, but if the bike matched the tyre, they'd need deep pockets. Putting those tyres on a cheap bike would be like putting lipstick on a pig.'

Blunt continued. 'Sold any of these tyres lately?'

Dolly sniffed. 'Might have. What's this all about?'

Blunt tried brute force. 'Have you sold any of these tyres?'

Dolly decided the rudeness of the cop didn't deserve an answer.

'Nup,' he said and wouldn't budge. The police departed. Payne squibbed telling Blunt his attitude was counter-productive.

'Right, we hit bike shops, schools, and houses around the crime scene showing photos of bikes with these tyres.'

'But we haven't got bike photos, sir, only tyre photos.'

Blunt hated a lowly Detective Senior Constable highlighting his mistake and the DI's anger boiled.

'Shops and schools,' he snapped and got in the car.

Hughes and Fleming knocked on the widow Grovene's door. The widow wasn't short of a quid, and her mourning was done and dusted.

'What do you know about your late husband's enemies, Mrs Grovene?' asked Billy.

'How long have you got?'

'Anyone stand out?'

She shrugged. 'Anyone who was owed money.'

'Where you were on the day your husband was murdered, madam?' asked Fleming.

She returned serve. 'Here with my in-laws, all day.'

'Were they upset at their son's violent death?' continued Billy

'Upset definitely but not surprised.'

The detectives were interested. She appeared to taunt them.

*I know something you don't and I'm not going to tell you.*

'Despite your husband's considerable debts, you would appear to be well off, madam,' said Billy with a straight face and monotone voice.

'Are you investigating his murder or researching for tabloid TV?'

Clearly the widow was no mug and the officers took their leave.

'I reckon she and the in-laws conspired to bump him off,' said Fleming as they walked to the car.

'That's a bit wild even for you,' replied Billy.

'Grovene's trashed the family's good name, has plenty of life cover, so a hit kills the bad publicity and lands the family a motser.'

'Why aren't you an inspector, sergeant?' she asked. 'Now where do her in-laws live?' They drove to the victim's parents.


Derek and Gemma Grovene were retired and not on Struggle Street. They still mourned their son. Billy made all the right noises about the tragedy and backed the police to bring justice to the Grovene family.

'Is there anyone who wanted to harm your son?' asked Billy.

They played a straight bat with no suggestions. Derek lived under petticoat government so Gemma took over. 'Do you know about Simon's wife's family and the agent who found his body?'

'No we don't,' replied Billy fascinated yet calm.

Mrs Grovene enjoyed a good gossip. 'Our daughter-in-law's sister and the man who discovered Simon's body are an item.' Silence. Gemma milked the pause. 'They're both married.'

'But not to each other,' added Derek hoping to please his wife.

'I see,' said Billy and asked for details. Fleming took notes. 'And is there anything else you feel we should know?'

'Derek and I believe Simon's money woes were not a factor in his death. Have you looked into our daughter-in-law's family?' She turned to her husband. 'Derek agrees with me, don't you Derek?' He did.

The police asked for more details none of which sounded helpful, thanked the couple and left. Fleming discussed the new lead.

'The affair is irrelevant. If it upset anyone, it would see Grovene kill the agent. There's no reason for the agent to kill the victim.'

'Why is it when I'm OIC, there are a million suspects?'

Charlie Baldwin worried. The CCTV camera at the bowling club covered the bar with the phone just in shot. He zipped through the footage to the first call. A man entered wearing a sunhat and dark glasses. Why? He made a call. So, no hair description and the man avoided looking at the camera. Bugger. He walked out of shot.

Baldwin hit fast forward. Just before the second call, another man entered who too was keen to avoid the camera. This bloke was short, stocky, with a flat cap and sunglasses. He used the phone. Baldwin let the disc run. Neither man returned the way he entered. Obviously they slipped out via the change room with its own exit from the clubhouse.

'Shit,' said Baldwin. He took still photos from the video and wrote a report. He needed to return the CCTV material and would ask at the club about the identity of the two callers.

Blunt led Payne into bike shops. The lack of a photo with the tyres on a bike made it tricky. Blunt hammered away. 'Have you sold a bike with these tyres?' They found no joy so started on schools.

Principals worried when meeting plainclothes police. 'Could we inspect the bicycles in your school grounds?' asked Blunt. The educators wanted to help but also to know if any of their students were in trouble with the rozzers. Blunt gave them nothing.

'We're interested in bikes with a particular tyre. May we get on?'

What principal would refuse to co-operate? None did but the searching was in vain. Blunt's anger grew. Finding no matching tyre made him mad but worse, he was, a DI stumbling through bike sheds on a wild goose chase on what he reckoned was a job for a rookie.

# 19

SOMETIMES IMAGINATION DOESN'T tell the true story. For example, what goes on in the mind of a child abused by an adult? When we hear about such behaviour do we know what the victim was feeling, enduring? We might think we know but thinking and knowing could be miles apart.

Understanding the suffering of the African teenage girl, Adamma, her betrayal and life as a sex slave may be beyond our comprehension.

Being lied to and tricked into leaving her family, her new life as a plaything for wealthy males, slobs to a man, forced her mind and body to suffer some of the worst degradation humankind can offer.

She was assigned to a pimp working for Laris Jlassi. His sidekick, Émile Bastien, enjoyed the perk of a free weekend with any of the girls and young, black flesh was his favourite.

What and how she suffered for Bastien's perverted pleasure does not bear repeating. We can but hope she finds freedom, justice and even revenge at some time in the future.

Michael was tucking into his muesli when Jo appeared. She yawned. He grinned. 'Sleep well?' he asked.

She poured a coffee. 'How come you're so bright-eyed and bushy-tailed? What's your cure for jetlag?'

'I'm not telling till I get the patent.'

She sat beside him in the quaint kitchen. 'We'll go and see that police officer this morning.'

'Do we have an appointment?'

'I think the less notice we give the better. Low-key are we.'

'You're the boss.'

She sipped her coffee then dropped the first of two bombshells. 'I've decided to go England this weekend with Little Lord Fauntleroy.'

'I see, and will you ever come back?'

She ignored his petty jealousy. 'And you're coming too.'

Michael choked on his muesli. 'What? Why?'

'I'll go to *Downton Abbey* while you interview an ex-Interpol cop in London.' Michael was told about the person and the plan.

'What about tickets,' he asked, 'and accommodation? And surely I'm not going to lob in London without first contacting the bloke and making sure he'll see me.'

'I'm Antony's guest but your costs will come out of the fund Pierre put aside for us.'

Michael wondered if Pierre knew how his funds were being spent. Did he know about Jo's cosy weekend with an aristocrat? Jo gave Michael details about the former Interpol officer, Silas Hornby.

'What do I say?' he asked. 'I'm IT, not Interpol.'

She looked at him and spoke sincerely. 'Michael, you're often better than me at solving crimes. You know Pierre's been framed. We have to find out how and by whom. This Silas guy knows the French criminal network and is our best lead.'

'Is he our *only* lead?'

'Unless Captaine Erec Bonnaire comes up with something. Now please call Silas and make an appointment. We're on the Eurostar on Saturday. I'll come back Sunday night; you can please yourself.'

He rang the London number—nothing. Not even an answer phone.

They arrived at Police HQ, approached *Reception* and asked to see Commandant Erec Bonnaire.

'Do you have an appointment?' asked the officer.

'We don't,' smiled Jo. 'But the matter's urgent and personal.' The officer and even Michael were hooked. 'Lieutenant Pierre Richelieu, once an officer of the Police Nationale, and a former colleague of Commandant Bonnaire, has been arrested and charged here in Paris on a trumped up charge. We are Australian police officers here to assist Detective Inspector Richelieu. Now ...'

'What name did you say?' Another officer, Lieutenant Dumont, standing nearby, overhead Jo's monologue and stepped forward. Jo explained again. 'Come with me,' he said. He asked for their names.

They stepped out on a floor where the corridors were wide and the décor ornate. 'Please wait here,' he said and disappeared.

'I can handle anything,' whispered Michael, 'but not being arrested.'

'Relax, we're the good guys.'

A door opened and the officer beckoned. They entered an outer office. 'Commandant Bonnaire will see you now but is a busy man.'

The Commandant's big office ran to a big desk. If size related to rank, they were dealing with a head honcho. Dumont introduced them then stood to one side. Bonnaire and his visitors sat in big chairs.

'I have heard about my former colleague, Pierre Richelieu and his troubles but did not know about his Australian visitors. Tell me your rank and why are you here, s'il vous plaît.'

Jo explained, referring to Dr Chan as a police consultant. They were here to liase between the prisoner and his lawyer. Jo finished with a plea. 'Commandant, if you are able to help in any way, we and Inspector Richelieu will be forever grateful.'

She paused looking hopeful. Michael reckoned violin music was required. Bonnaire spoke. 'I am not involved with the case but from what I have heard, Inspector Richelieu is in, how do you say in your country, deep shit?' Jo went from hopeful to hopeless. 'I can introduce you to the Officer in Charge, Brigadier Droit, but you must not interfere with the police investigation in any way. Do you understand?'

His look packed a threat.

'Oui Commandant and merci beau coup.'

'Please wait in the corridor.' They thanked him again and went outside. He spoke to Dumont. 'Take them to Brigadier Droit. Tell him what I told them—they must have no part in the investigation.'

'Oui, Commandant.' Dumont saluted and turned to leave.

'And Dumont.' He stopped. 'Put a tail on them. Do not let them know, and I want a daily report on where they go, who they see and what they do. And tell nobody about this order. Nobody.' He looked at his fellow officer. Their eyes spoke volumes. 'Dismissed.'

Brigadier Louis Droit was in charge of the case against Richelieu. Droit was Monsieur Tidy, and if solving crimes and winning promotion were down to the state of one's fingernails and the layout of one's paperclips, Droit was in for a glorious career. He welcomed the Australians and killed any hopes they may have harboured.

'Being police officers you will know I cannot provide information other than what your colleague's lawyer has already been told.'

'We understand,' replied Jo.

'The evidence is powerful and has recently been boosted with confessions from some of Monsieur Richelieu's associates.'

Jo and Michael felt their faces were slapped with a large fish.

'Pardon?' gasped Jo.

'The lawyer has not told you?' Both Aussies shook their head. 'Well I guess you will hear soon enough. Two drug dealers have confessed to their involvement in the scheme and named your colleague as the ringleader. I'm afraid it does not look good for your man.'

Jo struggled to think of anything she could ask. Michael spoke.

'And you say the lawyer has been informed of these confessions?'

'Some time ago.' Droit stood; for him this meeting was finished. 'I cannot spare more time. I suggest you speak with the lawyer appointed by your colleague. What is his name?'

'Antony Heron-Royhay,' said Jo.

'Ah yes, the Honourable Englishman. As they say in Blighty, jolly good luck with that, old chap.'

Still in shock, they were escorted out of the building by Dumont and set off not noticing the ordinary couple tailing them.

From his office window, Commandant Bonnaire looked down and watched the visitors and their tails walk into the Parisian sunshine. He showed a keen interest in what the Australians were doing. Sadly for them, he wasn't the only one.


Michael broke the ice. 'So Pierre has been grassed up by two fellow crims and his lawyer is either incompetent or compromised.'

'He'd better not be,' said Jo. 'Let's ask him.'

They caught the Metro and came out near the lawyer's office. As they walked, Jo broke away and headed to a shop. Michael caught up with her as she oggled the display.

'Detective, window shopping is not on the agenda.'

'Michael, we're in Paris and there's a sale on Gucci shoes. Two minutes,' she said and entered the shop. He followed, annoyed.

'Bonjour,' smiled Fabien, the toothy male assistant.

'Bonjour. Parlez-vous anglais?' asked Jo.

His smile expanded. 'But of course, Mademoiselle.'

'I was looking at the Gucci suede sandals with crystals.'

'An excellent choice, and what would Mademoiselle's size be?'

'Ah,' Jo hesitated. 'I'm Australian.'

'G'day,' said the young man in an accent sounding French and comical. 'Please take a seat.' Jo sat as did Michael still upset. Jo's trainers were removed and she prayed her socks were not whiffy. The measuring complete, the assistant disappeared.

'Michael, how much are they in Oz dollars?' He used his phone.

'Too much,' he said showing her the phone.

'Unbelievable,' gasped Jo. 'I'd pay double that back home.'

The shoes arrived. Jo became Cinderella and Michael fancied her something rotten. He read somewhere how Germaine Greer described Jo's new footwear as "fuck-me shoes".

'I'll take them,' Jo said.

'Merci Mademoiselle.'

The assistant left and Michael grew impatient. He whispered. 'We need to ask the lawyer why he hasn't mentioned the new evidence.'

'I know.'

'Your colleague has been fitted up and you're shoe-shopping in Paris.' She half looked at him. 'Are you listening to me?'

She pointed. 'Those boots are divine.' Michael blasphemed. Fabien arrived with Jo's purchase. 'May I see those boots, please?'

'Of course,' smiled Fabien thinking of his commission. Michael stood and moved to one side. He rang a London number.

'Silas Hornby,' said a voice.

Michael moved outside. 'Oh Mr Hornby, hello. My name is Michael Chan and Antony Heron-Royhay gave me your number and ...'

'You're an Aussie.'

Michael hesitated. 'For my sins, I am.'

'I know nowt about crime Down Under.'

'What about in Paris?'

'Ah, now there I can help. Who are you and what do you want?' Michael explained. 'Tomorrow afternoon suits me. Do you know the Warrington pub in Maida Vale?'

'I can find it.'

'Good, cos you're buying lunch. Say 1 for 1.30.'

'Thank you,' said Michael. 'Till tomorrow, sir.'

He felt warm inside then turned and felt sick. Jo Best stood there grinning holding a large carry bag with two shoe boxes.

'I couldn't resist the boots. Can you be a darling and pop them in your backpack?' *Now I'm the mule*, thought Michael as he stowed the shopping. 'I wouldn't want Hooray Henry to think I'm some bimbo with a shoe addiction.'

'Perish the thought.' They set off to see Antony. 'I've made contact with the ex-Interpol guy in London. We're having lunch tomorrow.'

'Brilliant,' said Jo as she switched to detective mode. Mind you, she did go back to thinking about her footwear purchases and tingled.

Antony seated them in his office. 'What news?' he asked.

Jo explained their meetings with two police officers and a planned meeting with Silas Hornby.

'Excellent,' he said. 'Now about tomorrow.'

Jo interrupted. 'And what of your news, Antony?'

'Ah, not good I'm afraid. A couple of ne'er-do-wells have confessed to their role in the drug activities of Monsieur Richelieu.'

'So we heard,' said Michael not liking Antony for several reasons.

'Oh, from whom?' enquired the lawyer.

'Brigadier Louis Droit,' replied Jo, 'the officer in charge.'

Michael tried to provoke the Englishman. 'He seemed to think their testimony would be the final nail in the Inspector's coffin.'

'He would.' Antony relaxed. Jo and Michael worried.

*Is this man taking this seriously? What are his plans to rescue Pierre? Has he even got a plan?*

# 20

KARL BENEDEK WAS ONCE the pimp for Maggie Stephens and a prime suspect in her 1996 killing. He conned two uni students to give him an alibi and their word got Karl off the hook.

'I never liked him,' said Robbo to Rose as they drove to interview the suspect, 22 years after the murder.

'And how is that relevant in this case?' asked Rose.

Robbo fell silent. That was the sort of comment she would have made as a new Homicide detective. He was out of practice. He worried that policing techniques had changed and he was now out of his depth.

Benedek was in his 60s and a doting grandfather. All three of his wives left him and his only pleasure in life was caring for his toddler granddaughter, Sami. Her squeals of delight drew the detectives to Karl's backyard and when they appeared, the look on his face was worth bottling. Robbo loved that look of fear and surprise.

'Hello Karl,' said Rose, 'long time no see.'

He knew who they were. 'Piss off,' he sneered. 'This is private property. You can't come in here.'

'We can if we're making an arrest,' said Robbo.

Benedek took up silence.

'We can talk here or at the station,' said Rose. 'You choose.'

His daughter came from the back door. 'Dad?'

'It's all right. Take Sami inside. This won't take long.'

Karl's daughter and granddaughter disappeared. Robbo pulled up a plastic chair which groaned when even a fly settled on it. Rose stood over the former pimp.

'We've got news, Karl. Those two vulnerable uni students who gave you an alibi for the day Maggie Stephens was murdered have retracted their statements.'

'So? The boyfriend confessed.'

'We reckon his suicide note is suspect.' Karl went quiet. 'Your DNA was all over Maggie's kitchen, you admitted she dumped you, and you no longer have an alibi.'

Benedek worried. Talk about a nightmare out of nowhere.

'I want a lawyer.'

Robbo and Rose smiled. Karl was arrested on suspicion of murder.

Danny Farr was once a boyfriend of Maggie Stephens. He enjoyed domestic violence and went to jail for one of the beatings he gave Maggie. When he heard she'd been murdered, he knew the cops would come for him. With no alibi, he asked his mechanic mate, Ricky, to give him one. 'He was with me,' confessed Ricky, 22 years ago. Not any more. Ricky retracted his original statement.

Tuck and Melk traced Danny to a building site in Rosebud.

'Danny Farr,' said Tuck, 'remember us?' He did but pretended otherwise. 'Homicide cops in 1996.'

'I'm busy,' he said and turned away.

'Five minutes,' said Melk, 'three if you use short sentences.'

Danny stared at them, a mix of fear and anger. 'What?'

Tuck enjoyed this next bit. 'Bad news, Danny. We're investigating the murder of your former girlfriend, Maggie Stephens.'

'Nothing to do with me. I had a cast-iron alibi.'

'*Had* is the key word, my son,' said Tuck. 'Your bosom buddy Ricky has given us a new statement in which he swears you asked him to lie and what he said was bullshit.'

'I don't believe ya.'

'Wanna see Ricky's revised statement?' asked Melk.

Tuck kept at Danny. 'So what about another mate? Anyone who can swear you were with them the day your bird was bashed? I mean fatally bashed as opposed to the times when you slapped her for fun?'

Danny chose to say nothing. Smart move. He wasn't arrested. Tuck and Melk avoided using the magic words, but Danny reluctantly went with the retirees to a cop shop where DI Rose waited. The cold case got warmer.

Rose interviewed Benedek first. She wanted Robbo to sit in but he recommended Tuck. 'He was the best for picking up anything I forget or glossed over,' said Robbo. So Tucky it was.

Karl didn't want a brief. He wanted out, a crim who wanted a quiet life. He fathered kids from all three of his marriages with grandkids everywhere. His income came from real estate he bought years ago. Now, out of nowhere comes this shit. Yes, he threatened the uni students to give him an alibi but so what?

'You were never charged Karl because of your alibi. Now it's gone and you're back in the frame.'

'You've got nothin'.'

'We've got *you*, Karl,' said Tuck, 'that's gotta be something.'

Rose continued. 'So where were you on the day Maggie Stephens was murdered?'

'You're joking. Where were you on Day X 25 years ago?'

'When did you stop being Maggie's pimp?'

'Sorry, I lost me diary for that decade.'

'You said at the time you warned her not to work on her own. Why?'

His anger peeped out. 'Because without me looking after her, she was in danger. And guess what? Some moron strangled the bitch.'

'Strangled?' Tuck pounced. 'Who said she was strangled?' Karl worried. 'We didn't tell you. Only someone in the house with Maggie would know that. How do you know that, Karl?'

Rose liked Tuck's approach. 'Answer the question,' she said.

'I'm sayin' nothin',' replied Karl and folded his arms.

Rose went for him. 'Your DNA was all over the kitchen and your alibi is crap. There's a lot of circumstantial there, Karl. Tougher men than you have gone down for less.'

The pause was loud. Benedek leaned forward and spoke softly—for him. 'Then charge me—I dare ya.'

Karl returned to a cell and Danny Farr arrived to face the music. Danny reckoned a lawyer was needed but with his budget, the best on offer was a washed-up alcoholic who'd forgotten more than he'd learnt.

'Mr Farr,' said Rose who was stopped by the lawyer.

'My client wishes to make a statement, officer,' he said and paused. 'May I proceed?' Rose nodded and sat back. The lawyer took out a document and read. 'My client admits to asking a friend for an alibi for the day of the murder. My client acknowledges his guilt regarding domestic violence issues against the deceased when they lived together. My client cannot provide an alibi for the day in question. My client states he was not in Melbourne on the day in question and had nothing to do with the death of Maggie Stephens.'

The lawyer pushed the statement towards DI Rose.

'Thank you,' said Rose picking up the document.

'And my client will not be answering any questions. Please charge or release Mr Farr.'

They did neither. Danny returned to his cell while Robbo and Melk joined DI Rose and Tuck to discuss the interviews.

'It's the old story, Elly,' said Robbo. 'They don't have to prove their innocence. Both could be guilty but no prosecutor will proceed on what we've got.'

'So we get more,' said Melk, 'we dig deeper.'

'Or we look elsewhere,' said Tuck.

They did that but for now, Messrs Benedek and Farr were released.

Billy asked the squad for reports. 'To misquote Mr Orwell, "Suspects good, convictions better". So without a prime suspect, let's eliminate those who *didn't* do it. Who's on first?'

The older detectives smiled but Blunt knew nothing about Abbott and Costello. He reported on his Tour de France adventure.

'We identified the bicycle tyre. We know its name, that it's expensive but there's no sighting of a bike with those tyres in the streets around the crime scene, in local schools or bike shops.'

'Thanks Callum. Charlie?'

'The club manager identified the two guys who made a call to the victim and to the estate agent. Both callers were big on pathetic disguises and we have interviews today.

'Thanks Charlie. Take DS Fleming.' Blunt fumed. 'Now, Justin and I called on the widow Grovene. She's not in mourning, appears cashed up, and is using her in-laws as an alibi. They in turn told us the widow's sister is having an affair with the agent who found the body.'

'The soap opera lives,' said Fleming.

'I can't see it's relevant,' said Rose, 'but we check everything.'

'I'll do it, Sarge,' said Blunt defying Billy to refuse him.

'Right, thanks, Callum. Take your sidekick, Senior Payne. And while you're there, a polite follow-up of the widow might be helpful. Why is she flushed with funds when her dead husband kept going bust?'

Baldwin and Fleming went to interview the phone callers. The first was retired and at home in his Hawthorn maisonette.

'Mr Kenneth Ingram?' asked Baldwin.

'Yes,' was the uncertain reply.

'Police,' said Baldwin showing his ID. 'Might we have a word?'

'What about?'

'We can explain inside.'

Ken surrendered and the trio sat in what used to be called the parlour here known as antimacassars anonymous. Baldwin began.

'You made a telephone call from the Riversdale Bowling Club last week at five past ten. Who was it to and what was it about?'

Ingram took a deep breath. 'I can't remember.'

'Do you often make calls from the bowling club?'

'Not often.'

'Apart from last week, when was the last time you used that phone?'

Ingram shook his head. 'I'm not sure.'

Baldwin pointed to a landline phone beside Ingram's chair. 'Why not make the call from your own phone?'

'I was out.'

'Do you have a mobile?'

'Yes.'

'Why not use it?'

Ken cracked. 'Look, what's this all about? Why are you here?'

Fleming ramped up the pressure. 'Who did you call, Mr Ingram?'

'I can't remember.'

'We know the number you called, sir. We want to know why you called that number and what was said.'

'Do I have to answer these questions? Am I in some kind of trouble? And shouldn't you give me a warning?'

'Of course, sir,' said Baldwin. 'Kenneth Ingram, you are not obliged to say or do anything unless you wish to do so, but whatever you say or do may be used in evidence. Do you understand?'

Ken wished he hadn't asked. 'I rang a wrong number.'

'What number did you mean to ring?' asked Baldwin.'

'I can't remember.'

'Who were you meant to ring?'

'I can't remember.'

'Who asked you to make the call?'

'No-one.'

'Mr Ingram,' said Baldwin, 'we're investigating a murder. If you played any part in this murder, even as an accessory, you will be charged.' Baldwin paused.

Fleming spoke. 'Ever been to jail, Mr Ingram?'

Ken seemed to grow taller. 'How dare you bully an old man, a returned serviceman. I've done nothing wrong and if you don't get out of my house immediately, I'll call the media and report you for elder abuse.' He stood, pointed and defied them. 'Now get out of my house.'

Fleming looked at Baldwin who gave a mini shrug. The police left and discussed their experience.

'Waste of time with the second codger,' said Fleming.

'Sarge?' queried Baldwin.

'They've both been put up to help arrange the murder. The killer didn't want to be traced so had mates, relatives or even complete strangers make the calls he couldn't or wouldn't make. Caller 2 will give us the same palaver as Caller 1. We need whoever hired the callers.'

'And he's our killer?'

Fleming shrugged. 'I'll be surprised if he's not.'

'I'd still like to have a go at the second caller.'

'Fair enough.'

They went to interview Graeme Farquhar who wasn't surprised when the detectives arrived because his mate Ken Ingram rang and gave him the lowdown. Fleming was right. It was a waste of time.

# 21

THE TRAVELLERS GATHERED at Garde du Nord. Antony was full of it—bonhomie to him, bullshit to Michael. They found their seats with Michael keen to sit facing the locomotive. Jo sat opposite with Antony beside her. The weekend as a planning exercise to save Pierre started like a trip to the seaside. No bucket and spade but life was grand.

Pierre Richelieu lay morose in his prison cell. His team didn't want to risk talking openly and leaning forward to whisper was ridiculous. Michael suspected Antony was more interested in Jo's body than her brain. He was right and jealousy took root.

'You'll enjoy meeting Silas,' said Antony. 'He knows everyone.'

'And what do I do after meeting the great man?' Michael asked. 'Take in a West End show? Join a Jack the Ripper tour?'

'Michael,' protested Jo in a restrained moan.

'Jolly good idea, old man. Miss Best and I will be hard at work planning our campaign but having one of Pierre's team enjoying a spot of R and R sounds like a damn good idea.'

Rather than swear or punch Antony, Michael went in search of coffee. He didn't re-appear until the Eurostar emerged in Kent. Jo was angry with Michael while Antony buzzed with anticipation. He planned to work closely with the detective from Down Under down under.

At St Pancras they said goodbye and Michael headed off for the Tube. He took the Bakerloo line to Maida Vale, surfaced and discovered it was raining. He pulled up his hood and wandered along Randolf Avenue.

He couldn't miss the pub. It was big and bold with proper architecture, and inside its atmosphere gave you a friendly touch up. Michael knew what Silas looked like according to a photo online. But the former police and Interpol officer now sported white whiskers.

The chap with the beard subtly waved as Michael was spotted. They shook hands, Michael disrobed and joined his luncheon pal.

'I've enjoyed fish 'n chips here on a Saturday since Adam was a boy but you please yourself. After all, you're paying.'

'Sounds good to me,' said Michael. 'Can I get you another drink?'

Silas knew his pomme frites English style and Michael hoped the information was as good as the grub. Silas asked a few questions. They finished their meal when Silas' phone trilled.

'Apologies, dear boy, damn rude.' He answered the phone and immediately became agitated. 'Not again,' he snorted and stood. 'Must dash, old man. Tha'ars trouble at t'mill.'

He headed for the exit with Michael stunned. 'But what about ...?'

Silas called back. 'Come on.' Michael fumbled to gather his gear. 'Don't forget to pay.'

Michael placed 40 quid on the bar. 'Enough?' he asked.

'Go,' said the barman and Michael did. The staff regarded Silas as a member of the family. Outside the pub Michael lost his host then saw him waving. Michael ran. Silas was twice his age, more, but set a cracking pace. He disappeared. Michael scrambled. Then a jeep reversed onto the road and nearly hit the Aussie. Silas was frantic. 'Get in,' he cried and the vehicle moved with Michael not fully aboard.

'These bastards want me out,' barked Silas, jamming the gears. The jeep was dirty outside and worse inside. Michael reckoned he'd be safer *not* wearing the seat belt.

'I gather this is an emergency,' said Michael considering prayer.

'I moor my narrowboat *Blodwyn* on Regents Canal. Some bastards want me out so they try sabotage. They hope I'll move to the sticks— anywhere. Now if *Blodwyn* sinks, it'll cost me a packet.' Michael didn't know what to say. 'Hang on,' said the driver and with good reason.


Antony and Jo's train left from St Pancras heading north. Once seated, Jo put her foot down.

'Antony, a weekend in the country is fine for Mr Sondheim but I'm here to have my colleague set free.'

'Of course,' responded Antony not happy to discuss legal matters in public. 'We'll have tons of time to work once we get to the Hall.'

Jo worried. The further they travelled from Paris, the less hopeful she felt for Pierre.

In the carpark at Kettering Station they walked to a 4WD vehicle with a driver standing by its side. Michael travelled in a ramshackle jeep, while Jo was helped into the latest Range Rover with hot and cold running wipers.

Maurice was the estate manager and gofer, here to fetch the Earl's second born and his bit of rough, home for the weekend. 'How do, Miss,' said the driver miming tugging his forelock.

The trip through Northamptonshire was enchanting. Jo saw how Antony could charm the birds out of the trees.

'We're coming to our local village of Blessingford,' said tour guide Antony. 'The church is on your right and Maurice's family has been residing in the churchyard for centuries. Right, Maurice?'

'Indeed, sir.'

Jo would have loved to explore the village but couldn't believe it when a few locals nodded in her direction. She looked at Antony.

'The estate car is well known and one can't be sure if the Earl is aboard. If we stopped, you'd be given the royal treatment, Miss Best.'

Her mind raced. *I'm here to rescue Pierre and instead am being treated like a bloody royal!*

They swung into the estate, seemed to take forever to traverse the drive and then, through the trees, Bulwer Hall appeared. Jo tried hard not to gasp. It was not magnificent with the size and granduer of Chatsworth or Blenheim but well named as the chocolate-box of stately homes. Its grounds were immaculate, and sweeping in by the rear, the Range Rover came to an effortless stop.

Maurice was out in a flash opening Jo's door. 'Welcome to Bulwer Hall, Miss,' he said doffing his flat cap. Jo wondered if Antony paid the staff to behave like so.

He guided her. 'Sorry about the tradesman's entrance, Joanna, but we Brits often slip in the back way.' He opened the back door which had more architectural merit than a million McMansions. 'Straight ahead,' he said and Jo entered a stunning kitchen. Remove the island, grab your tennis racquets and play. Pots and pans gleamed, hanging ready for action. An elderly woman chopped vegetables in a corner.

'Hello Annie,' shouted Antony. Jo assumed she was deaf.

'In about an hour, Master Antony. Thankee.'

'This is Miss Best who's come all the way from Australia.'

'Welcome, Miss,' smiled Annie who called every female Miss.

'Hello Annie,' smiled Jo.

Antony led the way. 'Come and meet the Countess.' The corridor was good for a coach and horses' race and the interior doors could easily repel boarders. Antony opened one of many and entered. 'Hello Mother,' he said. Jo followed thinking *he's a mummy's boy.*

She was tempted to call the woman Mrs Earl but did as tradition demands. 'How do you do, My Lady,' said Jo determined not to bob.

Countess Jonquil was slim, too slim, wore a white pants suit, and sported a head scarf so colourful it started a trend. She smoked a cheroot and her ashtray was worth an earl's ransom. Despite her wealth, Her Ladyship dismissed all airs and graces and said *shit* within 30 seconds.

After some boring small talk, Antony understood the mater and excused himself. Jo was alone with the Lady of the house.

'What's your accent?' asked Jonquil. 'Canadian? I can never tell.'

'Australian,' said Jo.

'Please don't tell me you're an actress from *Neighbours.*'

Jo smiled. 'I wish.'

'Well the Saxe-Coburgs are overrun with divorced foreigners and B Grade celebs so why not an Australian chorus girl?' She changed horses mid stream. 'Oh did Ant show you the downstair' s loos?'

'He didn't but I'm fine for the moment.'

The Countess took a final drag on her cherot. 'So where did my son find you? Earls Court is where you Ausssies hibernate isn't it? '

'At the risk of sounding rude, My Lady, there seems to be some confusion about the relationship I have with your son.'

'Confusion? It's perfectly clear. Whenever Ant pops in from Paris, it's always with bimbo in tow. He's like clockwork. So where, pray tell, is the confusion?'

Jo pondered her answer. *Will mine be the shortest ever stay at Bulwer Hall?*

'I'm a lawyer, madam, turned police officer.'

Lady Jonquil blanched. The woman's qualifications were a shock but more so was being addressed as madam. Jo continued.

'A police colleague of mine flew to Paris for a family funeral. He was arrested by French police on a trumped-up charge. Your son is his lawyer. I flew to Paris to help my colleague and the only reason I'm here this weekend is to work on a plan to set my colleague free. Does that, My Lady, clear up any confusion?'

She lit a fresh cheroot. 'Bloody marvellous,' she said. 'Now when you're taken upstairs, insist on a room with a bath with a view. If asked, say something about having always dreamt about lying in a bath looking at the English countryside. Understand?'

'Yes and no.'

The Countess groaned. 'I'm trying to save you, darling. When the amorous males come knocking, one particular room is your salvation.'

'Did you say males, plural?'

'Indeed, like father like son.' It was Jo's turn to be shocked. 'Do as I say and you'll be fine. Bathroom with a view.'

Jo couldn't remain silent. 'May I ask why?'

'It's the only room with a priest hole.'


Michael saw the sights of north London but not from the top of a double-decker bus. He was in a tip on wheels being driven by an ageing weekend sailor panicking because his vessel was apparently sinking. Silas' narrowboat was moored at Wenlock Basin on Regents Canal, about five miles across London. What a journey.

'You speak as if this is not the first time,' said Michael.

'I bought a residential mooring years ago but because I go ashore, some locals reckon I should move. I refuse, so some are getting nasty.'

'You mean they sabotage your boat?'

'They cut the electricity meaning no bilge pump, they put the weed hatch on the wrong way, they even pour water into the engine room.'

'Can you get the police involved?'

Silas blasted his horn in frustration. 'It's green, mate, green,' he shouted at a driver. Back to Michael. 'Sorry, what?'

Michael changed the subject. 'I hope you haven't forgotten why I've tracked you down.'

'Of course not.' He blasted his horn again.

'I will be able to pick your brains about organized crime in Paris?'

'Of course, tonight. There's a brilliant pub near *Blodwyn* and the landlord's a former villain. Between us we know every major crim and crooked cop in Paris. And you can kip on the boat.'

Michael looked at Silas. 'But will I need my waterwings?'

He growled. 'I bloody well hope not,' and blasted his horn.

Jo followed Her Ladyship's advice and settled in upstairs. The view from the bath was spectacular. The luncheon gong sounded and Jo joined Her Ladyship and offspring in the adjoining sitting-room. Jonquil complained about Brexit, the weather, and the parish council.

*Why aren't we eating?* wondered Jo. Then she discovered why.

The Earl of Eynesbury arrived. 'Father,' said Antony, 'this is Miss Joanna Best.'

The Earl strode towards Jo, took her hand and kissed it. She thought him better looking than his son and saw where Antony learnt his flattery. The son inherited the father's come-hither eyes.

'Welcome my dear, how delightful to meet you.'

Luncheon was served and Her Ladyship was quick off the mark. 'Miss Best is a police officer, my dear,' she said, warning her husband.

'I say, how fascinating.'

'From Australia no less.'

'A rozzer from Bondi Beach,' he grinned. 'Now there's a first.'

Jo didn't correct the Earl and noted Antony said far less with his pater present. Eating ensued with multiple questions aimed at Jo.

Over coffee, his Lordship ramped up his charm offensive. 'We shall give you the tour of the estate, Miss Best. Do you ride?'

'It's been a while, My Lord. I fear one's posterior would pay a high price.' *One's posterior* she thought. *I'm even talking like them.*

'No problem, my dear. And Antony's the family expert on bottoms.'

His Lordship displayed an upperclass leer, and Antony, not for the first time, pondered patricide.

Her ladyship saved the day. 'You're forgetting, my dear, Miss Best is here to work on a case with Ant. Some high-flying policeman's been arrested in Paris and Ant and his guest are charged with setting the poor chap free.'

'Of course,' said His Lordship. 'Well, all work and no play, as they say. Come and find me when your business is done. We can drive out and see the deer.' He stood and left.

Her Ladyship stood and Antony rose. Jo wondered if this was when the ladies went to an adjoining room leaving the men to their port and cigars. It wasn't. Antony showed Jo the library and suggested they meet there in ten minutes.

She went to her room, the one with the bath with a view, freshened up, collected her bag of tricks, returned to the library and set out her stall on the biggest table. She was alone when the door opened and Her Ladyship appeared. She hurried to Jo using a terrible French accent.

'Now listen very carefully. I shall say this only once.'

Jo wanted to giggle but became serious as Her Ladyship passed on details of Catholic families in large houses in the Midlands some 400 years ago. Priests were hunted like animals. They hid in secret places.

'Any questions?' asked the hostess.

'Only one. Why you are telling me this?'

'Because some so-called gentlemen in the ranks of English nobility, believe they have certain rights when it comes to females.'

'No, ma'am, I mean why tell me in particular?'

'Because you're the first eligible female who's turned up here *not* wanting to marry into the aristocracy. Every bimbo who arrives with one of my sons is set on succeeding me as Lady of the manor. You're different. So when, not if, you get a tap on the door tonight, follow my instructions to the letter.'

The door opened and Antony appeared. 'Mother?'

'Just going. Good hunting, sleuths.' She left. Antony sat beside Jo.

'So what's our approach, Mr Lawyer?' she asked.

'Account for every moment Monsieur Richelieu spent since arriving in Paris, up to his arrest, thus proving his innocence.'

'Too difficult, too slow and too polite.'

'Pardon?' Antony looked peeved.

'The traditional methods take forever. We need to hit the police hard and immediately.'

Antony frowned. 'So Australian police *are* gungho and crazy.'

'The only people we know who are involved in this set-up are the two who confessed to being part of Pierre's drug distribution. Who are they? And how do they know Pierre?'

'We may not know that until the trial.'

'Far too late. We need immediate action. We find a sympathetic journalist and have them run a story about police corruption.'

'What?' Antony recoiled. 'I'm a lawyer, Joanna, not a private eye.'

'Antony, this whole affair is rotten to the core. Pierre told us about former police he put away for corruption. Surely they're in cahoots with criminals and corrupt serving officers out to punish your client.'

'But even so, going to the press could backfire.'

'There are no phone or email records between Pierre and these two crooks. When did they meet? What do they know about Pierre? I bet they don't know him from Adam. What are their real names? They're stooges being paid or threatened to confess and implicate Pierre. We need to get the media and politicians asking questions.'

'Politicians? This is insane.'

'And if Michael has found any criminal contacts through this Silas chap, he and I can investigate them.'

'My God, woman, you're supposed to liase with the Australian Consulate and your colleague's lawyer. Nothing else.'

'Well two out of three ain't bad.' She looked at him. 'Come on, Antony, get with the programme.'

Silas knew short cuts through north London but many were no faster than the main roads. In London in 1901, the average vehicular traffic speed was about 8 mph. A century later it was still the same. Today it was worse. After an hour of frustration they arrived at Wenlock Basin, off Regents Canal. The jeep was parked and Michael followed Silas to his mooring.

'Thank Christ,' he said seeing his narrowboat above water. The owner jumped aboard, connected his power and started a pump.

Michael stood on the jetty. Silas opened hatches, disappeared below, fiddled then reappeared.

'We're okay, I think.'

'Who tipped you off?' asked Michael.

'I have my spies. Well don't just stand there.' Michael stepped onto a narrowboat for the first time. 'Stow your gear then come and inspect.'

Silas was like a proud father but Michael remembered his mission. Fine pub grub, a crazy drive across North London, and a narrowboat did nothing to help Detective Inspector Pierre Richelieu.

It was late-afternoon when the two men sat at the stern of *Blodwyn* and discussed the Melbourne detective's dilemma. Silas was great value. He knew about corrupt police in Paris and Émile Bastien in particular. Michael took notes. His knowledge grew. Antony's tip about Silas was a winner. Finally Silas suggested they take a break.

'Let's have a drink.' He pointed. 'There's my watering hole when I'm on the boat.' He pointed to a pub *The Lock Keeper*. They crossed a bridge and settled in a corner of the bar.

Mine host was Ronnie "Gruesome" Grayling, former major crim but now Mr Law-abiding Softie. He was cooking when told Silas was in the bar, so arrived in chef's attire.

Michael was introduced and his mission explained. 'We can have a chat later son, after you've enjoyed my farm sausages with spring onion mash,' said Ronnie.

*This is the life*, thought Michael. Great food, fascinating company, and best of all, inside information on how and who may have fitted-up Pierre Richelieu.

After Jo's plan for all-out war was discussed in detail, Antony improved. They set out how the Richelieu sting may have worked. They needed data. Michael's research was key. A media expose might get results but much depended on Michael's information.

The meeting ended when his Lordship arrived insisting Jo come for a spin around the estate. Off they went with the pater driving, Jo beside him, and the second son smarting in the rear. The deer were fabulous, the folly fascinating, and the autumnal leaves gorgeous.

Jo was relieved they didn't dress for dinner but did make herself a tad glamourous sporting her new Parisian pumps. Her ladyship nodded her approval. There was more of Annie's cooking, finishing with coffee in front of the fire. Talk about the life of Riley.

Jo was a hit. Intelligent, non-grasping females were rare at Bulwer Hall. But her mind was not what father and son were contemplating. Having the damsel under the same roof inflamed their carnal desires.

The guest decided to retire. Genuine thanks for the hospitality flowed from her lips. Genuine admiration for her presence flowed from the males. Her Ladyship slipped in a wink. Jo left.

She wondered about sleeping in the suit of armour standing outside her room. *Don't be silly*, she thought, *nothing will happen.*

After closing time in *The Lock Keeper*, Silas stood to leave. Michael was confused. *What about my chat with Gruesome Grayling?*

'Must away to feed the children,' said Silas. By children he meant cats. He handed Michael the keys to the narrowboat. 'Sleep tight, dear boy. I'll pop over for breakfast.'

Gruesome came into the bar, unlocked the door for Silas then sat with Michael placing two steaming mugs on the table.

'A nightcap with a kick. Now, son, wotcha wanna know?'

Like Silas, Gruesome was a treasure trove of information. In his bad old younger days, he ruled parts of London with a cosh and steel-capped boots. He worked with and fought against villains mainly in London. But across the Channel in Paris, he knew the man to avoid was one Laris Jlassi. Gruesome told all.

Michael thanked mine host, stepped aboard the narrowboat, opened his Notebook and typed—names, occupations, reputations, networks, crimes. He searched for more details using the names given by Silas and Gruesome. He linked possible partners in crime. He felt weary. He wondered about sleeping in his clothes in case of emergency. *Don't be silly,* he thought, *nothing will happen.*

# 22

THE THREE IDIOTS gathered at Robbo's with DI Rose arriving late. 'Apologies gentlemen but we have a tricky homicide and we're short of ideas and detectives.'

'You've got three experts right here, ma'am,' said Melk.

Rose looked at him. Melk's grin kept growing. 'Thank you, *For Sale*.' Everyone roared, even Melk. 'Now we're agreed Messrs Benedek and Farr are still in the frame, so how should we tackle them?'

'Leave them,' said Robbo. The others looked at him. All three still regarded him as the boss. 'Let them stew. As you suggested, ma'am, we need to look at those we never interviewed.'

'Go on,' said Rose behaving like she did when Robbo was her boss and she a beginner.

'For years I kept asking myself why we didn't chase up the families of people involved. Take the boyfriend who killed himself. How hard did we follow up his letter or talk to his family and friends?'

'You couldn't, boss,' said Tuck. 'You retired.'

'Who else?' asked Rose.

'What about the old girl next door?' asked Robbo.

Rose explained. 'We took her statement and she died in 2006.'

'Did we interview her family? Did they visit? Did she visit them? Did she say something to family or friends?' The others fell silent. 'And what have we done about Maggie's family; her parents, grandmother and obnoxious uncle? If we're serious, we should look at everyone.'

More silence. It was as if Robbo was DCI again and the others were his squad being given a bollocking. Rose responded.

'Maggie's family was, is dysfunctional. She never knew her father and rarely spoke to her mother. The grandmother had dementia and died in care, and the uncle, Harold Whipsnape, is residing in the same Ballarat nursing home and may not be fit for interview.'

Rose struggled. Tuck addressed Robbo. 'So what do you recommend, boss?' Rose was disappointed but relieved. She wanted Robbo to steer the ship.

'Let's divide into two teams. Elly and I can tackle the Watson family and Tucky and Colin concentrate on Maggie's mob.'

'Sounds good,' said Melk.

'Thanks Robbo,' added Rose, 'I needed a wise head.'

He continued. 'We look at friends and family who knew old Mrs Watson or Maggie. We keep Benedek and Farr on the back burner.' The others agreed. 'Right, who's for a cuppa?'


DI Blunt was not happy working with Stephen Payne. The feeling was mutual. Payne was doubly worried because Billy Hughes expected him to tell her stuff. 'You want me to spy on him?' moaned Payne. Billy gave him a look and he agreed under sufferance.

Blunt and Payne headed for the office of the estate agent who found the body of chisel-wearing Simon Grovene.

Ethan Marvel was 40 and unhappy. Being involved in a murder was not good for his image. The police found him at work and Ethan's displeasure grew. He wished he'd never found the stiff.

Blunt lived up to his name. 'Tell me about your relationship with the dead man's sister-in-law.'

'Christ almighty,' expelled Marvel. 'What's that got to do with anything?'

'So you *are* banging her?' taunted Blunt and both Ethan and Payne reckoned the DI was a serious candidate for *Prick of the Year*.

'Who is running this investigation?' demanded Ethan.

'Ah, DS Hughes,' said Blunt, 'although as DI I outrank her.'

Ethan fumed. 'Look, I've given the police a detailed statement on what happened. My private life is none of your fucking business.'

Payne tried to douse the flames. 'Who was the man who rang and told you about the house in Kew?'

Ethan took his time in calming down. 'Can't remember. He gave a name and number but you lot reckon they're false.'

Blunt wanted control and stood over Payne. 'So what did Mr Grovene say about you and his sister-in-law being an item?'

Ethan looked ready to explode. Payne looked for a fire extinguisher. 'God, if that's your best trick question, no wonder the case is unsolved,' sneered Ethan. Blunt boiled and Payne cheered inside.

'Well?' asked Blunt.

'For the record, Inspector, I didn't know Natalie's brother-in-law, I never met him until I walked in on his corpse, and I never spoke to him. No, not true. When I met him, I swore but apparently he wasn't listening at the time. The man was nothing to me. Now, I have a living to make so you lot can piss off.'

'Temper, temper,' mocked Blunt, departing. He walked out without a backward glance leaving Payne to act like a lapdog.

In their car, Payne allowed his anger to boil over and argued with his superior officer. 'I'm sorry, sir, but winding up a possible suspect is counter-productive.'

'Drive,' ordered Blunt.

'How can we find out if the guy had anything to do with the murder if you treat him like an arsehole?'

'I was told you're a pain, Payne. Now the grieving widow's next.'

'Would you mind, sir, if I led the questioning of the widow?'

'I wouldn't mind cos it ain't gunna happen. You can stay in the car or come inside and take notes—your choice.'

They drove in silence.

Robbo and Rose drove to meet Christine Cordner, daughter of the late Dot Watson, former next-door neighbour of the murdered Maggie Stephens.

'What do we know about her?' asked Robbo.

'She's 67, divorced and lives alone.'

'Was she close to her mother?'

'She was.'

'I can't believe she wasn't interviewed.'

Rose despaired. 'Boss, you're sounding like we're to blame. The old lady couldn't have killed Maggie, her daughter lived in Woop Woop and was nowhere near the crime scene, so what possible value was there in talking to her? Not forgetting we scored a confession from the boyfriend.'

After a pause, Robbo continued. 'The old girl may have said something to her daughter.' It sounded like he was clutching at straws. He was but desperately wanted to solve this one last case. So did Rose.

Christine shuffled to open her door. She was glad of the company and they settled in her humble abode. Robbo opened the questioning. 'Did your Mum ever talk about the murder, you know, over the years?'

'It was the only thing she talked about when it happened but as the years went by, not much.'

'Who used to visit your Mum; family members or friends?'

'Well I did and my son, Kevin sometimes if he could be bothered.'

'Where's Kevin living now?'

Christine sighed. 'God only knows. He married again and silly old me, I see his first wife more than me own son.'

'What's her name?'

'Dianne.' Christine gave family details and Rose took notes. Christine pointed. 'There's a photo album on the dining-room table.'

Rose handed it to Robbo. He flicked through it. He could walk and chew gum so kept questioning as he looked.

'Would Kevin's first wife ever have visited your Mum?'

'Yes, Dianne was good like that. Dunno what she saw in Kevin.'

'And Kevin's second wife?'

'Nah, Mum was dead when Julie come on the scene.'

Robbo handed the album to Rose who looked at the photos. 'Was your Mum a drinker, Christine?' Both women looked surprised. 'If she enjoyed a sherry at Christmas she might have let slip some gossip.'

'Not Mum. Dad was the drinker but he carked it years ago.'

Robbo smiled. 'I think we've run out of questions, Christine.'

'So, you think it wasn't Maggie's boyfriend who killed her?'

'We're not sure, but would like to be. And if everyone was as helpful as you've been, we might get Maggie some justice.'

The visit was a highlight for Christine's day, and one of the police left feeling a hunch coming on.

Blunt and Payne arrived at the Grovene estate. Mock Georgian was all the rage in this part of Deepdene. They rang the doorbell. 'Go easy, boss,' said Payne, 'please.'

Blunt looked at his colleague and was about to utter something derogatory when the door opened and the widow Grovene appeared.

Showing their IDs was enough to get Mrs Grovene's eyeballs rolling.

'Sorry to intrude, Mrs Grovene,' said Blunt in a polite manner. Payne froze. 'May we trouble you with a few questions, please?'

Such manners gave Anika Grovene little choice. She ushered the police inside. Her parents were seated on the imported furniture.

'Terrible business, officers,' said Anika's father.

'Terrible,' replied Blunt. He paused and when he next spoke butter wouldn't melt. Payne was in shock.

'I understand your grief must still be raw, Mrs Grovene but alas I'm obliged to ask certain questions.' Anika and her folks grew nervous. 'We've received some information. I hate to be the bearer of bad news, particularly at this dreadful time.'

*What the hell is he on about?* thought Payne, Anika and her folks.

'A member of your family may unfortunately be drawn into the reporting of your husband's murder. We will do everything we can to keep your family's name out of the public eye.'

Payne froze as Blunt went from slanderous to submissive.

'What on earth are you talking about?' asked Anika's father.

Blunt paused. An actor would have applauded his timing. 'The man who found Mr Grovene has confessed to being in a sexual relationship with your sister, Mrs Grovene; your other daughter sir, madam.'

Silence. Payne held his breath. Blunt faked shame and contrition.

'Is that it?' asked Anika being rude. 'Is that your terrible news?'

Her response stunned Blunt. Unlike him, Anika wasn't pretending.

'For God's sake, man,' said her father. 'The whole world knows Pippa's sleeping with Captain Marvel. How can you keep common knowledge a secret?' The pause was followed by the tag. 'You moron.'

Payne mentally celebrated. Blunt was too clever by half. His performance was designed to upset the family and have them panic, possibly revealing who killed their son-in-law and Anika's husband. His plan bombed—spectacularly.

The police left with the family laughing them off the property. The real joy for Payne was Blunt's grovelling. He begged Payne not to repeat what happened. Payne milked it and left Blunt hanging.

# 23

JO COULDN'T SLEEP. Her jetlag faded but the constant travel, unusual food and seriously loopy people made shut-eye tricky. She sat up in her Northants bed and on her tablet wrote an article she would like to see in the French media.

### *The Invented Crime*

*Pierre Grégory Richelieu grew up in France and became a police officer in Paris. In 2014 he moved to Australia where he works as a homicide detective, a Detective Inspector for Victoria Police.*
*Recently his mother died in Paris. DI returned to France to bury her. Soon after his arrival in Paris, he was arrested and charged with Class A drug offences. French police claim to have found commercial quantities of illegal drugs in the home of the late Madame Richelieu.*
*However, police have since arrested two men who confessed to being associates of M. Richelieu in his alleged drug empire.*

*A number of issues arise from these facts.*

*1. Inspector Richleieu's arrest record when serving in the French National Police.*
*2. Inspector Richelieu's record as a serving officer both in France and Australia.*
*3. The relationship between Inspector Richelieu and his two alleged accomplices.*

*1. Inspector Richelieu served as a police officer in Paris between 1999 and 2014. He made many arrests some of which included fellow officers. Several were found guilty of corruption, dismissed from the force and sent to prison.*

*2. When serving as an officer for the French National Police, Inspector Richelieu received a number of commendations for bravery. He left the French Police with an unblemished record and received a glowing testimonial from his superior officers. He was welcomed by Victoria Police in Australia where he continues to produce excellent results.*

*3. The men who confessed to being co-conspirators with DI Richelieu have never met their partner in crime, there is no record of any communication between these men and Richelieu and, when quizzed, if the matter comes before a court, will be shown to be fraudsters who have been paid and/or threatened to confess as they have.*

*What do the French police say about the information in this article? Are the claims true?*

She read her article making changes. She knew her idea carried risks. If it appeared online or on a traditional media platform and backfired, Pierre would be worse off. But waiting months for a trial would kill his spirit. Knowing he'd been set up and refused bail would crush him.

She closed her tablet, turned out her bedside light and slid deep into her comfortable bed. The room was dark. Jo closed her eyes.

Michael couldn't sleep. He had little problem with jetlag but London pubs, a scary road trip, two whacky characters in Silas and Awesome, plus a bed on a narrowboat, meant sleep was tricky. He listed names and occupations of people who might be involved in the Richelieu drug bust. Two prominent names were Émile Bastien and Laris Jlassi.

Michael searched these names. He built profiles. The more he discovered, the more he worried about their power and influence. Tiredness kicked in. He backed up his notes, turned off the Notebook and decided to sleep. He removed his jacket and boots, turned out the light and slept on *Blodwyn's* only narrow bed. He closed his eyes.

Jo was a light sleeper and in a strange bed in a strange location she woke thanks to a soft knocking. She froze. A voice whispered.

'Hello, Joanna. It's me, Antony. Are you asleep?'

She thought to whisper, "Yes", but didn't. The lawyer persisted.

'Do you fancy a midnight feast? I'm starving.'

Jo remained mute. *Surely he'll give up and go away.* He didn't. In the darkness she heard a key being pushed into the door. She flicked on her phone. The glow from the screen shone on the door. She'd locked it from the inside and her key blocked his.

She hopped out of bed. The floor creaked. She froze. She moved to the fireplace and the noise stopped. Then came a whisper.

'If you fancy some famous Belgian chocolate and cocoa, I'm the last room on the left in the West Wing. Good night.'

*He lives in the White House!* She waited then heard soft footsteps walking away. She exhaled and returned to bed thinking about an escape. *Have I enough sheets to reach the ground?*

Michael too was a light sleeper and as his cat Alan often requested room service at 0300 hours, when two humans stepped aboard *Blodwyn* at 0315 hours, Michael was awake. Neither visitor tried the door to the interior. Michael slipped out of bed and put on his footwear.

Michael thought. *Do I ring Silas? The police?* A clanging sound was followed by a curse. Michael thought about sabotage. He reckoned the interlopers were sinking the narrowboat and Michael had no floaties.

He crept past the kitchen and the lounge and paused at the door. It was glass. He could see out. He reached for the door handle. As he opened the door, a woman turned, nearly died of fright, and screamed.

Residents on both sides of the water, if awake, would have heard the cry. Light sleepers awoke. Certainly the gent trying to flood the engine heard it. The female grabbed a pot plant and took aim. Michael remembered his vow to never strike a woman, and to always allow an OAP to win. He stepped forward and grabbed her wrists. She screamed again with Michael yet to open his account.

He carefully turned the septuagenarian, and lowered her and the plant to the deck. With his back to the stern, Michael was about to advise the woman to stay put when her husband, an octogenarian, arose and struggled to stand. Brandishing a monkey wrench, the attacker charged. The martial arts expert from Down Under stepped aside allowing the OAP to head for the stern railing where he overbalanced, screamed, as did his missus for the third time, then toppled into the Regents Canal—well the Wenlock Basin offshoot thereof. His plunge scored a zero from Olympic diving judges.

In the water he floundered and yelled. On the narrowboat, his wife copied him. She was well warmed up by now. Lights came on from dwellings. People looked down from highrise apartments. Stickybeaks appeared. Several 999 calls were made.

Michael grabbed a life buoy and landed it beside the drowning man. Mind you, if the old geezer stopped thrashing about, he could have stood up and walked to the wharf as narrowboats like supermodels have flat bottoms to sail in shallow water.

A young hero arrived and guided the old man to dry land. His wife scrambled ashore and went to comfort him. More locals came out for a gander. Two uniformed cops arrived and the pantomime began.

Pointing at Michael who stood on the *Blodwyn* a la Captain Horatio Hornblower, the expert screamstress declared. 'There's the man. He attacked us and pushed my husband into the canal.'

Michael remembered a somewhat different version but the narrowboat invaders convinced the Bobbies to arrest Dr Chan. Before being led away by the constabulary, he asked a simple question.

'Would you check the engine, officers? If this vessel sinks ten minutes after we've departed, you might have a bit of explaining to do.'

They checked and found nothing astray and as they checked, Michael rang Silas, woke him and relayed the events. Silas rang Awesome and the narrowboat was guarded overnight.

Jo drifted towards sleep when she heard a soft tapping. *Not again,* she thought. This time she'd tell Antony to take a running jump but froze when a new voice spoke. It sounded like a pantomime character.

'Oh Miss Best. It's your favourite Earl. Is everything tickety-boo?'

Jo opted for the previous tactic—say nothing and wait till the philandering bastard gives up.

'Miss Best?' repeated the pantomime Dame.

The sound of the key in the door followed and was again jammed by Jo's key. Then a change of routine. Jo used her phone to observe. *The Times* appeared beneath the door, and some jiggery-pokery saw Jo's key wobble then dive forward and land on the newspaper.

Jo adopted Her Ladyship's emergency plan. The detective grabbed her phone and scampered to the fireplace. She reached in, felt for the tiny lever and pushed. The Earl's key settled in the door and clicked.

Jo dived into the newly opened hidey-hole, killed her phone and closed the secret panel. She stopped breathing and froze in the pitch black space. She heard the door open and close.

'Hell-o,' cooed the Earl now in his Modern Major-General's voice. 'Room service.'

*Room service?* thought Jo praying he would trip and fall. She heard his footsteps and pathetic entreaties.

'I've got you a nightcap, officer—the best single malt in the land. How do you like it?'

Jo lay there thinking her family, colleagues and friends would never believe this situation. She would never tell them.

She heard him opening wardrobes, bending to look under her bed, even opening windows. He hated missing a drink with the gorgeous young woman who wandered into his domain. He swore. 'Damn. No idea where you are, my dear. Righto, Detective. Sleep tight.' He fumbled with the key then left leaving the door wide open.

*Great*, thought Jo. *The creep was born in a tent.*

She lay still for ten minutes or more. Her plan was to sneak out, re-lock the door only this time add a chair beneath the door handle.

She felt for the lever in her cubby hole and pushed. Nothing. She tried again. Still nothing. *Oh brilliant. I'm stuck in a 400 year-old hiding place and need to pee. Did the last priest leave a chamber pot?*

Michael stood in front of the desk sergeant while the arresting constable explained the charge. When asked if he understood, Michael nodded and asked if he could put his side of the story.

'You can in the morning, sir. Now please empty your pockets.'

Michael was super cool. He'd rung Silas but wondered if the sailor would come to Michael's rescue? Placing the contents of his pockets on the counter, Michael's phone rang. He looked at the desk sergeant.

'Go on,' said the police officer, 'but make it quick.'

Michael checked then answered his phone. 'Hello Senior Constable,' he said which grabbed the attention of the police.

'Michael, I'm in trouble. Where are you?'

'I'm in Reception at the Stoke Newington Police Station in ...' He looked at the sergeant.

'Hackney.'

'In Hackney.'

Jo gasped. 'What? Why?'

'I've been arrested for allegedly throwing an old age pensioner into the Regents Canal.' He put his phone on Speaker.

'Michael, stop being ridiculous. Where are you?'

'It's true. I've been arrested. But where are you?'

'Stop being funny. I'm at Bulwer Hall and stuck in a priest hole.'

The police were hooked. On a relatively quiet night, this arrest was interesting getting better.

'You're in a priest hole in a stately home in Northhamptonshire?'

'Yes.'

'And you reckon *I'm* ridiculous.'

Jo snapped. 'Michael, this is serious.'

'Well you've got your phone. Ring His Lordship. He'll rescue you.'

'I can't.'

'Can't? Why not?'

'Because His Lordship's the one who invaded my bedroom, and I'm in the priest hole to evade his evil clutches.'

The police moved to incredulous. Michael took his phone off speaker much to the dismay of the rapt coppers and dropped his voice. 'We're supposed to keep this low key,' he said sounding angry.

She fired back at him. 'Don't you think I know that?'

'Imagine what the Chief Commissioner is going to say?'

Now Michael was no mug. The cops could only hear his half of the conversation but the words packed a punch. *Lordship, evil clutches* and *Chief Commissioner* all piqued the police officers' interest.

'Will you please ring Lady Jonquil and tell her I'm stuck. Use some witty code. She'll understand. Please Michael, I'm desperate.'

'I'll do what I can but it may have to wait till sunrise and only if I get bail.' Michael looked at the cops. They were hooked. 'You could ring 999. Between the police and the fire brigade, you'll be fine. Bye.'

'Hey,' demanded the desk sergeant. 'Is that a genuine emergency?'

'Of course.'

'Give me your phone.' Michael did. The line was dead.

# 24

TUCK AND MELK went looking for the sister of Maggie's boyfriend, Trevor Hastings. He killed himself in the house where he and Maggie lived, and where Maggie was murdered. Surprisingly the house still stood. Doubly surprising was the fact Trevor's sister, Gina, still lived in the same high-rise flat in Richmond. She was 22 years older and looked it. Mind you the two detectives were no spring chickens.

'G'day Gina, you won't remember us but we were detectives when your brother and his girlfriend ran into a spot of trouble.'

She pointed at Tuck. 'I remember you,' then at Melk, 'but not you.'

'Story of my life,' said Melk.

She let them in, heard their story, and spoke. 'Well I hope you find who killed Maggie but it sure wasn't my brother. He made me promise to tell no-one but after all these years, it can't do him no harm.'

'Exactly,' said Tuck. 'But it could help him and even Maggie if we can solve the case.' He paused. 'What did he say, Gina?'

'I can still see his face, white as sheet he was. "Maggie's dead, sis," he said. "She's dead".'

'From the beginning Gina, please,' said Tuck.

She told them how Trevor saw Maggie's uncle coming out of the house. 'Trevor reckoned the man was super scared like something terrible happened. Trevor waited for the uncle to leave then went inside. He found Maggie dead. There was a lot of blood. The baby was asleep so Trevor ran. He came here and made me promise to tell no-one. And I've kept my promise till now.'

The detectives wondered if they'd cracked the cold case. Gina looked and sounded sincere, even relieved to have told her story.

Tuck paused. 'Why do you think Trevor killed himself, Gina?'

'Because he let Maggie down. He should have been there to protect her. He should have stopped that bastard of an uncle.'

Melk was gentle. 'What did Trevor mean in his note, "I'm sorry, Maggs. Sorry for what I done to you. I never meant to hurt you."?'

'What it says. He let her down. I mean why kill the girl who gave you a home? She helped get him off the gear. She cared about him. And he was weak, never violent. He saw what happened to Maggie, and who killed her, and his depression came back.'

Tuck too paused. 'Why didn't you tell us this twenty years ago?'

She shrugged. 'Trevor made me promise. He was dead. She was dead. What was the point?'

Tuck spoke in a soft voice. 'Because Maggie might have got justice and the killer might have been punished.'

She nodded. 'Maybe. But who would've believed me?'

'Will you sign a statement, Gina, repeating what you've told us?' asked Melk. He paused. 'Please.'

She hesitated then gave a small nod. The retired detectives took her statement, left and immediately Tuck was on the phone.

Rose was driving Robbo. She used her speaker-phone. 'Tucky?'

'We have a statement, boss. The boyfriend who topped himself told his sister he saw the uncle, Harold Whipsnape, coming out of the house looking agitated. Trevor waited for the uncle to piss off, went inside and discovered Maggie's bloodied body.'

'Which contradicts what Harold told us and if your witness is correct then Uncle Harold's our man.' She looked across at Robbo who wore his poker face.

Tuck was a practical man. 'I reckon we'll need the uncle's death-bed confession. This statement ain't gunna get any murder charge.'

'We'll see,' said Rose, 'and well done, both of you. We've started on the family of the elderly neighbour. Let's meet at Robbo's tonight. The pizzas are on me. Ciao.'

She looked across at Robbo. 'Your thoughts, sir?'

'I haven't eaten pizza this millennium.'

DS Billy Hughes addressed the squad. 'News time, ladies and gentlemen, and make it good, please. Who's first? Detective Senior Constable Baldwin I think. Phone callers—where are we?'

'Good and bad news, Sarge. We've found the two callers who it seems were set up to set up the murder. Their response was simple. Deny everything and remember nothing.'

'Is that it? Justin?'

'It's like Charlie said. They claim they rang a wrong number.'

Billy persisted. 'So one rings the victim sending him to the property where he's murdered, and the other rings the estate agent asking him to visit the property where he finds the corpse.'

'That's about it,' replied Fleming. A two-minute wrong number call.'

'And the estate agent is sleeping with the dead man's sister-in-law,' added Blunt.

Billy stressed. 'This is not good. We have to get those two guys to talk. They were recruited by the killer or by someone the killer recruited. They're our best lead. What do we know about them?'

Baldwin replied. 'Retirees, bowling club members, no criminal records, and the last people you'd think would be involved in murder.'

'Oh come on,' argued Billy. 'They're pensioners not bikies. Get 'em in here and rattle their zimmer frames.'

Blunt offered. 'I'd be happy to have a go, Sarge.'

She paused. Payne had told her about Blunt's aggressive behaviour, and she didn't trust the new DI with counting paperclips. 'Okay,' she said. 'But I have to tell the boss where we're at. What can I tell her?'

'We're up a certain creek without a paddle,' offered Baldwin.

'Where is the boss, Sarge?' asked Payne.

'I told you, on special assignment filling in for Jo Best.'

'And what's the latest with the ace detective?' asked Baldwin. 'Not a single postcard I notice.'

'Shut up, Charlie.'

Billy's phone rang. She stepped to one side while the others discussed the missing Senior Constable and her Parisian adventure but everyone stopped when Billy shouted.

'What! You're kidding?' She waved to the others to get their attention. 'And who else have you told?' The others were hooked. 'No, leave it with me. We'll send someone straight away. Thanks.' She ended the call and beamed.

'Good news, Sarge?' asked Baldwin.

She stared at them. 'We may have our killer.' You could feel the release of tension. 'Bradley Devlin walked into his local nick and confessed.' Officers buzzed. Some looked at photos on the board to check who he was. 'He was one of our no-alibi, fab four.'

'His wife was arrested for threatening Grovene's wife,' said Fleming.

Billy explained. 'I was half right. I thought his wife, Donna, did it. She's short and wiry, capable of stabbing from a low angle.'

Payne turned practical. 'Where is he and has he been interviewed?'

'He's at Kew, awaiting interview.'

'I'll get him,' said Blunt sounding like the kid who volunteers to be the class monitor.

'Thank you, Inspector. Take Senior Constable Payne with you.' Blunt was chuffed. 'And when Mr Devlin is fit to be interviewed, DS Fleming and I will lead the team.' Blunt wanted to spit.

'Have you told the boss?' asked Fleming.

Billy punched her phone. 'I'm doing it. She'll be rapt.'

Blunt and Payne left as Billy relayed the news to DI Rose who was driving with Robbo.

Now usually when a case is cracked, the detectives let off steam, various frothies are consumed and general mayhem ensues. For some reason, the news of nailing this killer didn't produce such happiness.

'Great news, ma'am,' said Billy. 'Bradley Devlin confessed to killing Grovene.'

'What? When?' exclaimed Rose and pulled over.

Billy explained and Rose insisted on being in on the interview.

'No problem, ma'am. I'll call you when he's ready.'

The call ended and Rose felt good inside. She resumed driving.

'Congratulations,' said Robbo. 'How's it feel?'

'I'm not sure. I didn't think we'd crack it so easily.'

'You haven't yet.' She looked at him. 'The interview will tell all.' They reached Christine's son's home. 'If it's okay with you, sir, I'd like to be back for the interview.'

'Elly, you're the boss of Homicide. Your three musketeers are mere lackeys. We do as we're told.' They walked to the front door.

'With respect, sir, you're speaking complete bollocks.' Rose smiled as the door was opened by Julie. Rose explained their mission.

'Kevin's not here.'

'May we come in?' asked the DI.

Julie was Kevin's second wife. There was a wedding photo and Rose asked about it. Julie showed it to her and Rose handed it to Robbo. Kevin looked like a coal miner put through a car wash.

'Did you ever meet Kevin's grandmother, Mrs Watson?' asked Rose.

Julie only knew Kevin's mother, Christine. Things went nowhere fast and the police prepared to leave when the man of the house arrived. Kevin looked worse than on his wedding day.

'Did you ever visit your Gran in Collingwood, Kevin?' asked Rose.

'Not a lot,' he said. 'Me Mum took me there when I was a kid.'

'What about when you were a big kid?'

Kevin shook his head. 'I was too busy chasin' girls.' Julie sighed.

'Do you remember your Gran or your Mum talking about the murder next door to your Gran's place?'

'Yeah, it was talked about. I remember me Mum being worried the man who killed the woman might have hurt me Gran.'

'And you have a daughter, Rachel?'

'Yeah, with me first wife.'

'And her name is?'

'Dianne.'

'Did Dianne visit your Gran?'

Kevin shrugged. 'Might have. You'd have to ask her.'

'And would your daughter Rachel have been to visit your Gran?'

He became annoyed. 'How could she? She wasn't even born. Anyway, Margie's boyfriend confessed.'

*Margie?* thought the detectives. *Did he mean to say Margie?*

Rose looked at Robbo. 'Anything else, sir?' He shook his head. Rose stood. 'Well thanks for your help, both of you.'

They left and, in the car, Rose rang Billy where at Homicide they were still waiting for Bradley Devlin.

'More interviews or back to Homicide?' asked Robbo.

'He's not arrived and the first wife is close.'

They drove to meet Dianne, Kevin's first wife.

'Did we learn anything from Kevin?' asked Robbo.

Rose worried. *He's testing me, like the old days.* 'I had the feeling he was lying.'

'About what?'

'I'm not sure. Copper's instinct I guess.'

'Instincts can be good.'

Dianne welcomed the detectives. 'How is the miserable slob?' she asked referring to her former husband.

'Fine,' said Rose, 'and he sends his love.'

Dianne laughed and they chatted about old Dot Watson. Dianne did go to visit Kevin's Gran with her then husband but didn't think he went much once they married. Dianne couldn't remember Kevin or his mother talking much about Maggie's murder.

Robbo asked for any family photos and the ones of Kevin and Dianne's wedding day were good for a laugh.

'Tell us about your daughter, Rachel,' said Rose.

Dianne boasted. 'She's a brilliant girl, a wonderful hairdresser and real good to her Mum. And she's engaged. He's a lovely boy so I'm hoping I'll have some grandkids in my old age.'

Rose and Robbo were given the engagement photos. They studied them then thanked Dianne and left.

In the car, Rose's phone rang. It was Billy Hughes with news. 'I'm on my way,' said Rose.

'Suspect ready to be interviewed?' asked Robbo.

'I'll drop you home, sir, but I think we may have to cancel tonight's soiree. Can you ring Tucky and Colin and put them off?'

'I could but maybe I won't.'

She looked at him. 'Sorry?'

'This whole *New Tricks* thing has given us a new lease of life. We were hardly shut-ins but working as detectives means a hell of a lot.'

'I'm glad. And please, meet as often as you like.'

'And rather than drop me home, why not the beauty salon where Kevin's daughter works?' Again Rose looked at him. 'Assuming you trust me to work alone.'

'You *are* keen.' She dropped him in South Yarra.

# 25

AT THE POLICE STATION IN LONDON, Michael was booked in. As he was about to be led to his cell, Silas Hornby arrived and addressed the desk sergeant.

'My name is Silas Hornby, the owner of the narrowboat, *Blodwyn*.' He pointed to Michael. 'That gentleman was a guest on board my vessel and he it was who disturbed the people attempting to sabotage it. In short, officer, you've arrested the wrong man.'

'That's as may be, sir,' said the sergeant.

'And if you won't take my word for it, kindly call the Commissioner of Police of the Metropolis on this private number and ask her to describe my good self.'

Oh, shit.

The first pitch from Silas was arguable, the second not so—no way. If what the new arrival said was true, ringing the top cop in London (in the land) at 0300 hours did not appeal to the officer of the watch. Michael was released with a weak warning not to interfere with the two complainants. As if.

In Silas' wreck of a jeep, Michael was again driven across London. 'Terribly sorry, old man,' said Silas, enjoying driving in the wee small hours. 'Fancy my boating buddies being the bad guys.'

'You know them?'

'They're the ones who promised to keep an eye on my boat when all along they're the saboteurs trying to make me move.'

'I'm sorry,' said Michael.

'Not your fault, old man. And by way of saying thanks, I thought we'd make a call on some of my old police chums.'

'At 4 am?'

'Crime never sleeps, old man. Interested?'

'Does the Regents Canal flow into the Thames?'

Silas laughed and Michael's face said it all. His quest to help Pierre Richelieu copped a boost. Silas knew the right people and in the wee small hours, the young man from Northcote met some heavy-duty security officers fighting crime in London, across the English Channel, in Gay Paree and across the globe.

Jo tried not to panic. She couldn't believe Michael would leave her in the priest hole. He didn't. The police, having heard part of Jo's dilemma and his instructions for her to call 999, agreed to Michael making a call. Before Silas arrived at Stoke Newington Police Station, Michael rang Buwler Hall.

Maurice, asleep in the gatekeeper's cottage, took the unusual message from Michael then rang Her Ladyship. This was not the first time the Countess was woken at such an hour.

'Strange message, Your Ladyship,' said Maurice. 'Damsel stuck in Catholic closet.'

'Thank you, Maurice,' said Lady Jonquil and set off for Jo's room. She tapped the panel and whispered. 'Father, are you in there?'

'Very funny.'

The women wandered downstairs, enjoyed coffee and a chat. 'I must admit my Lady, in the days of #MeToo and calling out sexual harassment, I found your family's behaviour to be appalling. A less capable woman might well have been assaulted.'

'I agree, and I didn't want you to use the priest hole.'

'Then why tell me about it?'

'To be used as a last resort. I would have preferred you to accidentally place your knee in a certain sensitive spot.'

'What twice? There were two of them.'

'Quite so.'

Jo looked at her hostess. *Are all upper-class families like this?* 'Can you help me leave earlier for London?'

'Oh don't go, please. The so-called gentlemen are cowards and won't say a thing, and you have to work with Antony to save your friend. Besides, it makes a change to have a feisty female on board.' Jo wanted to go. 'We'll go to church, have brunch and then you can go.'

Jo hesitated but agreed. 'Okay but under protest.'

'Thanks.'

Jo wanted as little fuss as possible. What would DI Rose say if she read the headline? *Aussie policewoman attacks English Earl* with the sub-heading *Family jewels damaged.*

During coffee, Jo's phone gave a tremor as a text arrived from Michael. *I'm OK. You?*

She replied. *I'm good. St Pancras 1530 hours?*

His reply was immediate. *Roger that.*


Maurice drove the women to the village church. The service summed up today's society. A congregation of 14, average age 71, the priest only here once a month and the rest of the village given over to sleep, sloth or the telly. The Lady of the Manor attended as it was the done thing.

Annie's brunch was little short of sensational and Antony was Mr Polite. His old man sent his apologies being called away on estate business. Liar. Coward.

Maurice drove Jo and Antony to Kettering. Jo didn't show Antony her article. She reckoned what he didn't know, he couldn't stop. On the trip up to London, Jo mentioned Michael's interesting experiences without naming names. They arrived at St Pancras, met Michael and caught the 1601 Eurostar non-stop to Gare du Nord.

Back in Paris, Jo and Michael were due back in Melbourne in 10 days. The clock was ticking. An article and some details about crims and crooked cops were all they had. Would it save DI Richelieu?


As the trio alighted in Paris, Yousef Jlassi was hard at work on his bomb-making. Now living in a cellar in his brother Laris' house, Yousef was out of sight, out of mind and preparing for death. He was no terrorist but a warrior, fighting a holy war, seeking vengance for the countless believers killed by infidels.

Yousef nervously packed the bomb in his rucksack. He wore the suicide vest back to front. Sweat trickled into his eyes. He couldn't stop his hands shaking—only small tremors but the pressure to become a martyr kept building.

He was running low on food and toilet paper and dared not go upstairs fearing his brother's wrath. The old toilet he used was blocked and the stench reached out and slapped him. Tomorrow would be the day he flew to Paradise. The bomb and the suicide vest were ready. Glorious martydom beckoned.

'Where are you?' Yousef heard his brother and panicked. The bomb was in his rucksack but not hidden. Anyone could find it. If Yousef told his brother about the bomb, Laris would explode more than the device. If Yousef said nothing, his brother might accidentally detonate the device or find it and detonate Yousef.

The trapdoor in the roof of the cellar creaked open and Laris peered inside. 'Where the fuck are you?' Yousef stood, numb and dumb. Laris scrambled down the stairs. 'What stinks?'

'I'm leaving tomorrow, brother,' squeaked the bombmaker.

Laris approached the rucksack. 'What are you doing down here? Making a fucking bomb or something?'

Yousef needed the stinking toilet. Laris pulled back the flap of the rucksack and peered inside. 'What's in here?' He reached inside.

'No,' screamed Yousef but his cry was drowned.

'Laris,' roared one his goons. 'The cops are here.'

'What!?' Laris lost interest in the rucksack and headed upstairs. 'I'll be back,' he called. He closed the hatch and told the goon to cover it.

Yousef panicked. He needed a hiding place. Gingerly he removed the bomb and placed it on the concrete floor. He picked up some empty tins of food and stashed them in the rucksack. He grabbed the old towel Laris removed and covered the new contents. Now, where to hide the bomb?

Outside, the yard was overlooked. Then Yousef knew. He moved to the toilet and carefully placed his weapon of death in the pan. No way would anyone look in there. He closed the seat and as the cistern didn't work, trying to flush the mush would fail.

*This is too dangerous* thought Yousef. *I need to venture out to busy Paris. I need to become a soldier.*

Upstairs, anti-terrorist officers searched. Furious, Laris arrived.

'Hey!' he yelled enraged. 'What the hell are you doing?'

'We're looking for your brother,' said the OIC.

'My brother?'

'Where is he?'

'How the fuck would I know?'

'He's wanted for murdering a police officer so hiding him will bring you serious pain, Laris.'

The criminal was stunned. 'Murder? My brother's a weed, scared of his own shadow.'

'Is he here?'

'No, and you have no right to be here. I'm calling my lawyer.'

Showing Laris the warrant, the officer gave an order. 'You lot upstairs, you lot downstairs.' The men departed.

In the cellar, Yousef heard the heavy boots above. He picked up the bomb and prepared to detonate it. He would wait until the last moment. But they would shoot first. He began to cry.

The footsteps went away and the bomb was returned to its putrid hidey-hole. Yousef didn't fancy the next visitor.

The cops left empty-handed and Laris and goon #1 headed for the cellar. 'I'll kill him,' breathed Laris. The cupboard was dragged away and the trapdoor opened. Yousef automatically prayed. 'Come here, you little prick,' snarled big brother, descending the stairs.

Yousef was terrified. 'I promise I'll go tomorrow.'

Laris grabbed the bomb maker. 'The cops reckon you murdered one of them. I know it's impossible but why were they here?'

'No idea. It's not true,' pleaded Yousef.

'What are you doing? Where's your bag?' Laris let go of his brother, and moved to the rucksack. He lifted the towel and found empty tins of food and dirty laundry. He ordered his thug. 'Check outside.'

'Tomorrow, Laris, I promise.'

'What happened with the safecracker?'

'Nothing. I saw him but my friend paid off the blackmailer.'

'The cops seemed sure it was you. Did you kill a cop?'

'Me? I couldn't kill a fly.'

The goon returned and shook his head. Laris pointed a finger at Yousef. 'F'get this blood-is-thicker-than-water shit. You fuck with me, brother, and our parents will be short one son.' He went to slap him but found the stench overpowering. 'What is that smell?'

'It's the toilet, it's blocked,' said Yousef starting to tremble. Laris moved to the toilet. 'No!' screamed Yousef stopping his brother who grew suspicious. 'I've got blood in my stools.' Laris stared at him. 'I need to take them to my doctor. I'm not well.' Yousef begged. 'Please don't tell Mum and Dad. I'll tell them. Please Laris.'

Big brother looked at his pathetic sibling. Of sympathy was there none. Laris headed upstairs followed by his goon. Laris spat at his brother without a backward glance. 'Piss off.'

In Paris, Jo and Michael farewelled Antony, and took a cab to Rue Crémieux. En route, they spoke little about their English adventures but once inside, both had tales to tell.

They opened the door, tossed their luggage on the floor and prepared to make coffee.

Jo grabbed Michael's arm and whispered. 'Wait. What's that?'

'What's what?' he whispered. Then he too heard it. Someone or thing was upstairs. A criminal or a crooked cop?

'My kingdom for a gun,' whispered Jo, looking for a weapon.

They crept up the stairs when a woman appeared. Shock spread across her face. 'Who the hell are you?' she demanded.

'Who the hell are you?' replied Jo. 'And what are you doing here?'

'Get out now or I'll call the police.'

'Suits us,' replied Jo, daring the woman to act.

Michael intervened. 'Look, we're staying here. What's your excuse?'

'I'm part of the family. I'm Pierre's sister.'

Jo and Michael froze. They remembered. At his mother's funeral, Pierre met a sibling he never knew existed.

Jo slipped into her detective role. 'We're Pierre's friends. He knows we're staying here. Does he know you're here?'

'Of course not. He's in jail. I was fetching his mail.'

Another stalemate. 'I'm Jo and this is Michael. What's your name?'

'Michelle,' she said and headed down the stairs. She wasn't going to stop. Jo and Michael moved to one side. 'I'll tell Pierre I met you,' she called, opened the front door and disappeared.

'Interesting,' said Michael. 'Did you notice her hands?'

Jo whispered. 'She was wearing disposable gloves.' Jo put a finger to her lips and headed upstairs. On the first floor landing she leant close and whispered in Michael's ear. 'Listening devices, cameras. Anything missing or out of place.' Once a detective, always a detective. He understood. They separated and searched.

At his home, Commandant Erec Bonnaire answered his phone. 'Oui?'

'Good evening, Commandant. Renaud reporting on the two Australians, sir, who are back in Paris.'

'Yes?'

'In London the male was arrested and released without charge. The female reported an incident in a stately home in Northamptonshire.'

'Details?'

Renaud repeated what he'd been told. 'They've returned to the Richelieu house in Rue Crémieux.'

'And?'

'Shortly after they arrived, a woman came out of the house.'

'Who is she?'

'No idea, Commandant.'

'Find out. And excellent work, Renaud.'

'Merci, Commandant.'

Having searched high and low, Jo and Michael found nothing suspicious and settled in the kitchen.

'Was she Pierre's sister?' asked Michael.

'Possibly. Remember he met a woman at the funeral who said Pierre has five siblings all, except her, living in the US.'

'Let's ask Pierre about her tomorrow. Now I want to know about your hanky panky with the aristocracy.' She glared at him. 'Or we can go over whatever plans we have for your imprisoned colleague.'

'I will never tell you about my shenanigans with the toffs.'

'So something *did* happen.'

'Just as I will never ask about your run-in with the Met.'

He grinned in a sort of "ha ha" sort of way. 'So what have you and His Highness come up with?'

She showed him her article. 'This is my work. Antony hasn't seen it. He wants the staid approach. I like to crash or crash through.'

'Typical Joanna Best, and I like it,' he said giving Jo a boost.

'And you?'

He showed her a list of names. 'These are prominent crooks in Paris. Two in particular. Bastien is Pierre's former colleague sacked and sent to jail for corruption thanks to Inspector Richelieu.'

'Great motive,' said Jo feeling excited.

'Laris Jlassi is the Parisian drug and vice king who uses Bastien to launder his profits. If Bastien wanted to get back at Pierre, knowing Jlassi would make a sting so much easier.'

Jo was super impressed. 'Trust you, Dr Chan. Is there anything you can't do?'

*Make love to you* thought Michael.

'I also heard,' he said, 'Jlassi and Bastien are friendly with at least one high-ranking officer in the French police.'

'Shit,' spat Jo with feeling. 'Name?'

'Don't know.'

'So, what now?'

'Let's have a chat with Pierre in the morning, tell him what we know and see what he thinks of your article. We should also have a plan, something he could approve or reject.'

'Great. Thanks heaps, Michael. I could never do this by myself.'

'We haven't done anything, yet.'

She paused. 'What should we do about the Honourable Antony Heron-Royhay?'

He paused. 'Put him on the mushroom diet.' She didn't understand. 'Keep him in the dark and feed him manure.'

# 26

RETIRED DCI JOHN ROBERTSON stood outside *Henri's Hair Stylist* in trendy South Yarra. Robbo was an octogenarian with thinning hair arranged in a pudding basin style in vogue in 1963. He was not the usual client who popped into *Henri's* for a cut and blow-dry or a splash of semi-gloss colour. When Robbo entered, everyone in the salon stopped and stared. A Martian would have made less of an impact.

Robbo smiled. 'Good afternoon. I'm a retired detective investigating a cold case. May I speak with Miss Rachel Cordner?'

His statement answered several questions but raised even more. Rachel came forward. 'I'm Rachel and it's Ms not Miss.'

'Hello,' said Robbo smiling. 'I'm John Robertson. I've been talking to your Mum about your great-grandmother, Mrs Dot Watson.' Rachel was intrigued with the rest of the staff and their clients hooked. 'Can I buy you a coffee and have a chat? It won't take long.'

Rachel looked at Henri. 'Five,' he said and returned to work.

Robbo was his usual avuncular self, making Rachel feel at home. He explained the case sans the gruesome details. 'Can you remember your parents talking about Grandma Watson?'

Rachel shook her head. 'I've only seen her photo in albums.'

'Did you know about the murder next door to her house?'

'My Mum told me about it when she saw something on TV about the 20th anniversary. It all happened before I was born. I'm only 19.'

'And I believe felicitations are in order.' She didn't understand. 'On your engagement.'

'Oh, yes,' she beamed and showed Robbo her engagement ring.

'It's beautiful. I hope my granddaughter's getting engaged. May I ask where you got your ring?'

She looked puzzled. 'From my fiancé.'

'No, sorry, I mean where did *he* get it?'

'He won't say but he said he got a great deal.'

'My granddaughter would love it. May I take a photo?'

Rachel loved the attention. Robbo used his phone and discreetly snapped. They chatted some more then he stood. 'Well you must get back to work. Thank you so much for your time.'

In the street, Robbo held out his hand which she took then leant in and kissed his cheek. He smiled enjoying his moment of bliss before coming back to Earth with a thud wondering how he would get home.

DI Rose arrived at Homicide trying to keep a lid on her excitement. Tackling a homicide as head honcho is tough. Sometimes you get lucky. Out of the blue, a suspect confesses but Rose knew the dangers. Ask the wrong question and she could damage, even destroy the police case. Rose thought of her early days working with DCI Robertson. 'Draw them out, never demand,' he would say.

Billy Hughes spotted Rose. 'Glad you're here, ma'am.'

'Are we all set?'

'We are. He's with his brief and seems keen to talk.'

'Good.'

'Who do you want sitting in with you, ma'am?'

'You, of course. And I want you to lead.'

Billy was pleased and explained her plan. Rose asked questions, probing possible weaknesses in Billy's approach. Once their discussion finished it was time to go.

'First I need a pee,' said Rose and departed.

Bradley Devlin looked sad. His expression was "pre-tears". His solicitor was an elderly gent who looked after Bradley's father's estate. Ralph Gems was a wills and conveyancing old-school solicitor and this was his first client involved in murder. After Billy's meticulous preliminaries, the interview proper began.

'Why did you go to the Kew police station, Mr Devlin?'

'To confess to killing Simon Grovene.'

'I assume you've discussed this matter with your solicitor.'

'I have.'

Ralph didn't know what to say. 'He has,' was his contribution.

'Can you tell us what happened on the day Mr Grovene was killed?'

Bradley kept calm. He was emotional but calm. He explained how he got a friend to call Grovene and invite him to the empty house. When there, Bradley asked Grovene several times for the money he was owed. Grovene laughed at him. Bradley admitted he threatened Grovene and his wife did the same to Grovene's wife.

'Let's talk about the murder,' said Billy. 'How did it happen?'

'I shot at the wall to frighten him. He panicked so I stabbed him.'

'What gun did you use?'

Bradley looked at his solicitor who was more worried than his client. Bradley addressed the police. 'No comment.'

That threw the detectives. Up until then they were in cruise control. Billy recovered. 'You told us you stabbed Mr Grovene. With what?'

Bradley didn't look at Mr Gems. 'No comment.'

Billy looked at Rose who mouthed the word 'Break'. The recording was stopped and the detectives departed.

'I don't like it,' said Rose. 'He confesses but without details. Why?'

'Because he didn't do it and is covering for the killer.'

'That's a big cover—20 years for something you didn't do.'

'I've always suspected his wife. She's got a temper. She went for Grovene's wife. She has the build to stab a low blow.' They looked at one another. 'I think we have to charge him, ma'am. If a man with the motive, means and opportunity to kill Grovene confesses to the crime, we'll look bloody stupid if we let him go.'

Rose wasn't sure. 'But why the "no comment"?'

'He's acting under instructions.'

Rose scoffed. 'From *that* solicitor?'

'Why don't we charge him, oppose bail, and go hard on his wife? Depending on what she says or anything new, we prosecute or release.'

Rose blew hard. She desperately wanted success. If she released him and it turned out he murdered Grovene, she'd look a goose. If she charged him and his confession was false, she'd look a bigger goose.

'Okay, we charge, oppose bail and test his confession.'

Devlin was charged and Mr Gems went back to writing wills.

The three retired detectives sat in Robbo's lounge room where the host's tea and biscuits were disappearing. Melk complained.

'Did Elly really say she'd bring pizza tonight?'

'She did,' added Robbo, 'but she's about to solve a big homicide so may not make it. Let's crack on. What news?'

Tuck reported on the girlfriend of Trevor Hastings. 'If what she says is true then Trevor didn't kill Maggie but her lowlife uncle did.'

'But he's in care and away with the pixies,' said Melk.

'We need a trip to Ballarat,' said Robbo. 'You two have a statement that puts Harold in the frame. I have photos that might free him.'

'What?' exclaimed Tuck and Melk.

Robbo explained the visits to Dot Watson's family members.

'I think our case is solid, boss,' said Tuck. 'Yours is speculation.'

'And if Harold is non-compos,' added Melk, 'he won't be able to answer your questions.'

'True,' replied Robbo, 'and he won't be fit to stand trial.' Silence.

'Bugger,' said Tuck.

'Damn,' said Robbo.

'Phooey,' said Melk.

They were upset but relieved their frustration by swearing politely. This was a hangover from their Homicide days when Robbo's predecessor, a Methodist who, when upset, only ever said *drat*.

'Baloney,' said Tuck.

'Shoot,' said Robbo.

'Bummer,' said Melk.

Their voices grew louder and the tempo increased.

'Darn,' said Tuck.

'Shucks,' said Robbo.

'Doggone,' said Melk.

'Narf,' yelled Tuck.

'Pluck it,' roared Robbo.

'Banana shenanigans,' screamed Melk.

Tuck and Robbo paused then yelled as one. 'Banana Shenanigans?'

Melk went defensive. 'What's wrong with that?'

It was a mixture of protest, laughter and mockery interrupted by the doorbell. They fell silent.

Tuck looked at Robbo. 'You said she wasn't coming.'

'It might be someone else,' suggested Melk.

A familiar voice was heard. 'Do you want these pizzas?'

All three headed to the front door.

# 27

'HOW DID PIERRE'S SISTER get inside the house?' asked Michael over breakfast. 'And why was she keen to avoid leaving fingerprints?'

'Because she wasn't who she claimed to be.'

'Ouch,' winced Michael.

'This will kill Pierre. He thought he had a family.'

Michael opened his Notebook. 'I've constructed some plans.'

Jo forgot her toast and read with interest. 'Michael, this is brilliant.'

'That's Plan A. Plan B is further down.'

'What?' She scrolled and read. 'God, Michael, you are a genius. If you ever become a crim, you could make a fortune.'

'We leave it to Pierre to say yea or nay. He'll know which plan has the best chance of success.'

Jo turned serious. 'He won't accept either.'

'What? Doesn't he want to get out?'

'Michael, Pierre will not want either of us placed in harm's way.'

'You pinched that line from an American movie.'

She ignored his limp humour. 'My article is not dangerous. Your plans take us into conflict with men who think nothing about killing. Forget Pierre giving permission, *I* won't let us take these risks.'

'So you want to go with the Honourable Antony Heron-Royhay's plan and have Pierre rot in prison for months before any trial?'

She shook her head. 'You know I'd hate that.'

'We could re-visit the police and pressure them.'

'The best way to pressure them is through widespread media coverage using my article.'

He knew she was right. They finished their breakfast barely speaking then prepared for prison. Jo came out of her room ready to roll. Michael stood waiting for her. 'A moment, Miss, if you please. May I steal two hairs from your lovely head.'

She liked Michael and sometimes thought he wanted their friendship to develop into a more intimate relationship. He did. He stood behind her and carefully selected two hairs from her long ponytail. 'You might feel a little prick.' He yanked and Jo lost a miniscule amount of her dark auburn locks.

'Are they for your locket?' she asked.

'I wish,' he said and moved to her bedroom door. Standing on a chair, and using clear sticky tape, he attached a hair to the top of her door with the other end on the door frame. He did the same with his bedroom door then closed both doors and replaced the chair.

'You were in the Scouts.'

'Cubs actually but I saw it in a James Bond movie. It's to tell us if any more of Pierre's family drop in.'

'Duh,' said Jo, secretly pleased.

En route to the prison, she rang Antony. 'Good morning, sir.'

'Good morning, Miss Best.' He was quiet, worried his weekend behaviour would come back to bite him.

'Michael and I are on our way to see Inspector Richelieu. Is there a message you wish us to convey?'

'Thank you, no. I'll visit my client later this morning.'

*Your client,* thought Jo. *My colleague. Our friend.*

The call ended and they entered the prison. Pierre looked worse. Apart from his lawyer and two friends, he was alone. He knew the trio were in the UK on the weekend, and longed for news. He longed for company and clung to the hope his nightmare would end.

When he saw Jo and Michael, his heart sang. He and Jo wanted to embrace and kiss, not only because of their romantic feelings but because of Pierre's tragic circumstances.

The trio sat and spoke quietly. Jo explained their three suggestions and Pierre looked at their written ideas.

'You cannot consider these two plans.' Jo and Michael were not surprised. 'The people who 'ave framed me, 'ate me with a passion. I put them in prison and they will stop at nothing to make sure I am found guilty.'

'Is Émile Bastien behind your arrest, Inspector?' asked Michael. Pierre's silence spoke volumes.

'Possibly,' he said in a whisper. He meant "yes".

'So what about my article?' asked Jo. 'Surely it's a way to have you released without dealing with dangerous men.'

'Per'aps,' he conceded. 'But I do not want either of you to face any danger. Nothing dangerous.'

Silence. Pierre was determined, Jo and Michael felt flat.

Michael tried. 'Antony gave me a contact in London, a former police officer with contacts in Interpol. He gave me those names in my plans. He took me to meet some current officers. They believe there is a top police officer, here in Paris, who is corrupt.'

'Per'aps,' said Pierre.

'We have met Commandant Erec Bonnaire, and the man heading your case, Brigadier Louis Droit,' explained Jo. 'What can you tell us about these men?'

Richelieu shrugged. 'Bonnaire and I were colleagues. I knew Droit but never worked with 'im.'

'Could either be corrupt?' asked Michael.

The question hurt Richelieu. The psychological pressure he endured since the day of his mother's funeral was immense and building. Tears came to his eyes and his hands covered his face. 'I do not know.'

Jo and Michael exchanged glances. This was going nowhere. Then Jo remembered.

'Pierre, we met your sister, step-sister Michelle.'

He came alive. 'What? When?'

'Last night. We returned from London and she was in your house.'

Pierre struggled. 'That cannot be. She left for America.'

'Did you give her a key to your house?' asked Jo.

Pierre shook his head and the visitors were floored. 'Please describe your sister,' said Michael. Pierre's description of the woman he met at his mother's funeral matched the woman Jo and Michael confronted.

The trio endured horrible thoughts. Jo explained the conversation with the woman. Michael asked, 'And you're sure you didn't give her a key?' Pierre shook his head. The dark mood grew darker.

Jo tried to pull things back into focus. 'Okay, the woman is not your step-sister, so who is she and why was she in your home?'

'Obviously she's working for Pierre's enemies,' added Michael.

'That could be our lead,' said Jo, again thinking like a detective. 'Do you have her address or phone number?'

'They'll be fake,' added Michael, rubbing salt into Pierre's wounds.

He slumped. 'Three strikes and I am out. My mother is dead, my career ruined, and my new family non-existent.' The others said nothing. He was pathetic. 'What does our learned lawyer recommend?'

Jo and Michael paused. They didn't want to kick Pierre when he was down. They lacked confidence in Antony's approach and attitude.

'He's playing by the rules, Pierre,' said Jo, 'and even if he does get your charges thrown out, it may take time ... like months.'

Michael tried to coax the prisoner. 'Jo's article posted anonymously online could flush out your enemies and put real pressure on the police to question your two phoney accomplices.'

Jo appreciated Michael's support. Pierre knew the article idea was sound but procrastinated. 'Let me think about it. When is the lawyer coming?' They told him. 'I'll ask his advice.'

'No!' said Jo and Michael as one in too loud a response.

Pierre went pale. Jo explained. 'He doesn't know about my article. We think it best to keep it secret.' She looked at him. 'Okay?'

Pierre nodded. He struggled and was easy to manipulate. The pressure battered him. A guard arrived. 'Stay strong, Inspector,' said Jo and threw him a dazzling smile. It fired his heart and Michael's too.

Bastien's phone rang. This time it didn't involve coitus interruptus. 'What?' he said and listened.

Using a disposable phone, the caller disguised his voice. 'The goods move this week.'

'When it's done, tell me.'

'There's something else.'

Bastien hated problems. 'What?'

'Two international tourists are helping our friend.'

There was a pause. 'Trouble?'

'Could be.'

'Send details.'

Bastien ended the call then rang Laris.

He was furious. '*Another* favour?'

Bastien explained and later, at the agreed dead letter drop, Laris Jlassi's goon collected an envelope. It contained a photo of Jo Best and

Michael Chan, taken in Paris, and their current Parisian address. Both photos featured an X crudely drawn on each head.

Bastien's plan was simple. Using his corrupt police officer chum, he would swap the drugs seized in Richelieu's mother's house. When the swap occurred, Bastien would return Jlassi's drugs, please him and thereby get a better cut on their deals and his perks.

One perk being the black teenager from Nigeria, the beautiful but shattered Adamma. She was in peril and despair. Being summoned by M. Bastien pushed her feelings of dread to the red zone.

She arrived and was greeted with creepy words and touches, the warm-up to the disgusting sex games solely for the benefit of the middle-aged man caring nothing for the devastated girl.

Bastien plied her with fine French champagne. Adamma hated it. She loathed his grubby activities. He led her to his bathroom. Naked, he joined her beneath the bubbles where his tongue became a loose cannon. She hated the man and his behaviour. But what could she do?

She pondered killing Bastien. *How? Drowning? But he would need to be unconscious first. Smashing his head would do the trick.* As she attended to his carnal desires, she looked for a suitable weapon. *But once he's dead, where do I go?* It was a plan doomed to fail.

His hands invaded her every orifice accompanied by vile flattery. They left the bath, dried and headed to the bedroom. For Adamma there was a Dantesque sign above the door. "Abandon hope, all ye who enter here". They continued his games on the massive bed. She was made to delight him without restraint.

Her idea about killing Bastien became a goal. As he copulated and dwelt on pleasure, she endured and dwelt on death.

The heavies who worked for Jlassi got their orders. Assault the two tourists helping Richelieu. Don't kill them; no international incident. Rough them up making them desperate to leave.

The news pleased the thugs. One's a woman—too easy. The man's an Asian nerd. Slap them hard.

The thugs went to Rue Crémieux and rang the doorbell. They were to burst in and do the business. No-one home. They left to return later.

Jo and Michael were eating sandwiches on a park bench trying to figure out what to do next. Michael wanted action.

'If we wait for Pierre's approval, we'll do nothing, and doing nothing, Detective, is not an option.'

'Michael, I'm under strict instructions. Work with the Australian Embassy and assist Pierre's lawyer—no heroics.'

They ate in silence. Both knew if left to Antony, Pierre was finished.

Across town, Yousef Jlassi examined his suicide vest. He was rapt. All he needed was the venue, date and time.

The plan was to place the bomb in a crowded area—the more the merrier—move away then detonate the bomb. Those who survived would run towards Yousef and be greeted with a second explosion.

He carefully tried on the suicide jacket. It felt good. He walked around the cellar holding out his arms feeling as if he could fly, trying to get the right stance to cause the most deaths and injuries. He held no fear only eager anticipation of life in Paradise with his multiple virgin brides.

Jo and Michael headed to the Australian Embassy, sat in reception and waited ages.

Jo studied her article, wondering when she should post it.

Having failed to attract the Ambassador, the duo cracked it for an officer clinging to the bottom rung of the public service.

'How can I assist?' was his opening pitch.

Jo explained the situation in words of one syllable. It produced a less than useless response. It was the usual line of allowing the French justice system to run its course—blah, blah, blah.

Michael had a go. 'With Inspector Richelieu holding both Australian and French passports, could the Australian government support the lawyer's request for bail?'

Rupert was clueless. 'I would need to take advice from my superiors, I'm afraid. Could you put your request in writing and I'll push it along for you. But these things do take time. What is your schedule?' he asked, pronouncing schedule as sked-ule.

'We leave on Friday week,' replied Jo.

'Oh God,' exclaimed Rupert. 'That's impossible.'

Michael persisted. 'But could you make representation without us being here?'

Rupert pondered. 'It might be possible. Again I'll need to consult a senior member of staff. Can you come back tomorrow?'

'Definitely,' said Jo rising but meaning, "over my dead body". She held out her hand. 'Thank you for your time.' Both visitors shook hands with Rupert and left. Being a drongo, Rupert thought he'd handled the situation with aplomb.

The duo walked in the Parisian late afternoon sunshine. Jo shook her head. 'The lawyer is useless and the Embassy worse. We are stuffed, Dr Chan. Our trip has been, pardon my French, a fucking disaster.'

'I like it when you're so upbeat,' he said without smiling. Jo liked his sarcasm and wit. 'How about we treat ourselves to a slap-up French feed?'

'At Pierre's expense?'

He shrugged. 'I reckon that's exactly what he'd want us to do.'

Jo agreed. They found a busy restaurant and indulged in typical French cuisine—Soupe à l'oignon, Coq au vin and Pompe aux Pommes du Perigord. The repast was to die for and with each course they thought more of Pierre Richelieu and his awful fate. They dined like aristocrats while he moped, probably wept in his cell.

They were a little worse for wear when heading to Rue Crémieux. Neither were drinkers but a Rosé cocktail or three gave them a feeling of invincibility. That would prove a blessing in disguise.

It was dark when they alighted from a taxi. A man walked towards them. Another approached from behind. Two goons, employed by Laris Jlassi, were on a mission and feeling confident.

Rue Crémieux at night was not the tourist hot spot it was during the day. Jo and Michael noticed the approaching goon because he was alone in the street. Behind them, his mate was too slow and needed to scamper to reach the couple at the same time as his mate. Big mistake.

The footsteps behind were a giveaway. Jo and Michael turned and the sight of the running goon rang alarm bells. The one in front went for the kill. He chose Jo leaving the second assailant to whack Michael.

'Look out, Michael,' was all Jo said as Goon #1 went to punch her in the face. This was 101 training in self defence for Jo. She evaded the fist, tripped the thug and knelt on his spine dragging one of his arms up his back. That hurt.

Goon #2 went for the rabbit chop on Michael's neck. Dr Kung-fu handled the attack with precision. He stepped forward meaning the blow simply grazed Michael's back. He turned, grabbed and twisted the goon's fingers. That hurt; really hurt. Screams rent the Parisian air.

Jo ripped a trailing handkerchief from the thug's jeans, tied his hands, and then dragged him to his feet. She planted a foot in his back and pushed. The thug staggered forward before falling. His hands, being tied, meant the thug's face kissed the cobblestones. Ouch!

Michael's attacker suffered two dislocated fingers and the pain was red hot. A boot helped #2 lurch forward. His mate needed help to stand. With only one pain-free hand, lifting the bound-hands thug was tricky. Both Jo and Michael feinted towards the men who staggered and stumbled their way to safety. Not a successful mission. "You should see the other guy, boss," would not work with Jlassi or Bastien.

Jo and Michael hurried inside. 'Get your gear,' said Jo.

'I never picked you as a moonlight flit kinda gal,' called Michael.

They ignored the hairs stuck to the doors and stuffed their belongings in their rucksacks. Jo called. 'We have to get out, Michael. They know where we live. They'll be back with reinforcements.'

'Where are we going?' he cried.

They met in the corridor. 'Anywhere safe—a hotel, under a bridge, in Antony's sodding apartment.' She headed downstairs. 'Come on.'


It took them a while to find a dingy, cheap hotel. Michael paid. 'Third floor,' said the night manager. 'Lift's out of order.'

They entered the room. The overhead light didn't work. The bed was hard against the wall. The bathroom had an unknown smell.

'You have the bed, I'll take the chair,' said Michael being noble.

'Other way round,' said Jo, searching her rucksack. 'I'm going to work.' She pulled out her article.

He looked at her. 'You really do want to send that.'

'It's this or nothing, Michael. We could have been killed tonight. They're playing for keeps. We fight back or die and Pierre'll rot in jail.'

'How did they find us? How do they know who we are?'

'Corrupt cops, criminals or both—who knows?'

'Where will you send your article?'

She looked at him. 'That's where you come in, maestro. How about you find me the ideal blog?' He did.

# 28

THE TRIO OF RETIRED DETECTIVES drove to Ballarat. Over pizza the night before, Rose agreed that Harold Whipsnape was a major contender for the murder of his niece, Maggie Stephens. The main problem was the suspect's health. Harold was reportedly close to death and thus probably incapable of being interviewed.

Tuck rang the nursing home, told them of their proposed visit, and asked for a health report. Staff expected Harold to enter palliative care in the next week or so.

'If we left it another two weeks, we might have been chatting to him in a coffin,' said black humourist Tuck.

He drove, Robbo beside him and Melk, the junior officer, relaxed in the back. En route they discussed alpacas, Puffing Billy, and Robbo's granddaughter and her Parisian adventure.

'What is she actually doing there?' asked Melk.

'Trying to save her DI who's been framed on serious drug charges.'

'Who framed him?'

'They think corrupt police are involved with organized crime.'

'Bloody hell,' said Melk. 'Dealing with bent cops is hard enough in your own backyard but in another country, that's tough.'

'And dangerous,' added Tuck.

'Thank you gentlemen,' said Robbo. 'I'm worried enough without you two adding to my woes.'

They apologised and the discussion turned to Harold Whipsnape. They planned their attack. Tuck would start with Robbo to follow. But it all depended on the man being willing and able to speak.

They pulled into the nursing home carpark. 22 years ago they parked here waiting for Harold who was inside visiting his ailing mother. He came out and was arrested on suspicion of murder. Not this time.

'You have some visitors, Harold,' said the nurse leading the trio into his room. Only Harold's eyes moved.

'Hello Harold,' said Robbo. I bet you don't remember us.' The trio waited. Harold said nothing. 'We investigated the death of your niece, Maggie, more than 20 years ago.' He paused. 'Do you remember?'

Harold spoke with his face. The retired cops knew he knew. Now they needed his lips and vocal cords to work.

Tuck pulled up a chair and sat beside Harold. Robbo and Melk sat at the foot of his bed.

'G'day, Harold, I'm retired DS Tuck but you can call me Tucky. Now the other day, with the now retired Detective Senior Constable Melk—he's the hairy one—I took a statement from a woman.' Tuck produced the statement. 'She reckons on the day of Maggie's death, her brother saw you come out of your niece's house looking like you'd seen a ghost. The brother said he waited for you to leg it, then went inside and found Maggie's bloodied body. Now if that's true, Harold, you were the last person to see Maggie alive before you killed her.' Tuck paused. Harold kept talking with his eyes. 'So, Harold, all those years ago when you said you left the house with Maggie still alive, did you lie?'

No reply, nothing. It was worse than "No comment". They waited. Maggie Stephens has been waiting for 22 years. She deserves a break.

The trio agreed if Harold's response was no response, they would not put pressure on a dying man. Tuck reckoned his time to interview was up so put the statement away and stood.

'Yes,' said Harold.

Tuck froze and Robbo and Melk exchanged glances. Tuck sat. Harold's diction and projection were lousy but everyone heard him.

'Thank you, Harold,' said Tuck, keen to continue. 'So in your original statement you said Maggie was alive when you left. Now you say she was dead when you left. Correct?'

'Yes,' from the man in the bed.

The retired detectives were buzzing. Finally, the cold case could be solved. Tuck kept an even tone and tempo to his questions.

'Why did you lie?'

The trio anticipated Harold's answer to be, "Because I killed her". Instead they heard, 'Because you would think I killed her.'

Big difference. Huge difference. The atmosphere crackled.

Tuck pondered his next question. 'So, is this right? You left the house with Maggie dead inside but you didn't kill her?'

'Yes.' His voice was hoarse but his meaning crystal clear.

Wow. Harold was on a roll. It was time for the $64,000 question.

'Harold, do you know who murdered Maggie?'

Drum roll. Harold unintentionally milked the moment. He was not a well man. The detectives held their breath. 'No.'

Tuck looked at Robbo. It was time to swap positions. They did and Robbo placed his satchel on Harold's bed.

'Harold, I'm retired DCI John Robertson. You told us you took your Mum's rings when she came to this nursing home. Correct?'

'Yes.'

'Why?'

'Dementia.'

'Because your mother had dementia?'

'Yes.'

'What did you do with those rings, Harold? Did you sell them?'

'No?'

'Did you give them to someone?'

'Maggie.'

'You gave your mother's rings to your niece Maggie Stephens?'

'Yes.'

Robbo opened his satchel 'I want to show you some photos. If you recognise your mother's rings, will you please blink? Can you blink?'

All three visitors looked at Harold. He blinked both his eyes.

'Thank you,' said Robbo and took out the A4 sized photos showing them to Harold, one at a time. No blinking. Robbo showed the last of six photos. Harold showed no reaction. Then he spoke.

'Go back.'

'Go back?' asked Robbo.

'Go back.'

Robbo produced the last photo. No response. Then the second last photo. No response. Then the third last photo. Harold blinked.

'Thank you,' said Robbo, his heart working overtime. 'To be sure, Harold, did these rings belong to your mother?'

Harold didn't blink, instead he spoke. 'Yes.'

He coughed and it wasn't nice. Whatever lay buried inside his chest was doing its best to end Harold's life. A nurse arrived and helped him. Robbo stood and moved to his colleagues. They watched.

The nurse turned to the visitors. 'I think Harold should rest now.'

'Certainly,' said Robbo and indicated the door with Tuck and Melk departing. 'Thank you, Mr Whipsnape,' he said and meant it.

Robbo followed the others who stopped when Harold spoke. 'Wait.'

Robbo moved back. 'Do you want to say something, Harold?'

'Just you,' he said looking at Robbo. He looked at the nurse who understood and left. Robbo looked at Tuck and Melk who understood and left. Robbo stood beside the bed.

'They've gone, Harold. It's only me. What did you want to say?'

Harold paused and spoke indistinctly.

'I'm sorry, I can't hear you,' said Robbo.

'Closer.' Robbo twigged and bent over. 'Closer,' said Harold. Robbo sat on the bed and put his good ear an inch from Harold's mouth.

'I'm listening, Harold.'

The uncle took what for him was a deep breath. 'I did it.'

Robbo had witnessed dying confessions from villains who'd been shot. But here was a man Robbo's age and clearly on the way out due to natural causes. Did Harold want to die with a clear conscience?

Robbo sat up and looked at Harold's unchanged expression. There was no sign the confession made him feel better. 'Thank you, Harold. I think Maggie and her boyfriend would appreciate that.' Robbo put a hand on Harold's shoulder. 'Goodbye.' Robbo stood and was about to walk away when Harold spoke.

'I didn't kill her.'

Robbo was confused even angry. *The old bastard's playing games.* Robbo stared at the man in bed then froze when Harold spoke again.

'But I did rape her.'

Robbo understood. Maggie told her girlfriend about Uncle Harold the rapist. He claimed it was consensual sex and with Maggie dead, and no witnesses, the police chose not to prosecute.

Robbo spoke. 'Thank you.' He wanted to leave the man in his misery but something pricked his conscience. 'Do you remember Maggie had a little boy, your great nephew, Kaiden?' Harold nodded. 'He's a fine young man, a chef. You'd be proud of him.'

Harold absorbed the news. Robbo walked straight out of the room and kept walking past his colleagues who scampered to catch up.

Rose walked away from the cold case and worked hard to ensure Devlin's confession was watertight.

She addressed the squad. 'We need to start afresh. Everything about Devlin needs to be reviewed. His confession was clear until asked for details. Why won't he tell us *how* he killed Grovene?'

'He didn't do it,' said Fleming.

'He's covering for whoever did,' said Blunt.

'He wants to cut a deal,' said Billy Hughes. 'Take my suffering into account and I'll give you chapter and verse on what happened.'

'Right, he's either telling the truth or lying. We need to find the answer and prove it. Billy will lead one side and Callum the other.'

Blunt rejoiced. 'He's lying. I can prove it.'

Rose looked at Billy who nodded. 'Okay,' said Rose. 'Let's do it.'

The detectives broke into teams with Blunt cajoling a few to join his side. Rose was interrupted by a phone call from Reception.

'There's a Donna Devlin to see you, ma'am.'

Rose grabbed Billy and departed. The others were confused and Blunt furious at being ignored. Rose popped her head back inside.

'Callum.' He was rapt and joined the females.

'What's up?' asked Billy as the trio headed to the lifts.

'Devlin's wife is downstairs and wants to speak to us.'

'She's not going to confess? Don't tell me my hunch was correct?'

They found Donna in an interview room. She didn't want a lawyer.

'So what do you want to tell us, Donna?' asked Rose.

'Bradley didn't kill that bastard, Grovene.'

'How do you know?'

'Because he was with me when the murder happened.'

'With you, where?'

Donna paused. This was the tricky part. 'We were doing a break and enter in a house in Caroline Springs.'

The detectives were shocked. 'I think we'll need more details,' said Rose who warned Donna about her position.

'I know what I'm saying,' she said. 'Bradley confessed to the murder 'cos he's covering for the person who done it.'

174

# 29

JO WROTE HER FINAL final version. Michael found four popular blogs based in France. They were anti-corruption, pro-democracy blogs ideal for exposing corruption. The duo discussed the options.

'Why not send to all four?' said Jo.

'Because publishers want an exclusive. If we send the article to one saying it's theirs until midnight, we have some control.'

'And if they don't publish we move to the next blog.'

'That's the plan.'

She looked at him, sitting on the bed, in a dimly lit room in a budget hotel in Paris. The walls were thin and graphic sounds outside left little to the imagination. They were not in The Ritz.

They listed the four blogs in order and Michael prepared to post. 'Say the word, Skip.'

'The word,' she said and Michael hit *Send*.

Silence settled, at least in their room. Neither knew what to say. Michael stared at the blog's web site. 'Anything?' asked Jo.

Michael smiled. 'Hardly. The article needs to be opened, read, translated, discussed and moderated. And if they won't publish, they won't tell us.'

She looked at her watch. 'So we wait till midnight then try blog two.'

'Something like that.' More silence in their room. More noise from next door and down the corridor.

She changed the subject. 'So you rated the blogs, how would you rate our adventures?'

He was surprised at this question out of the blue. 'Sorry?'

'There's been my mother, your parents, child abduction, revenge porn, lost dog, religious nuts, international corrupt cops and crims.'

'You're forgetting the priest hole and piracy on the high seas.'

She laughed. 'What?'

'I fought off pensioners and saved a narrowboat from sinking.'

More laughter this time from both. 'So come on,' said Jo. Give me your Top 10 Best/Chan incidents starting with number 10.'

He paused. 'There's been a few.'

'Answer the question.'

'It hasn't been boring.'

'And we're still friends.' She paused. 'Aren't we?'

'Possibly.'

'Possibly?'

She threw a small cushion at him. He caught it then collected a toilet bag and clothes from his rucksack. 'I need a shower. May I?'

'Good luck,' she said stretching out on the bed. 'If the plumbing's as good as the lighting, enjoy your ice bath.'

He navigated the miniscule ablutions wing, enjoyed a lukewarm shower, shaved because he could, and changed his smalls, socks and shirt. When he emerged refreshed, his friend was asleep. He tiptoed to his rucksack, re-packed then looked at the blog. Nothing.

He sat still, watching Joanna knowing his romantic feelings were not reciprocated. Plighting his troth would not go down well—for him. As friends and crime-busting partners, they were brilliant. As lovers, well, it was never going to happen.

Michael lifted the eiderdown and folded it carefully over the sleeping detective. She barely moved. He returned to the chair and tried to sleep.

At 2341 hours his laptop pinged. There was an email from the blog moderator. *Thanks for the post. It's live. What more can you give us?*

Michael smiled then sat on the bed. He looked at Jo who he regarded as the epitome of a fabulous woman—feminine, beautiful, intelligent, funny, caring and sexy. He squeezed her shoulder.

'Jo,' he whispered. 'Jo.'

She woke in an instant, panicked momentarily then rejoined the living. 'What's happened?'

He showed her the screen. 'We have lift-off.'

Her excitement bubbled. She devoured the online response. 'The first blog accepted us. So what now?'

'We wait. Your article's available to every police officer, lawyer, politician and criminal in French France, not to mention the rest of the world. What we want is the viral experience.'

'Reposting our post?'

'And what will help is if a TV network or multiple Twitter feeds pick it up. That means huge coverage with the genie out of the bottle and tap dancing.'

'Wow.' She looked at him. 'Are you excited, Michael?'

'Hmmm, more worried than excited.'

'Worried? Why?'

'If Inspector Richelieu is innocent and ...'

She shouted. 'If?'

'There are some high-flying people who will soon be shitting bricks. They took a big risk framing Pierre, never expecting two bumbling Aussies would stir the pot. Remember, they can eliminate us.'

'They can try,' interrupted Jo. 'And who's bumbling?'

'Having the media, politicians and a mass of angry citizens asking questions, is their worst nightmare.'

'So what now?'

'For me, sleep.'

She pulled back the covers, plumped a pillow, and indicated. 'Sorry there's no chocolate on the pillow, my Lord, but your boudoir awaits.'

He slid across the bed, turned his back to Jo and fell asleep. Jo sat in the chair and checked her phone. Texts were unanswered. From DI Rose. *We are surviving without you. Are you surviving without us?* From Dr Jack Carr. *G'day Jo. Hope you're well. Grace keeps improving. Harry misses you. Love Jack.* Both messages gave her a fillip. Then from her mother. *Joanna. Your sister is back in hospital. The cancer may have spread. Call me. Mother.*

Jo was slapped. Terrible news when she should be celebrating. She checked the time. It was about mid-morning Down Under. She stepped into the bathroom and rang her mother.

'Joanna? Where are you?'

'Hello, Mum. I'm still in Paris.'

'We need you back here. *I* need you back here.'

'What's happened with Caitlyn?'

'She's back in hospital. They think the cancer has returned.'

'But she's only just out of surgery. Surely it would take months even years to come back, if at all.'

'All I know is she's back in hospital and I'm minding the kids along with Malcolm X and Jeremy's useless parents. So when are you coming home?'

'As soon as I can, Mum, I promise.'

'I can't believe you care more about your job than your family.' Jo wanted to scream. 'And there's another family disaster.' Jo died inside. *What now?* 'Your grandfather's rejoined the police force.' *Is that all?*

'I'm booked to fly home next week, Mum, maybe sooner.'

'Stop that.' Jo didn't understand. But then there was a lot about her mother she didn't understand. 'Put it down.' Jo finally understood. 'The kids have a day off school and I'm going nuts, here.'

'Mum, I have to go. I'll ring you later today, tonight, soon. Bye.'

She came out of the bathroom, heard Michael snoring then ever so carefully climbed onto the bed beside him and fell asleep.


Commandant Erec Bonnaire was an early riser. He checked his phone and saw message after message. It looked bad. He switched on his TV. The facts and questions in Jo Best's article were front page news. It looked worse than bad. His phone rang. He knew the number and dreaded taking the call.

'Bonjour, Minister,' said Bonnaire.

The Minister of the Interior was blunt. 'What the hell is happening, Bonnaire? The press are in the street screaming at me.'

'We're still coming to grips with it, Minister,' said Bonnaire lying.

'The President and Prime Minister are demanding answers. Tell me, for Christ's sake, what it's all about?'

More calls came across Bonnaire's phone. 'May I call you straight back, Minister?'

'What? All right.' He raged. 'Five minutes, do you hear?'

'Yes Minister.'


'What?' snarled Bastien struggling from his slumber.

'The shit has hit the fan,' said the corrupt cop.

'What shit? What are you talking about?'

'Look at your TV.' Click.

Bastien watched the morning news. As the mastermind behind the arrest of his former colleague, Pierre Richelieu, Bastien saw events unfolding and swore. If his corrupt cop contact rolled over, Bastien was dead. If the drugs were not returned to Jlassi, Bastien was dead.

He rang and woke Laris. 'This better be fucking good.'

'Trouble, Laris. The stitch-up has gone tits up.'

'Not my problem—nothing to do with me.'

'True, but if our friend rolls over, we're cooked.'

Silence. Heavy breathing. 'You maybe, but not me. Screw me matey and you'll crawl over broken glass to get back inside.'

Click.

It's fair to say, the article written by Jo Best and uploaded by Michael Chan set a supercharged moggie among the Parisian pigeons.

Jo and Michael shared a bed and slept soundly. Jo's phone rang; both woke and didn't have time to be embarrassed. Jo grabbed her phone and stood while Michael slid across the bed and popped into the loo.

'Good morning, Antony,' said Jo stretching and yawning.

'What the hell have you done, Miss Best?'

'I'm fine, thank you,' said Jo. 'How are you?'

'The press have gone bonkers on my client's case. Is this because of something you've done?'

'Possibly.'

Antony's voice modulated. 'Possibly? I can't defend my client if you interfere with French law and my campaign to free your colleague.'

Jo wanted to ask "what campaign?" but instead said, 'Sorry, Antony. Can we discuss this later?' Michael emerged from the bathroom. 'Michael and I are off to breakfast. Bye.' Click.

'Was that the Honourable lawyer?'

'And he isn't happy.' She changed tack. 'Michael, with all this publicity for Pierre, is it safe to show our faces in Paris?'

'I hope so. Anyway I'm starving.' He started to sing the opening song from *Oliver!*

'Give me five,' she said diving into the bathroom.

Bonnaire was driven to work fielding phone calls. He rang Droit and demanded an immediate meeting. The media frenzy kept growing because of the lack of response from the police.

Bastien saw his life ending. If the drugs he borrowed from Laris to stitch up Richelieu were not retrieved, Bastien was cactus. Even if he could retrieve the drugs, it now seemed Richelieu might worm out of his predicament. The honest cops would come after Bastien. *Shit.*

Jo and Michael found a snazzy café and tucked into some fine French fare—orange juice, coffee, and croissants with butter and jam. People hurried past en route to work. The news about possible police corruption captured the headlines and the two people responsible sat incognito enjoying their *petit-déjeuner*. Who would have thunk it?

Yousef Jlassi decided. Today was D-Day. He placed the bomb in his rucksack then filled it with nails and broken glass. He put on his suicide vest and double-checked everything. His loose jacket covered the vest. Gingerly he picked up the rucksack and eased it onto his back. No bouncing to put it in place.

He knew his destination. There was a busy shopping centre not far from his brother's house. He left via the back lane and headed for Paradise—heart rate, a million plus.

Upstairs, his brother was filthy. Watching the breaking news about police corruption and knowing his stash of drugs was sitting in a secure police building waiting to be destroyed, ignited his blood pressure.

'Boss,' said his main thug.

'What?' snapped Laris.

'You told me to remind you about your brother.'

Laris was busy with other matters. 'Get him.' The thug left and Laris made some calls. The thug returned.

'He's gone.'

Laris fumed. 'Gone? How? Where?'

'He opened the old door to the lane.'

'Find him.'

'What?'

Laris moved into screaming mode. 'I don't trust the little shit. Find him and bring him back.'

'But he could be anywhere, boss.'

'There's CCTV out there. Find him!'

Droit arrived at Bonnaire's office looking calm but worried like hell. His case against Richelieu resembled a train wreck. 'An explanation, Brigadier, and make it good.'

Droit could explain everything. The fact Richelieu was involved in drugs was well known. It was the reason he left the force in Paris and fled to Australia. His two accomplices were mules and did what Richelieu or his stooges told them. Sure they got a good deal for giving up their boss but why not? It would halve their sentence.

'But Richelieu was the detective who uncovered corrupt officers,' argued Bonnaire. 'I worked with the man.'

'What better way to hide your own corruption than by arresting your crooked mates. It makes you look like a saint.'

Bonnaire shook his head. 'Incredible,' he muttered. 'Double check those two mules and report back as soon as possible.'

Droit saluted and left, heading for the police evidence storage building.

Jo and Michael finished breakfast. They were in no hurry and Michael again showed Jo the blog on which her article first appeared. There were masses of comments and reposts.

'I think this is what you call a smash hit, Detective,' he said. 'You've done it again.'

'*We've* done it again,' she corrected him. 'But it's not over, Dr Chan, until the corpulent contralto croons.'

He groaned. 'You just made that up.'

She smiled. 'Let's go and see the reason why we came to Paris.'

As a language fanatic, Michael followed, querying whether you could "see a reason".

They caught a cab and arrived early at the prison and were not alone. A scoop of journos with cameras and the ubiquitous phones were camped outside the entrance.

'Bugger,' said Jo. 'I forgot the paparazzi. It's a no go, Michael.'

'Unless,' he said. Jo looked at him and he subtly pointed. Striding towards them was the Honourable Antony Heron-Royhay. He didn't see them, being too busy being noticed by the media.'

'Good morning, sir,' called Jo.

He stopped and saw them. They hurried to him. 'I'm not speaking to you,' he said in an upper-class huff.

Jo teased. 'Oh come on, my Lord.' She took his arm. He felt good. Michael didn't. 'We'd love to see your client before we fly home. Please.'

He relented, signing them in as associates. The waiting press gang and the prison officers were aware the case against Richelieu was front page news and not looking good for the prosecution but had no idea the extra visitors were responsible for the whole darn shooting match.

As the trio waited for Pierre to be delivered, they realised he may have no idea about the ruckus happening all over the city and the country. When he appeared it was obvious he knew nothing.

'Bonjour, Detective Inspector,' said his police colleague. 'You're looking well.'

His heart copped a jolt at the sight of three smiling visitors.

# 30

THE THREE IDIOTS headed back to Melbourne. Tuck and Melk were desperate to know what happened when Robbo was alone with the dying man.

'He did confess,' said Robbo, 'but not to the murder.'

'To the rape,' said Tuck, who remembered Maggie's girlfriend's testimony.

'To the rape,' repeated Robbo thinking of young Maggie and the wretched life she led.

'So tell us about the photos, boss,' said Melk.

'Maggie wasn't murdered by someone in her family or circle of friends. It was a stranger, someone she didn't know.'

'And those photos are the key,' said Tuck.

'They're part of strong circumstantial evidence but unless the killer confesses, we can't prove a thing.' The others wanted more.

'You need to start at the beginning boss,' requested Melk.

Robbo leaned back in the front passenger seat and told the tale.

'Harold took his elderly and demented mother to the nursing home. He reckoned someone would pinch her wedding rings and the old lady would never know. So Harold pinched them, well, saved them might be kinder. He abused Maggie and as a sort of penance, later gave Maggie her grandmother's jewellery.'

'Keep it in the family, like,' offered Melk.

'When Maggie was murdered, the killer stole the rings, and decades later, the engagement ring and soon the wedding ring will finish up on the finger of Rachel Cordner, a young hairdresser, and the great-granddaughter of Mrs Dot Watson.'

'The old girl who lived next door to Maggie,' added Tuck.

'So how did this kid get the rings?' asked Melk.

'Good question. My money's on Rachel's father, Kevin.'

'I bet you've got four pieces of evidence to nail him,' smiled Tuck.

'Five,' cried Melk wanting to support his former boss.

Robbo explained. 'At Kevin's first marriage, on his wedding day he's sporting a beard. Not much of a beard but it's there. He was married not long after Maggie's murder and if she scratched or whacked him, one way to hide any scars or scratches is to grow a beard.'

'One piece of evidence,' said Melk.

'Circumstantial, Colin,' said Robbo. 'Now Kevin's first wife, Dianne today is ring free. No jewellery on her fingers at all. But her daughter, Rachel, is wearing a ring identified by Harold this morning.'

'Two,' said Tuck.

'Rachel's fiancé won't say where he obtained the ring but claims he got a good deal. My money's on his future mother-in-law as vendor. Kevin's given them to Dianne who sold or gave the rings to the young lad. He's had the engagement ring cleaned, maybe a minor change, and given it to Rachel when he popped the question.'

'Three,' said Melk.

'Kevin's DNA is likely to be in storage from Maggie's kitchen although he'll say he was a punter who paid Maggie for her services.'

'More circumstantial, boss, and you're stuck on three.'

'We need a way to encourage Kevin to confess.'

They drove in silence.


Rose told the squad what Donna told her, Billy and Blunt. 'If Donna's telling the truth, Bradley's lying. He's not the killer.'

'I can follow this up, ma'am,' said Blunt. He was so up for glory. 'You asked me to disprove Bradley's claims. I reckon he's covering for the real killer and I think I know how to prove it.'

'Thinking's not good enough, DI Blunt,' stated Rose. There was no way she was giving him carte blanche to wreck her latest homicide.

'Give me an hour to chat with Mrs Devlin and I'll have the real killer named and shamed ready for your inspection.'

Rose was in trouble. How could she turn down a DI, her rank, when a short time ago in front of the squad she'd said, 'Okay, let's prove or disprove this as soon as possible.'

'Right but no heroics, DI Blunt. Take DS Fleming and Senior Constable Payne and keep me posted.'

'Yes ma'am,' said Blunt, heading off to make a name for himself.

Tuck turned to Robbo as they reached the outskirts of Melbourne. 'You'd better tell the DI, boss. She'll be chuffed with our news but you know what she's like on unauthorised activity.'

Robbo rang Rose and put his phone on speaker.

'Robbo,' she answered. 'Where are you?'

'Almost back from Ballarat, ma'am having just about solved the murder of Maggie Stephens.'

'Just about? Is that the same as being a little bit pregnant?'

'One interview, ma'am, and we can give you the killer.'

Rose was thrilled. The Grovene murder was close to resolution and now the cold case too.

*Can I crack both cases on the same day? If so, it will be a huge boost for my status and career.*

'Okay but nothing dangerous. Clear?'

'Clear, ma'am,' said Robbo.

'And are your mad mates there?'

'Here ma'am,' echoed Buck and Melk.

'The same goes for you two only double. Oh and listen. Solve this cold case and you'll do a lot better than pizza. Good hunting.'

There was restrained joy in the car as Robbo gave directions.

Blunt was on a mission to nail the killer of Simon Grovene. He headed for the Devlin household.

'What's the plan, sir?' asked Fleming.

'Simple—I lead, you follow.'

Fleming and Payne felt sick. Blunt was a loose cannon. Rose made them tag along to stop the DI arresting the wrong suspect or starting World War 3 or both.

The trio stood on the Devlin doorstep. Donna opened the door.

'What?' she asked.

'Mrs Devlin, we'd like a chat about your husband and his ridiculous claim to be a murderer.'

She turned and walked inside followed by the detectives. She resumed food preparation. 'You won't mind me doing some real work.'

'We're not interested in your little break-and-enter, Donna,' said Blunt. 'We're interested in who your husband is protecting—the real killer of Simon Grovene.'

'Dunno what you're talking about.'

'Come on, Donna, Bradley no more killed Grovene than I did. But you, now there's an idea. Low stab wound on victim—you're short. Attacker needed plenty of grunt—you're in great shape. Motive—you assaulted Grovene's missus in public. Opportunity—you provide a terrible alibi about being a crappy little thief on the other side of town.'

'It's true,' screamed Donna threatening with the knife she used to cut the vegies.

Fleming and Payne moved back from the furious woman although they feared Blunt more than Donna.

'Easy, Donna,' said the DI. 'You don't wanna make this worse.'

There was a Mexican standoff and Fleming and Payne dreaded Blunt drawing his gun. Before he could, old Ed Devlin, Bradley's father arrived in his wheelchair.

'Visitors again,' he said, 'and noisy too. You all right love?' he asked. The old man's presence calmed the scene. Blunt took advantage.

'We're fine, thank you sir. Why don't you go back outside and leave us to chat to Mrs Devlin?'

'Payne was anxious. 'Sir,' he said.

'Not now, Senior.' He addressed Ed. 'Off you go, mate.'

'What if I don't want to?' defied the Vietnam Vet.

'Sir,' said Payne in a more agitated voice.

'Shut up, Payne. I'm trying to solve a murder.'

'Look at his tyres,' said Payne pointing at the wheelchair.

Blunt stopped. What a strange request. He moved to look at the wheelchair. 'Jesus,' he said. 'They're the tyres from the murder scene.'

Before the police could move, Ed hit reverse and was out of the kitchen and heading for his bungalow.

'Get him,' shouted Blunt who moved but stopped when Donna brandished her kitchen knife with a piece of carrot lodged on the end.

'Leave him alone,' shouted Donna.

'Drop the knife,' roared Blunt drawing his weapon. Donna was scared but Fleming and Payne were terrified.

'Sir,' cautioned Fleming.

'Go on then, shoot me,' dared Donna.

Blunt froze. Donna threw open her arms giving Blunt a free shot at her chest. The knife was no longer in a strike position and Fleming grabbed her wrist. The knife hit the floor and Payne seized her other wrist and handcuffs followed. She swore. Blunt didn't wait.

'It's the old bastard,' he snapped heading outside with gun drawn.

'Sir,' yelled Fleming and Payne as one but in vain. Blunt was gone.

Donna swore and spat and was restrained. They tripped her, put her on the floor but still she screamed and struggled.

'Donna, stop,' said Fleming. 'We need to make sure the old boy doesn't get hurt. Stay still.'

Slowly she settled. Waiting for her to totally relax, took time. Meanwhile in the back yard, Blunt saw glory beckoning. First week in Homicide and here he was about to make the big collar.

With Donna settled, the detectives helped her to a chair. Fleming was about to tell her to sit still when ... Crack!

A gunshot rang out. Donna screamed, 'Dad!'

Fleming and Payne screamed, 'Sir!'


Robbo navigated Tuck to Kevin and Julie's house. 'What if he's not home?' asked Melk.

'What if he is and turns nasty?' asked Tuck. 'Elly'll go nuts.'

'We cross that bridge when we get to it, gentlemen.'

Tuck and Melk worried and more so when Kevin opened the door.

'Not again,' he muttered. 'What now?'

'Could we have a chat please, Kevin?' asked Robbo.

'Who is it?' called wife, Julie.

'You might want to talk out here,' said Robbo looking hard at Kevin. Something pinged in his brain and a thought he sometimes pondered over the last twenty plus years came alive.

'Be back in a minute,' called Kevin and closed the door. The quartet went into the street and stood on the nature strip. Robbo led.

'We've got some pretty hard evidence, Kevin.'

He defied them. 'What are you talking about?'

'You can do this the hard way or the very hard way but we reckon you murdered Maggie Stephens in the house next door to your grandmother's in Collingwood.'

Kevin shook his head. 'Bullshit.'

'Okay,' said Robbo. 'The uncle of Maggie Stephens identified an engagement ring he gave to Maggie before she was murdered. That same engagement ring you gave to your first wife and right now it's on the finger of your daughter.' Kevin looked like he'd been punched in the solar plexus. 'How do you think that happened?'

The detectives held their breath. Cracking a case produced this tension. Would the accused fold or fight. He folded.

'It wasn't murder. I knew she was a prostitute. I'd seen blokes going in there when I visited me Gran. I went in and asked for sex. I said I'd pay. She said she knew I was the old lady's grandson. I tried to persuade her. She slapped me so I slapped her back. We fought. She hit her head and looked a mess. I couldn't leave because she knew me. I had to make sure she was dead.' He looked pathetic. 'Isn't that manslaughter?'

Tuck looked at Kevin. 'Did you have to steal the rings?'

Kevin didn't speak.

'You'll have to come with us,' said Robbo.

Kevin hesitated then spoke in a childish voice. 'Will I miss me daughter's wedding?' The retirees said nothing and Kevin cried.


Fleming and Payne hurtled outside to the bungalow in the backyard. There was only one door. It was locked. They banged hard.

'Sir,' cried Fleming. 'Are you okay? Sir?' The silence was eerie. They heard sounds and then the door was unlocked. Both drew their weapons. The door opened and there stood Blunt looking as white as a sheet. A voice called from inside.

'Come in gentlemen. I was telling your colleague how I killed Simon Grovene.' Fleming and Payne entered. 'Take a seat if you can find one.'

What a scenario. The killer, without a French accent, became the little Belgian and explained how the crime was committed.

'I killed a few blokes in Nam. Once you've done it, it gets easier. But I'd only kill someone who deserved to die and Grovene was it. Oh, by the way, I've got emphysema so chargin' me's a waste of time really.' Blunt had to sit. 'I got a couple of mates to make a phone call. The first brought Grovene to the house. I told the bowlers I had a medical appointment and got a cab to Kew. I was waiting and told Grovene how he ruined my son. Grovene laughed at me so I pulled out my ancient service revolver and fired—like I did for your colleague just now.'

Blunt sat uncomfortably as his underwear needed changing.

'That put the fear of God up him—he was more frightened than you sir—and while he recovered, I produced my old man's World War 2 bayonet and stuck it in him. They don't like it up 'em, you know.'

Fleming wanted to ask questions but said nothing.

'I pinched a chisel from one of the tradies at some creditors' meeting and stuck that in the bayonet wound. Then I put the secateurs on his crotch and my valuable coin collection in his mouth—to make it tricky for you blokes. I pissed off, got a cab in the next street, and my mate rang the agent who rocked up and discovered the body.' Ed looked at the gobsmacked detectives. 'I think that's about it.'

'Thank you, sir,' said Fleming. Blunt still shook. So would you if someone shot at you from point blank range.

'My boy twigged it was me when he couldn't find me coin collection. I told him everything. I'd given him all me savings and he couldn't bear to see his old man go to jail. Now please make sure my lad is released. Bloody hero he is. So come on, slap on the bracelets, and read me m'rights.'

The best part of the arrest of the Simon Grovene murderer was that DI Callum Blunt refused to take credit for the capture of the elderly Ed Devlin on the understanding that neither Fleming or Payne would breathe a word about the DI who shat himself.

# 31

BRIGADIER DROIT ENTERED the evidence storage unit. The officers on duty stood and saluted. 'I need to check some evidence,' said Droit. 'There's uproar about the Richelieu arrest.'

'We heard, Brigadier. What's it all about?'

'God only knows. But I have to double check that everything on the forensics sheet is present and correct.'

'Of course.'

'Show me the record book.' Droit pretended to study the details when all he wanted was to get inside and swap the drugs. His career, his life was in the balance. 'Right, I need to inspect the items.'

'You'll need to sign in, sir,' said the senior officer beginning to feel uncomfortable.

'Quickly man, the Minister of the Interior wants answers.'

Droit signed the visitors' book, was escorted to the security door and waited for the officer to swipe his card. The lock was released.

'Do you need a hand, Brigadier?'

Droit's sarcasm flared. 'I think I know how to check evidence.'

He entered the secure facility, the door closed behind him, and the officer in charge looked at his colleague and spoke.

'What's that all about?'

'Someone's in trouble. Did he sign the book?'

'Yes.'

'Make sure he signs it on the way out.'

Inside, Droit controlled his panic. He searched for the Richelieu evidence. He couldn't find it. He couldn't ask for help as obviously he wanted to work alone. His panic levels rose. He couldn't remember the

190

location details. He swore under his breath. His language turned ugly. He spoke to himself. 'Think, Droit. Use a system. He went back to the shelves closest to the entrance. Again he looked, walking slower. 'Less haste, more speed,' he muttered.

In the third row, he found it. 'Thank Christ.' He put on surgical gloves, dragged the box from the shelf and placed it on a table. Inside he saw the primary piece of evidence, the drugs from Laris Jlassi via Émile Bastien. He took the evidence envelope from the box, carefully opened it and removed the bag of drugs. 'Shit,' he said seeing the attached label.

He opened his shirt and removed the bag of drugs taped to his vest. The value of these drugs was about 5% of the ones in the evidence bag. Droit's drugs contained a blank label. Using a marker pen, he carefully copied the details on the blank label—M18/319.

All this took time. His hands shook. He tried to hurry. A voice called over a PA system in the evidence room.

'Is everything in order, Brigadier?'

More whispered swearing from Droit. He called. 'One minute.'

He placed the bag of fake drugs back in the large evidence envelope and put that in the box. He returned the box to the shelf. He picked up the Jlassi drugs and attempted to stick the bag to his chest. He and his vest were damp. The tape wouldn't stick well. The bag of drugs was attached but only just. More four-letter words poured out in a whisper.

He did up his shirt and tucked it in his trousers. He buttoned his jacket. He stopped and took deep breaths then headed for the office.

He banged on the door. It opened.

'All done, Brigadier?'

'All done. And thank you. The minister will be pleased.' He headed out but stopped.

'Brigadier, you haven't signed the book.'

He gave a forced smile and left a signature which made a doctor's handwriting look like a 12th century priest's calligraphy. Droit walked to his car with his arms folded across his chest.

'Will we get into trouble?' asked the junior officer.'

'No idea,' replied his colleague. 'Do you think he knew he was being filmed?'

Bastien sweated. His pulse raced and his swearing flourished. His 2IC, a Baldrick lookalike, another former policeman called Balzac, interrupted. 'That black bitch is here.'

'What?'

'Why do I have to say everything twice?'

'Send her in.' Adamma entered looking subservient yet burning with hatred and revenge. 'What are you doin' here?'

'You told me to come back today, Master.'

'No I didn't. Fuck off.' With sadness, Adamma's face fell and she turned to leave. 'Wait. Get upstairs.' She smiled and bowed.

'Thank you, Master.' She headed upstairs. 'You might be useful,' he said to himself thinking hostage not sex.

She busied herself placing the items she had in her bag, hiding them ready for action. She waited. Bastien failed to appear. Then she heard him shouting. Unhappy was putting it mildly.

Swearing, he ran up the stairs. He burst into the bedroom where she sat submissively on the bed.

'I am ready, Master,' she said standing ready for his commands.

'Shut up and stay there,' he said not looking at her as he rummaged through a drawer. That was the last thing he said for a while as Adamma withdrew the marble ashtray she'd hidden under a pillow and belted the head of her tormentor.

The blow felled him and, as he dropped, he struck his head on the bedside table adding an extra serve of anaesthetic.

She locked the bedroom door.

Bastien was beside the bed but without a block and tackle, she faced the major task of lifting the brute off the floor. She sat him up against the bed, then straddled him and, with arms under his armpits, heaved. It was a super effort but her motivation was white hot. Once his bum was level with the bed she fell forward on top of him. She'd done that several times before when naked. He groaned. She panicked.

She leapt to the floor, grabbed his ankles and swung them onto the bed. She snatched the chains and ropes from under the bed. The chains went from each wrist to the bedhead posts and the ropes around each ankle went to a bed post. He was strapped to his own bed. He groaned and opened his eyes. They showed fear.

He swore. He was good at that.

She straddled him, again a familiar position, and whacked some adhesive tape across his mouth. He struggled, he bucked. His eyes spewed hatred. She ran more tape around his head and over the tape covering his mouth. Snot flicked in and out of his nostrils.

Adamma disappeared into the walk-in robe. She came out wearing one of Bastien's bathrobes and a pair of his expensive sunglasses. She opened her bag and removed a sealed plastic sandwich bag. Its contents didn't look or smell appetising, revolting more like.

She looked through his bedside table drawer and found a flick knife. She straddled him on the bed above his thighs. She'd been there before. Her mission was already a success. Bastien was terrified and incandescent with rage but best of all, helpless.

The flick knife flicked open and sneered. The knife was gently pressed on the victim's crotch. Bastien's blood pressure roared above the white-coat-syndrome range.

'Now Master,' she said, preparing for the main event. 'I wish to return the favour.'

His eyes bulged, his cheeks became scarlet, and his wheezing and grunting sounded like a mix of Welsh and Polish as spoken by drunks.

'You were kind to let me taste your shit. I'd like you to enjoy mine.'

If he could have said, "I'll kill you," he would. Alas his reply sounded like, "ill ryll ewe".

With slow and deliberate movements, Adamma opened the sandwich bag containing her poo, dipped the flick knife blade into the stinking paste and carefully withdrew the loaded weapon. She raised the piece of metal, took aim and flicked.

Her aim was poor and most of the excreta stuck to the bedhead. She apologised to the cleaning woman who would have to tackle that task.

She reloaded and adjusted her aim. An accomplice with field glasses would have said, "Ten degrees, south, Gunner Adamma". She fired. Excellent shot.

Bastien closed his eyes as the vile smelling material splattered against his face. Fortunately, with his mouth gagged, he couldn't taste it but the feel and smell dug their claws into his brain.

She reloaded. 'I hope you are enjoying this, Master. It gives me great pleasure to satisfy your needs.' His eyes fired knives and bullets as, instead of flicking shit, she leant forward and smeared her droppings over his face in an artistic manner. She painted with poo.

The razor sharp edge of the knife only added to his agony. His now brown painted eyebrows began to drip.

Her performance continued, humiliating her tormentor. She was almost out of bullets when loud sounds were heard.

Voices informed the "lovers" the Police Nationale were here. It meant absolute misery for Bastien who couldn't fight back or escape.

Rapid footsteps were followed by door banging. 'Boss,' shouted Balzac, 'it's the filth.' He tried the locked door. 'Boss! Are you in there?'

Bastien replied. 'Lyk en tha fyykin more!'

'What?' yelled Balzac not speaking Muffled.

Adamma finished. She slipped off the bed, collected her belongings sans shit, and raised the flick knife above her head. It was time for the coup de grâce.

Bastien felt compelled to exclaim, "Oh shit!" but couldn't bring himself to mutter or even stifle those words. The knife plunged towards the corrupt former cop's crotch as the bedroom door exploded and police officers piled into the room.

Their weapons were pointed and their dialogue well learnt but the sight which greeted them induced silence. They stared at the man tied to his bed, covered in what smelt dangerously like shit—it sticks to blankets, you know—with a knife protruding from the bed clothes, a bee's dick from the crotch of Mr Shitface.

There wasn't much to say and Bastien refused to join the talkfest.

Adamma stood there, butter wouldn't melt, smiling and asking by gesture, "What do you think, boys? How many stars?"

An hour later, an NGO set up to rescue victims of sexual slavery, collected Adamma and her next new life began.

Brigadier Droit lost it. The high-ranking corrupt cop panicked when the media exploded with questions about Richelieu. Crazy situations cause crazy reactions. *How can I get out of this alive?* he thought.

He knew if he survived any corruption investigation, his criminal associates Jlassi and Bastien would kill him in a heartbeat if he didn't return the drugs. So any police enquiry could wait. First he needed to return the goods.

He drove too fast to Bastien's fortress. He would hand over the real drugs, get the hell away and tackle whatever they threw at him as best he could.

Droit's car turned into Bastien's street. It was filled with a dozen police vehicles with flashing lights. Most of the occupants of these cars were upstairs arresting Émile Bastien who right now felt shithouse.

*Don't panic*, thought Droit as several police officers hurried towards him. The first to arrive saluted.

'Everything's under control, Brigadier.'

'Excellent. Who's been arrested?'

'They've got Bastien, sir, and his stooge. Apparently the big boy was captured by a girl. She tied him to his bed and covered him in shit.'

'What?'

'That's the word we heard on the radio.'

'Right, I'll leave you to it.' He reversed as quickly and as carefully as he could and drove away wondering what the hell he was going to do.

He hid the drugs in an abandoned factory owned by Jlassi. He buried the package as best he could. Strangely he felt relieved as if he'd carried off the great escape. He drove back to his office, blissfully unaware that IPGN officers, responsible for internal affairs, were watching footage of Brigadier Droit undressing and swapping a bag of drugs. The Brigadier was about to go the way of the criminals with whom he conspired.


Laris spat, words and saliva. He couldn't raise Bastien, the cops were all over the news, and now his little brother had disappeared. Laris couldn't believe the cops came looking for Yousef claiming he killed a police officer. Losing a shedload of drugs was the pits but being undone by his little turd of a brother was worse. Where is he?

The thug returned, breathless. 'I lost him. A cop car raced past siren blaring and he hid.'

'Bastard,' snapped Laris. 'Get the car.'

Yousef panicked when he heard the cops. He hid behind a bus shelter. The cops flew past. Yousef couldn't accept he'd come this far only to be captured before completing his mission. He resumed his journey.

'Where did you last see him?' yelled Laris.

'He hid behind that bus shelter.'

'Keep driving,' snapped Laris. 'No, stop.' The car screeched to a halt and Laris yelled at some kids. 'Hey. You want money?'

The kids approached. 'To do what?' asked the brave one.

'I'm looking for my brother. He's 30, short, thin hair.'

The interviewees shook their heads.

'With a black rucksack and large red jacket,' added the driver.

Bingo. 'Yeah, we saw him,' said the leader.

'Where?' snapped Laris.

They all pointed. 'He went into the shopping centre.'

Laris tossed a few notes out of the car which sped away.

In the shopping centre, Yousef knew what to do. He'd cased the joint as an innocent shopper. The plan was simple. He would subtly place the bomb by one of the large potted plants in the dining area where people gathered for coffee and croissants. He would then move to the main walkway and detonate the bomb. Survivors would rush towards him where he would detonate his suicide vest causing multiple killings and wounding, and all for the glory of the jihad. Yousef would become a martyr.

In the shopping centre car park, Laris and his thug parked and raced inside. For years, big brother evaded police capture and maintained his criminal lifestyle thanks to corrupt police. Now, out of nowhere, his pathetic pipsqueak of a brother killed a cop and brought the filth to Laris's door. How ironic is that? Where is the little prick?

Yousef tried to walk normally. He knew the shopping centre would have CCTV and some security guard was probably watching him right now. He bought a coffee and took it to a table next to pot plants. He removed his rucksack and placed it between him and the plant. It would need an overhead camera to see what he planned to do.

'Go that way,' barked Laris, 'and call me if you see him.'

The crowd in the eating area kept growing. Yousef was rapt. Between sips of coffee—*my last meal before Paradise*—he gently opened the rucksack and, lifting the towel, checked the device. In trying to adjust the bomb, he cut himself on broken glass. 'Shit,' he whispered sucking his finger.

He looked around. He was sure people were looking at him. He was the only solo diner in the food hall. But now it was time. He went to push the timer when disaster struck.

'Excuse me,' said an elderly man with a tray. 'Are these seats taken?'

Yousef was thrown. 'What? No,' he blurted.

'Thanks,' said the diner as three senior chums plonked their trays on the table, pulled out the chairs and sat.

Being alone and away from prying eyes, Yousef was good to go. Now three strangers sat with him. They chatted amongst themselves. Yousef failed to disguise his nervousness. One of the old gents made a polite enquiry.

'Are you all right, young man? You don't look well.'

Yousef fought to control his emotions. 'I'm fine.' He snatched at his coffee and drained the plastic cup. He raised the rucksack flap, slid the cup inside and hit the timer. It was preset for three minutes. He flipped the flap back, removed a handkerchief and wiped his nose.

The crowded walkway was forty metres away. It would soon be packed when the terrified shoppers fled.

Yousef was trying to kill time before he killed people. He wanted to remain beside the bomb until the last moment. He cursed himself for not having checked his watch. He thought about lifting the flap and looking at the timer. It barely made a sound. *How long to go?* His mind screamed.

Then he decided. He stood, carefully pushed his chair under the table and walked.

'Hey?' yelled a voice. Yousef ignored it. Then multiple voices were heard. 'Hey! You left your bag!'

Yousef died. He turned. The three fellow-diners pointed to his rucksack. Others diners watched. Some felt nervous, stood and hurried away. Fear spread. One of the old chaps said something to his mates. They realised.

The rucksack was deliberately left where it was. The young man didn't want it because it contained a bomb. Somebody screamed, 'There's a bomb.'

Fear swept through the food hall. Yousef panicked. This wasn't the plan. He wanted the bomb to explode and bring death to people. Now the people were running *from* death.

In his own panic, Yousef raced back to his rucksack. *I know. I'll throw the bomb after them.* He was almost at the rucksack when he heard the sound.

'Yousef!' roared a voice and the brothers froze, staring at one another. 'Stay there,' roared Laris heading towards his sibling. Yousef paused, not knowing what to do. Then he turned and ran. Laris roared at him and crashed through the plants and tables and chairs of the food hall. He spotted the rucksack. *That belongs to Yousef.* He turned to the bomb-laden item of luggage.

Yousef looked back and screamed at his brother. 'No, Laris, run!' Big brother opened the flap, saw the bomb and felt sick. It exploded.

Yousef would have scored a B+ for bomb-making but an F for victim impact. Yes, the device exploded. Yes, it killed someone but only one. Yousef's bomb was a dud in this Cain and Abel scenario.

Once the panic began, Security staff came running, the police were called as were the anti-terrorism experts.

Yousef, distraught, stumbled towards the remains of his rucksack and his brother. Yousef killed his own flesh and blood.

Security guards appeared with guns drawn. They screamed orders. Yousef ignored them. He was overcome with grief and anger.

The guards edged closer. One came too close and Yousef flipped.

'Stay back,' he screamed. He threw wide his arms revealing the suicide belt and the trigger mechanism in his right hand. The guards nearly died—literally. Yousef screamed. 'This is a suicide vest. Come any closer or shoot and this will kill you all. Now stay back!'

Yousef was convincing. He had a track record. One explosion already plus the sight of bomb-like material strapped to the madman's body, saw security back-pedalling fast.

It was a stalemate. The bomber was armed but without his target, the shoppers and workers having fled. Yousef looked ready to explode.

*I want to die but I want to kill as many people as possible.*

No sign of specialist police and Laris' thug vanished.

The plan for Security was to wait for the experts to negotiate or eliminate. For now their instructions were, "do nothing".

The seconds ticked by. Word in Security earpieces was that the cavalry were 60 seconds away. Then it happened.

A lost child, a toddler, a little boy called Salem came out of a toy shop holding a plastic dinosaur. The child was happy to have found a great place to explore and even happier to have acquired a new toy.

Looking for his mother, Salem wandered straight towards the only person he could see, Yousef. The guards froze and the bomber felt worse. Salem's smile had joy written all over it.

'Get him away,' said Yousef without shouting.

'Little boy,' called a guard. 'Come here, little boy.'

Salem ignored everyone. He looked at Yousef and grinned.

'Get him away or I'll explode this bomb,' said Yousef.

More fear from all four guards who hid behind pillars. Salem was thrilled with his new toy and wanted to show it to someone.

Unwittingly, Yousef encouraged the toddler to approach. Yousef's arms, in scarecrow style, told the child to "come to me". It was an adult beckoning a child to come and get a hug. Salem obliged.

The child could see the suicide belt. Everyone could. It meant nothing to Salem. Closer he came, holding out his toy.

Yousef spoke clearly. 'I must die now.' As he squeezed the trigger, a wild scream of terror filled the food hall. Everyone stopped.

The voice belonged to Salem's desperate mother. He entered the toy shop unseen, dived into a kids' wonderland and became lost.

Calling his name and asking others to help proved fruitless. She rushed to the shopping centre's office to have them announce a lost child. When there, the bomb exploded and Salem's mother died again.

She rushed back to the food hall where she last saw him. As she sprinted towards the scene of the blast, a security guard grabbed her. She fought. Two things happened simultaneously. The guard said the word *bomb*, and Salem's mum saw her son. No wonder she screamed.

The elite anti-terrorist force moved quickly and quietly towards the food hall. Two officers moved to the upper level.

The mother's scream changed to one word—'Salem.' He knew his name and he knew his mother's voice. Salem turned. The guard holding the mother copped elbows and kicks. He held her fast. If she ran forward, the bomber would panic and press the trigger.

Yousef stood still, his arms outstretched, the deadly device clearly visible, and the firing mechanism in his hand. He addressed Salem.

'Go to your mother.' The boy was confused. 'Go to your Mummy.'

'Salem,' screamed the woman. 'Come to Mummy. Please.'

Yousef made one final statement. 'Salem, go to your mother.'

There was a pregnant pause. Time stopped. Salem turned, then holding aloft his new dinosaur, ran to his mother. She grabbed him, a guard grabbed them as a cracking sound echoed around the food hall.

The police sniper's bullet hit Yousef a millimetre above the bridge of his nose. The suicide belt failed to detonate and Mr and Mrs Jlassi lost both their sons on the same day in the same food hall in Paris.

# 32

JO, MICHAEL AND ANTONY waited anxiously in the prisoners' meeting room. Richelieu appeared, shocked. 'Something 'as 'appened,' he said. 'Tell me, s'il vous plaît.'

'Please be seated, Monsieur,' said Antony, seeking to make the news he was about to declare the result of his handiwork. Jo's grin and Michael's half smile got Pierre's heart pumping.

To be fair, Antony did tell the truth, well, his version thereof. As the tale unfolded, Pierre became ever more emotional. He put a hand to his face, then both hands. Then tears welled and finally broke free.

His voice broke. 'Merci, merci,' he blubbed. The others were moved. This man had been to the gates of Hell and back. From the grief of his mother's death, and the lies about his new family to the appalling injustice of a false criminal charge, it seemed soon he would be free.

'We are not yet out of the woods, Monsieur,' added Antony trying to control the situation.

Two prison guards approached. 'We have been ordered to ask all visitors to leave. The governor wishes to interview the prisoner.'

'I insist on being present,' said Antony.

'I regret, Monsieur, that will not be possible.'

'I'm his lawyer,' protested Antony. Jo placed a hand on his arm.

She whispered. 'It's to limit their embarrassment.'

He whispered back. 'But we must sue for wrongful arrest.'

'Later.'

Antony despaired. His client looked like winning a great victory but with a limited contribution from his highly-paid lawyer. Antony wanted to ride on the coattails of the Aussies.

Jo whispered even more intimately so only Antony could hear. 'Let's get him out first, and then you can do your party tricks.'

Antony liked the closeness of Jo's lips to his ear. But in the cold light of reality, he knew she was right. He stood.

'I will expect to hear from the prison authorities today,' he said to the guards. Antony addressed his client. 'It has been an honour to serve you, Monsieur,' beamed Antony extending his hand. Pierre shook it.

He knew the real genius was Jo Best. 'Merci, Monsieur.'

Michael offered his hand. 'Well done, Inspector, bloody well done.'

The men shook hands. 'Thank you, mon ami. I will never forget what you 'ave done for me, Dr Chan.'

The homicide detectives looked at one another. The guards and Michael and Antony looked at the couple looking at one another.

'Congratulations, Inspector,' said Jo. He took her hand and kissed it.

'Ah, ma chérie, not only beautiful and brilliant but enchanting as well.' They kept looking at one another and then as if directed, embraced. It wasn't the plastic hug of two footballers before play, afraid to damage their masculinity. This was a coming together of two willing bodies. The onlookers were hooked and felt like voyeurs.

Then steam covered the shower screen as Pierre and Jo broke the intimacy of their hug only to rejoin their bodies via their lips. The guards were touched, Antony jealous and Michael heartbroken.

Pierre was escorted back to his cell, waving and calling his thanks with the prison officers treating him with respect.

Outside the prison, the scoop of impatient journalists saw the trio emerge and moved to them. These people might be involved. Let's find out. Jo and Michael went into escape mode. Antony didn't. He stood his ground and ignored their questions. He was like a schoolmaster waiting for noisy students to sit still and be quiet.

Jo whispered to Michael. 'C'mon, let's go.'

They left as Antony slipped into his "Look at me" routine. 'My name is the Honourable Antony Heron-Royhay, and I am the lawyer representing Inspector Pierre Richelieu. My client has been the victim of a grave miscarriage of justice and on his behalf I will pursue all legal avenues to punish those responsible for these vile crimes.'

He droned on turning to face different cameras to maximise the publicity. Antony fell on his feet with this case—not only was his client about to be set free but he, Antony, could put his face and name in front of the media. He milked his fifteen minutes of fame.

Jo and Michael went cab searching. She slipped her arm into his. They felt great. Their trip from Down Under was a smashing success. It was not over yet but with Pierre seemingly being released today, the celebrations would be long and lively.

'Face it, Michael, we have to be the best crime-fighting team, ever.'

'Maybe,' he said, hailing a cab.

'Maybe? We're the have-mystery-will-solve-it gang. Working alone, we're nothing; together we're superstars.'

They climbed into the cab heading for Rue Crémieux. Michael raised the dreaded topic. 'We can't ignore the elephant in the room.'

'Sorry?'

'Can you imagine the publicity from this latest escapade?'

Jo and Michael shared the same antipathy to the press. 'And worse, it'll be in two countries,' said Jo.

'I suggest we let Mr Heron-Royhay absorb the lot.' Jo agreed. 'Did you know his surname is an anagram of Hooray Henry?'

Jo looked at Michael's brilliant half smile. She roared with laughter.

From their cab ride, they enjoyed the sights of Paris then reached Pierre's home. Each went to their bedroom to sort their belongings. Jo appeared and knocked on Michael's open door.

'What would you like to do?'

'Do you mean today, tomorrow or for the rest of my life?'

'We could have some lunch then go and collect Pierre.'

'Lunch is fine but alas not the Inspector's collection.'

Jo paused. 'Sorry?'

'I'm on a flight to Marvellous Melbourne leaving in,' he looked at his watch, 'just under four hours.'

'Michael!' Jo was surprised, angry and confused.

'Oh come on, Jo. The corpulent contralto is caroling.'

Jo moved into his room and sat on the bed. 'Michael we've scored a fantastic result, arguably our best ever, beyond our wildest dreams. We have to celebrate. We have to let Pierre thank us in the way you know he would want us to.'

'Look, Detective, I'm rapt in the result, all due to your brilliant article, I've had a wonderful time both here and across the Channel, but I do have another life and my cat and clients need me.'

Jo wanted to probe deeper. 'Our success rate is so high Michael because of our honesty. Have we always been open and honest?'

'We have, and this conversation is getting way too serious.'

Jo came close to snapping. 'Michael.'

'Oh come on, Jo, two's company. I don't fancy a stroll along the Seine with you and Pierre. And if Antony tags along, I'll jump in the bloody river and swim home.'

They looked at one another. She stood, walked to him and put her arms around him. She didn't speak. He didn't struggle, sort of froze.

'If that's your best hold, Detective, I could disarm you in a second.'

She hugged him, kissed his cheek, laughed and let go. 'Well I'm coming with you to the airport.'

'What for? I'll see you back in Melbourne and we can ...' He stopped. 'You are coming home?'

She shrugged and wouldn't meet his gaze. 'I honestly don't know, Michael. I guess it depends on any offer I may receive.'

Michael took in a sharp breath. 'Right. Well we still have time for a final Parisian luncheon. How's that for an offer?'

'Perfect,' she smiled. 'Give me two minutes,' she said vanishing.

Michael spoke to himself in his empty room. 'Two minutes is a general expression in which speed equals distance divided by time.'

The lunch was lovely although both Jo and Michael were having thoughts they didn't wish to discuss. He was nosy wanting to know if she and Pierre were lovers. She was nervous wondering how she might respond to any offer made by Pierre. And with Michael off the scene, there goes the chaperone. How would Jo get through the night? Or rather, where would she sleep tonight?

They wandered back to Rue Crémieux where Michael collected his rucksack. She walked with him to find a cab. When it arrived, he opened the door and tossed his rucksack inside. He turned to face her.

Both enjoyed strong feelings for the other although from a different POV. She loved him like a friend. He just loved her.

He produced a reasonably good Humphrey Bogart. 'Here's lookin' at you, kid.'

'I hope we can work together again soon, Michael.'

'I'm off to Northcote, not the Moon.'

They stared at one another. The impatient driver spoke, 'Monsieur?'

He slipped back into his Bogart. 'We'll always have Paris.'

She smiled, hugged him, leant back and kissed his lips then turned and walked back along Rue Crémieux without looking back. Michael would relive that moment over and over as he set off Down Under.

Jo's phone rang. Antony told her Pierre was free with all charges dropped and one huge apology from both prison service and police.

'Monsieur Richelieu will attend my chambers shortly to plan his case for suing people and institutions. I have every confidence he will win a massive payment.'

'May I speak with him, please,' asked Jo.

'Of course. As soon as he arrives, I will have him call you.'

'Thank you, Antony. And despite our differences, I appreciate all you've done for Pierre.'

'Will I see you before you go?' She hesitated. He twigged. 'Well if not, thank you for helping Monsieur Richelieu, and bon voyage.'

'Goodbye,' said Jo to a disconnected phone. She wondered about her life. *Am I doing the right thing? Am I making a fool of myself? Does Pierre want a permanent relationship? What would Dr Gabrielle Strange recommend?*

With time on her hands, she checked the time in Australia. It was pushing midnight and calling her mother would not be kind. She rang her brother-in-law, a rare event. He answered immediately.

'Detective Best, how lovely to hear from you.' He sounded sincere. *Has his wife's serious illness made the man a human being?*

'Hi Jeremy. Sorry it's so late.'

'It's never too late to hear your dulcet tones, officer.'

*No, he hasn't changed.* Jo braced for some bad news. 'I'm ringing to hear the latest about my sister.'

'She's fine. Doing a lot of sleeping of course but she's okay.' Jo struggled to speak. 'You still there?'

'Yes, sorry, so no relapse or problems with the cancer returning?'

'She went back into hospital for a couple of days but she's fine. In fact the surgeon reckons she's doing better than expected.'

'That's fantastic. And you and the kids are okay?'

'We're good despite my mother-in-law being the biggest pain this side of the Eiffel Tower.'

Jo twigged. Her mother could worry for Australia. 'You're talking about my mother, Jeremy.'

He laughed. 'So how's Paris? And is it true all Frenchmen are fantastic lovers?'

'Good night Jeremy. Oh and give my love to all.'

She ended the call in haste. The thought of her sister dying young leaving two beautiful kids ate away at Jo. Now she felt enormous relief. Her phone rang again and her heart accelerated.

'Pierre? Is that you?'

'Oui ma chérie. It is your favourite Inspector speaking.'

'Where are you? How are you?'

'I am wonderful and 'ere with Monsieur 'eron-Roy'ay. We 'ave legal matters to discuss but soon I will be free to run to your arms.'

*Okay* thought Jo. *He's certainly keen to pick up where we left off.* 'We must celebrate your freedom, Inspector.'

'Naturellement. I will book the finest restaurant in Paris with you and Michael as my guests.' He dropped his voice. 'Do you think I should invite the 'onourable Englishman?'

Without thinking, Jo whispered her response. 'No,' she said with conviction. 'I mean, perhaps not.'

'Okay, ma chérie. I understand. I will call you when I am leaving. Au revoir, mademoiselle, until tonight.' Click.

'Oh shit,' said Jo. 'I didn't tell him there'll only be two for tea.'

She ran a bath washing with a purpose in case she might be subjected to an intimate investigation. She inspected her meagre wardrobe. The sight of her new Gucci pumps prompted thoughts of seduction. *Me or him?* She wasn't sure.

Eventually Pierre rang to say he was on his way. She dressed casually downplaying her appearance. He rang the doorbell before unlocking the door. She came down the stairs and their eyes met. Neither spoke.

He opened his arms. Jo wasn't sure if this was a sign of their legal victory or the beginning of their affair. She moved to him. His hug was powerful, lifting her off the ground. Back on terra firm, she smiled.

'Welcome to Paris, my beautiful detective.'

'Merci,' said Jo but nothing more because his lips prevented hers from moving, well from creating spoken words.

She managed to break free. 'I have some news, Pierre.'

His face dropped. 'Nothing sad. I forbid you from having sad news.'

'Michael has gone home.'

'Oh?' from the Frenchman who regarded this as fantastic news.

'Once he knew you were free, he wanted his family and work.'

'Michael is a gentleman and a scholar. I will personally thank 'im when next we meet. But now, ma chérie, you must prepare for a night on the town in the City of Light. I 'ope you are a beautiful dancer.'

'Me, no. Please Pierre, a quiet meal would be perfect. And you must be tired after your ordeal.'

'True,' he said kissing her hand. 'But the company of a beautiful woman can do wonders for any man—surtout un homme dans l'amour.' (especially a man in love). He brought her hand to his lips again and looked into her eyes.

*Jeremy is right,* she thought. *Frenchmen are fantastic lovers.*

Jo was glad Hooray Henry wasn't invited not because he was a bore, but because he'd seen her one and only upmarket outfit. This time her black slacks, roll neck sweater, Versace jacket, gold belt, gold necklace and earrings, were topped with her Gucci heels. She came down the stairs with enough makeup and Pierre stopped in his tracks.

'Oh mon dieu. Absoluement parfait. Be still my beating 'eart.'

*This man is a charmer,* thought Jo.

They went to a Michelin Star restaurant and Jo needed Pierre to translate the menu. The atmosphere, the service, the comfort, and the wine list were superb. Mind you the grub scraped a pass as well.

*Can they really make butter from seaweed?*

Jo was glad the restaurant made no provision for dancing.

*Surely he won't suggest kicking on to a nightclub?*

Over the meal, he explained the events since his arrival in Paris. He knew Jo and Michael had set him free. Then he changed topics.

'I am truly sorry, Joanna, you did not meet my dear mother.'

'So am I,' said Jo unable to eat another thing.

'But now we must think of the future.'

*The what?*

'We could take our time going 'ome—a trip down the Rhine or a few days on the Orient Express. We could travel from Paris to Venice and fly 'ome from there. What would you like to do?'

*Right now? This very moment? If I tell him, he'll think I'm easy.*

'You are too kind, Pierre. I think I was lucky to get leave in the first place. Now you're free, it might be wise to return as soon as possible.'

'As always, ma chérie, you are correct—damn you.' He smiled and she melted. 'Let us go for a final stroll around Paris.'

In the street, he offered his arm. They said nothing, enjoying the buildings, shops, the history of Paris, and their bodies touching. Jo pondered how events might unfold back at Rue Crémieux.

*Will he carry me upstairs? Surely he won't want to make love in his mother's bed? What if DI Rose again asks me if Pierre and I are lovers? Will I leave Homicide and become a kept woman?*

Pierre knew his way around town. He stopped when they turned a corner. 'A sight uniquely Paris, n'est-ce pas?'

Jo looked and saw the Eiffel Tower. She couldn't see it for long because Pierre put his face between the monument and her face. He kissed her without asking. She joined the party, and the people passing ignored the common sight of lovers doing what lovers do in Paris.

They found a cab and sat quietly, heading home. He held her hand and she felt nervous—excited but on edge. She decided. She wanted to be this man's lover whatever the consequences.

The cab stopped at Rue Crémieux, Pierre leant forward, paid then stepped out and offered his hand to Jo. She took it and life exploded.

It wasn't another arrest by French police although nearly as bad. A horde of paparazzi swarmed towards the cab. They came from all directions. They knew what Pierre looked like, where he lived, where the drugs were planted. They knew he was a former French detective and was set up. They wanted his photo, his story. They wanted him, and anyone with him was fair game.

Lights flashed, voices called and Pierre was ambushed. Jo pulled the door shut and yelled, 'Drive.' The taxi took off and stopped a few blocks from Pierre's house. She called him. He answered but couldn't be heard. She paid the driver and entered the budget hotel where she and Michael once spent the night.

The manager remembered her although not looking as glamourous.

'All alone tonight, Mademoiselle?'

She paid and took the key. 'No, I'm expecting my husband any minute. He's a boxer.'

She went upstairs, locked herself in, and tried calling Pierre again. Still cacophony. *Why doesn't he go inside? Maybe he can't.* She sent him a text saying she was safe and could he call her when free.

He rang. He was trapped with the media annoying his neighbours. The tourists were bad but journalists were worse. He wanted to know where she was. She wanted her location kept secret because it was a dive and because the media could find her through him.

'I'll call you in the morning, Pierre,' she said, 'au revoir.'

He was shattered. She went online and booked a flight to Oz tomorrow. She stripped, climbed into bed and fell asleep to the sounds she and Pierre may well have made had the media not been so keen.

She woke early, and rang Pierre. He was full of apologies. She asked about the media. A few were camped outside his front door. She broke the news about leaving. He begged her to stay. She politely stood firm and promised to call soon, certainly before she left Paris. She waited till the rush hour faded then left to buy coffee. She looked overdressed so went shopping. It was hard to shop downmarket in central Paris. She bought trainers, jeans, a jacket and a cheap holdall. She put her good clothes and shoes in the holdall, sat in a café and rang Pierre.

'I can still see them, ma chérie. I am so sorry. Are you okay?'

'I'm fine, Pierre but I have to go home.'

'Non, please wait for me, s'il vous plaît.'

'I need a favour, Pierre. My rucksack is upstairs in your house. Can you bring it back with you to Oz? Please.'

'Of course. But do you 'ave to go today?'

She paused. 'I'm sorry our wonderful evening ended like so, Pierre.'

'*You* are sorry? Mademoiselle, *I* am 'eartbroken.'

'I could not bear to become front-page news in France. It was bad enough back home with the kidnapped toddler and then those religious serial killers.'

'I understand, ma chérie. You must do what you want. I will bring your rucksack 'ome for you and then we can celebrate together, oui?'

'Oui, Pierre, I would like that.'

She heard what sounded like a kissing sound and he whispered, 'I love you, Mademoiselle Jo Best.'

She whispered 'Au revoir, Monsieur,' and ended the call. The great Parisian romance died a death. This is the way the love affair ends, not with a bang but a whimper. In the back of the taxi, she cried.

The train took her to the airport where she was back in cattle class. She sat in a corner of the public lounge and checked her phone. She sent a text to her mother, to Dr Gabrielle Strange, DI Rose and Dr Jack Carr. Each text was identical.

*Successful trip, leaving Paris, home soon. Jo xx.*

She closed her phone and it pinged. Wow. Someone from Down Under wished to welcome her home. No, it was a surprise, a text from the Honourable Antony Heron-Royhay.

*Wishing me a safe journey? Thanking me again for saving his bacon? What?* Jo opened the message and read. Her heart grew cold. Had it stopped? What the hell?

> *My Dear Miss Best,*
> *In preparing a case for my client, I came upon a fact of which you may not be aware. Monsieur Pierre Richelieu is married. His wife was convicted of homicide but found to be of an unsound mind. She resides in an institution for the criminally insane. With every good wish for your future,*
> *The Honourable Antony Heron-Royhay*

The waiting-lounge was packed. People chatted, kids played, PA announcements blared, and Jo Best sat in disbelief. Sure Antony was bitter after being rejected by Jo. She didn't care. One thing dominated her thinking and caused a sharp pain in her chest. DI Pierre Richelieu is a married man who never bothered to mention the fact.

*I was minutes away from becoming his lover.*

She couldn't move and forgot time. She thought about ringing him. "Pierre, are you married?" That didn't appeal. A face to face meeting was required and thinking about it made her sick. She typed a text.

> *Hello Michael. About to board Qantas at CDG Paris. Can you please collect me at Tulla? Love and thanks.*
> *Jane Eyre*

To Be Continued

# The Detective Joanna Best Mysteries

www.cenfoxbooks.com

The much maligned and misunderstood father of the famous Brontë sisters led an amazing life. Discover the Brunty (that's right) family tree in Ireland and how this man of sorrows survived horrendous sadness and inspired his daughters to scribble with stunning success.

*A splendid story, reading like a Victorian melodrama.* **Louise Joy**
*Portrays the life of Brontë in remarkable style giving a deeper insight into a famous literary family.* **Rev. Philip Higgins**
*Cenarth Fox has seized the day to revisit Patrick Brontë, an extraordinary man who encouraged his children to read, to think, and hence to imagine.* **Geraldine Starbrook**
*Wonderfully evocative.* **Steve Stanworth**
(Co-ordinator for the Brontë Bell Chapel)
www.cenfoxbooks.com

www.ingramcontent.com/pod-product-compliance
Lightning Source LLC
Chambersburg PA
CBHW071108100726

47908CB00008B/2307